M000012117

Letters between Forster and Isherwood on Homosexuality and Literature

Letters between Forster and Isherwood on Homosexuality and Literature

Edited by Richard E. Zeikowitz

palgrave
macmillan

PR
6011
.O58
Z489
2008

LETTERS BETWEEN FORSTER AND ISHERWOOD
ON HOMOSEXUALITY AND LITERATURE
Copyright © Richard E. Zeikowitz, 2008.

All rights reserved. No part of this book may be used or reproduced in any manner whatsoever without written permission except in the case of brief quotations embodied in critical articles or reviews.

First published in 2008 by
PALGRAVE MACMILLAN™
175 Fifth Avenue, New York, N.Y. 10010 and
Houndmills, Basingstoke, Hampshire, England RG21 6XS.
Companies and representatives throughout the world.

PALGRAVE MACMILLAN is the global academic imprint of the Palgrave Macmillan division of St. Martin's Press, LLC and of Palgrave Macmillan Ltd. Macmillan® is a registered trademark in the United States, United Kingdom and other countries. Palgrave is a registered trademark in the European Union and other countries.

ISBN-13: 978-0-230-60675-3
ISBN-10: 0-230-60675-X

Library of Congress Cataloging-in-Publication Data is available from the Library of Congress.

A catalogue record of the book is available from the British Library.

Design by Scribe Inc.

First edition: August 2008

10 9 8 7 6 5 4 3 2 1

Printed in the United States of America.

All letters by E. M. Forster are reproduced with permission from the Society of Authors as agent for the Provost and Scholars of King's College Cambridge.

All letters by Christopher Isherwood are reproduced with permission from Don Bachardy.

Cover drawings of Forster and Isherwood drawn from life by Don Bachardy.

For Don Bachardy and James White

University Libraries
Carnegie Mellon University
Pittsburgh, PA 15213-3890

Contents

Acknowledgments

I thank the Research Foundation of the City University of New York (CUNY) for a generous grant that enabled me to travel to Cambridge, England. I also thank the Huntington Library for a one-month residency fellowship. I was able to examine and transcribe the letters at both King's College Cambridge and the Huntington Library with the help of the very knowledgeable and friendly staff. I thank Patricia McGuire, the archivist at King's College, who was always very attentive to my needs. I also thank Peter Jones, the librarian of King's College Library, for his assistance in obtaining permission to publish E. M. Forster's letters to Christopher Isherwood. I am indebted to Elizabeth Haylett of the Society of Authors for granting permission on behalf of King's College, Cambridge. I am grateful to Sue Hodson, the curator of the Isherwood papers at the Huntington Library, for her enthusiastic support for this project. I also thank the staff of the reading room at the Huntington Library for their assistance.

I wish to express my gratitude to Chris Suggs, the former chair of the English department at John Jay College, CUNY, for his support. Without the one-semester release time I would not have been able to complete this project in a timely manner. I also thank Steven Kruger, Michael Shugrue, and James White for their support and encouragement.

Lastly, I would like to thank Don Bachardy for graciously permitting two drawings he made of Forster and Isherwood to be reproduced here. As far as I know, he is the only artist to have drawn both Forster and Isherwood.

Introduction

In the fall of 1932, William Plomer took Christopher Isherwood to meet E. M. Forster for the first time. Isherwood had long been an admirer of Forster's work. The two writers belonged to two different generations: Edward Morgan Forster, born in 1879, came of age during the late Victorian and Edwardian periods; Isherwood, born in 1904, was a member of the post-World War I generation.[1] Each, too, was in a very different stage of his writing career. Forster was the author of several highly regarded novels, particularly *Howard's End* (1910) and *A Passage to India* (1924), and was well established within the literary circles of the time. His professional acquaintances and friends included Virginia Woolf and other members of the Bloomsbury group. Isherwood had just completed his second novel, *The Memorial*, which reveals stylistic influences from Forster. Forster had read the novel, liked it, and expressed a wish to meet the young author. Isherwood recalls his admiration for Forster and excitement at meeting him that day: "It *was* tremendous for Christopher. Forster was the only living writer whom he would have described as his master. In other people's books he found examples of style which he wanted to imitate and learn from. In Forster he found a key to the whole art of writing.... A Forster novel taught Christopher the mental attitude with which he must pick up the pen."[2]

Often looking back at that auspicious meeting and Forster's kind words about *The Memorial*, Isherwood would say, "My literary career is over—I don't give a damn for the Nobel Prize or the Order of Merit—*I've been praised by Forster!*"[3] Isherwood also had a great deal of respect for Forster as a person. On a visit to Forster in 1947, Isherwood reflects that he was in awe of Forster not merely as his literary master but also because "Forster demanded truth in all his relationships; underneath his charming unalarming exterior he was a stern moralist and his mild babylike eyes looked deep into you. Their glance made Christopher feel false and tricky."[4] While their professional relationship was one of mentor and disciple, their personal relationship was cemented by an equal caring for one another. Forster was loyal to his intimate friends and expected the same from them. Isherwood was indeed loyal throughout the thirty-eight years of their friendship.

The letters are a personal record of these two writers' lives, both professionally and personally, over a period of more than thirty years. The substantial number of letters exchanged during the increasingly turbulent years of the 1930s reveal how Forster and Isherwood each came to grips with the rise of fascism in Europe and the threat of war as both writers and human beings helplessly caught in the midst of a world on the brink of disaster. On a more subtle level, the letters tell two parallel but very different stories of love and devotion between each writer and his respective male partner. The letters of the war years juxtapose the strikingly different worlds in which Forster and Isherwood were living: London and its environs during the Blitz, and the southern California community of exiled writers and artists, respectively. Each friend informs the other how his life—and view of life—is being shaped by events, whether unfolding within his midst or thousands of miles away. The postwar letters, although sparse, particularly after the early 1950s, record moments in the later careers of the two writers, such as Isherwood struggling to find a new voice in his novels, one that treats homosexual characters more openly and Forster embarking on new projects and fitting himself into the role of elder statesman. In these later letters, the two friends also continue their ongoing conversation to find a suitable ending for Forster's ground-breaking but yet unpublished novel, *Maurice*.

One theme that surfaces subtly throughout all three periods of the correspondence is each writer's life as a homosexual in a society where one could not openly express one's sexual preference. During the 1930s, Forster and Isherwood were both in committed relationships with younger men of the working class: Forster with the policeman, Bob Buckingham, Isherwood with Heinz. Both situations had their complications. Isherwood and Heinz were on the run from Nazi Germany; Forster was involved with a married man. Although Bob's wife, May, was Forster's rival for Bob's attention in the beginning, over the years he actually became close friends with May and an uncle figure for their son, Robin. The letters offer many clues that Bob regularly spent the night at Forster's flat in London and refer to occasional weekend trips they took together to the continent in order to visit Isherwood and Heinz. Yet Forster and Isherwood are both reticent—in their letters at least—about intimate details. One needs to coax out details from between the lines.

Nicola Beauman maintains that Bob was "the great love" of Forster's life.[5] Although normally reserved in his letters to Bob (of which more than one thousand exist!), on the eve of prostate surgery, Forster reveals his love for Bob and the suggestion that the love is reciprocal: "I feel gay and calm, but have an open mind as to whether I shall get through or not[.] I don't say this to anyone else, but I love you too much to say anything but the truth. I don't feel afraid of anything and it is your love that has made me be like this."[6] One catches a hint of this love in an uncharacteristically gushing remark Forster makes to Isherwood after dryly listing upcoming events on his engagement calendar: "and the evening after that will be best, for Bob comes." Although Forster does not actually live with Bob except for the nights they spend together in Forster's London flat and the occasional trip abroad—such as when Isherwood arranges for them to stay in the "Royalty Bedroom" when they visit him in Brussels—the letters suggest that Forster and Bob were a "couple" parallel to that of Isherwood and Heinz (who were in fact living together). Forster and Isherwood both regularly close their letters with, respectively, love to Heinz or Bob.

Isherwood never openly describes his love or affection for Heinz in his letters to Forster in the 1930s; yet it is implied in his desperate search to find a country where he could live with Heinz in safety. He envisions an ideal life with Heinz in Portugal: "I think we might quite possibly settle in this country if we can find the right house and if Heinz can get a reasonable assurance that he will be allowed to stop here indefinitely." The intensity of Isherwood's bond with Heinz during turbulent times—times that eventually overpowered their efforts to remain together—is revealed in several entries Isherwood writes in his diary after they are separated. Two weeks after Heinz's arrest in Germany, he reflects: "At first I didn't think about Heinz at all. Or tried not to. I felt like a house in which one room, the biggest, is locked up. There, very cautiously, I allowed myself to think of him in little doses—five minutes at a time: then I had a good cry and felt better."[7] Then, from the distant perspective of five months: "Never to forget H. Never to cease to be grateful to him for every moment of our five years together. Never to cease to hope that, somehow, some day, all will be well. And yet to find a real warm decent relationship for myself—something not of the same kind, but really worthwhile."[8] After losing Heinz, Isherwood had a series of relationships—some lasting several years— which he alludes to in his letters to Forster, but he was not to find another long-lasting relationship until he met Don Bachardy in 1953. On the other hand, Forster's relationship with Bob survived the war and another twenty-five years until Forster's death.

Forster's unpublished novel, *Maurice*, completed in 1914, is an ongoing topic of conversation in the letters from the 1930s through the 1950s. In the spring of 1933, Forster gave Isherwood the manuscript to read. Although some of the antiquated euphemisms, such as "sharing" for "sex," embarrassed him, Isherwood felt nothing but admiration for Forster's brave effort. He reflects later, "the wonder of the novel was that it had been written when it had been written; the wonder was Forster himself, imprisoned within the jungle of pre-war prejudice, putting these unthinkable thoughts into words."[9] Isherwood was honored that he was chosen to respond to it on behalf of his generation and recalls the scene where he was to give Forster his verdict on the novel—a scene that cemented Forster and Isherwood's personal relationship. Isherwood recreates the scene: "My memory sees them sitting together, facing each other. Christopher sits gazing at his master of their art, this great prophet of their tribe, who declares that there can be real love, love without limits or excuse, between two men. Here he is, humble in his greatness, unsure of his own genius. Christopher stammers some words of praise and devotion, his eyes brimming with tears. And Forster—amused and touched, but more touched than amused—leans forward and kisses him on the cheek."[10] To Forster's fear that the novel might seem dated, Isherwood replied, "Why *shouldn't* it date?" Soon after this meeting, Isherwood proposes that Forster rewrite the ending so that Maurice and Alec, instead of separating, settle into a permanent domestic relationship. But Forster, who, after all, came of age in the late Victorian to early Edwardian era, replies in a letter: "I daren't thus instal them, no, not even under a hay-stack."

Five years later, Isherwood rereads the novel and gushes in admiration for his mentor and friend: "have finished 'Maurice,' and am in a state of reverence which even my most irreverent moments of you do nothing to dispel." Isherwood himself was struggling with how to present homosexual characters in his fiction. Looking back at *Mr. Norris Changes Trains*, Isherwood realized that if he had made the narrator, William Bradshaw (Isherwood's two middle names), openly homosexual "[t]he narrator would have become so odd, perhaps so interesting, that his presence would have thrown the novel out of perspective," taking attention away from the title character.[11] He thus opted to keep the narrator's sexuality ambiguous both in this novel and in *Goodbye to Berlin*.

The young writers of the post-World War I generation resented and even hated the older generation whom they blamed for the recent horrific war. Forster, however, escaped the wrath of the younger generation and his novels were regarded as "modern." Isherwood describes Forster's "tea-tabling" technique, through the voice of Chalmers in his autobiographical novel, *Lions and Shadows*: "The whole of Forster's technique is based on the tea-table: instead of trying to screw all his scenes up to the highest possible pitch, he tones them down until they sound like mothers'-meeting gossip. . . . In fact, there's actually *less* emphasis laid on the big scenes than on the unimportant ones."[12] Forster was also respected and befriended by others within Isherwood's circle, namely W. H. Auden, Stephen Spender, and

William Plomer. But Isherwood's relationship with Forster was the most complex, one that was a combination of awed disciple, naughty son, and devoted friend. Throughout the 1930s, Isherwood kept Forster abreast of his current writing projects, writing in late 1932 that he was working on "an indecent bumptious stupid sort of novel about Berlin which I fear you won't like." Thirty years later he would no longer feel it necessary that Forster approve of his work, but at this stage in his writing career he sought Forster's praise.[13]

Like other writers of his generation, Isherwood was keenly aware of the growing menace of Nazism in the early 1930s. In "The Lost" Isherwood sought to portray some of the people he had met during his years in Berlin who were living in the shadow of the Nazi threat.[14] Though he was not writing a political novel, he was offering an interpretation of Berlin society in the early 1930s. His diary records are "The link which binds all the chief characters together is that in some way or other each one of them is conscious of the mental, economic, and ideological bankruptcy of the world in which they live."[15] Although Isherwood abandoned the project two years later, characters such as Mr. Norris, Bernard Landauer, and Sally Bowles were to fill the pages of his two famous Berlin novels, *Mr. Norris Changes Trains* (U.S. title, *The Last of Mr. Norris*) and *Goodbye to Berlin*, published in 1935 and 1939, respectively.

In 1934, Isherwood was also collaborating with Auden on a play, which was eventually titled *The Dog Beneath the Skin*. It makes a tentative antifascist statement but is not really a political play. Jonathan Fryer notes that the play "is very much a child of its time, urgent in its anti-fascism and aggressive in its overt suggestion that such things might also take place in England . . . yet its political position is not so clear-cut, its ardour for the left-wing cause ambiguous."[16] Part of the problem was Isherwood's and Auden's reluctance to embrace a political cause—even when they had a personal antipathy to fascism. Fryer suggests that in Isherwood's case, "his artistic temperament and interests would always prevent him from being a political mouthpiece."[17]

Though he worked quickly with Auden on the play, Isherwood was finding it difficult to work steadily on his novel. He was traveling restlessly around Europe with his young German lover, Heinz, trying to find a country where they could settle together. In May 1934 he wrote to Forster, "My own novel doesn't get finished and changes its form daily. I read chiefly books about what is going to happen in Europe and study maps." Forster, meanwhile, attempting to emerge from a dry spell, was beginning a new project: a biography of his Cambridge friend, the historian Goldsworthy Lowes Dickinson, who had recently died. He confesses to Isherwood, "It's so long since I've written a book that it feels like opening a tomb." Although each writer keeps the other up-to-date on his latest writing project, the letters become increasingly personal and intimate. Isherwood's letters to Forster from 1933 to 1937 are a travel diary of beautiful places inhabited by odd people. He entertains his mentor-friend with descriptions of mysterious ship passengers, Germans in the Canary Islands who "bow from the waist and say 'Permit,'" and Portuguese workers who sing loudly as they work. And wherever Isherwood and Heinz are, he coaxes Forster to join them for a visit, in one letter giving him rather hilarious directions of how to reach them on a remote Greek island.

But always present like a dark cloud threatening to pour down on a sunny, idyllic picnic is the rise of fascism in Europe. As early as April 1934, Forster writes to Isherwood of the "coming smash" and resigns himself that "nothing can be done." Forster notes that those whom he admires feel the need "to do something," but he only supports such action if one remains true to one's character and is not playing the role of political activist merely to gain admiration. He thus never suggests that Isherwood should become more politically engaged. Forster himself was decidedly apolitical and even when war was imminent did not add his voice to those who strongly advocated fighting the Germans. Although not overtly carrying a political message, Isherwood's works during this period are informed by the times. In August 1934, as he began the segments that will eventually become *Goodbye to Berlin*, Isherwood reflects that "they ought, at least, to form quite an interesting set of illustrations to a serious work on Fascism." The outcome is perhaps more in line with what Fryer writes about the companion novel, *Mr. Norris Changes Trains*: "The background of the Nazi rise to power is succinctly and powerfully evoked, without ever directly intruding on the private drama in the foreground."[18]

Isherwood's placing of his story within a background of the rise of the Nazis in Berlin is in keeping with his relation to political developments of the 1930s. The fascist threat is the active backdrop for the drama of Isherwood's life which was mainly concerned with keeping Heinz out of Germany and with him. His letters to Forster record his anxiety, fear, and desperation not about a future war per se but about the very threatening present situation he faces in his personal life—the fact that Heinz could any day be arrested and deported for failing to report for military duty in Germany. In the summer of 1936, after unsuccessfully seeking help from a famous Lisbon lawyer, Isherwood records in his journal: "I came out into the street feeling stunned. It was absurd, of course, to be so upset. What else had I expected?. . . Why shouldn't H[einz] go back? Everything seemed to be slipping away down into a bottomless black drain. . . . So absolutely doomed did I feel—wandering up and down the hot sunlit streets."[19] Shortly after, still in Portugal, Isherwood writes Forster that "Every time the door-bell rings, we jump out of our skins and the postman is awaited daily like an executioner." Isherwood's fears are realized but not in the way he imagined. Heinz was arrested by the German Gestapo in Trier, Germany, where Isherwood's attorney had instructed him to wait for a visa to return to Belgium. He eventually was found guilty and given a six-month prison sentence. His freedom would be denied for three additional years: one year working for the German government and two years military service.[20]

Throughout the 1930s, writers of Isherwood's generation struggled with the question of how to respond effectively to the increasing menace of Fascism. In 1935, John Lehmann felt that "time was running out for a new world war"; He asks, "How to defend oneself, to be active, not to crouch paralysed as the hawk descends?"[21] Stephen Spender, who joined the Communist Party in late 1936 and wrote articles for the party's newspaper, *The Daily Worker*, later reflects on his commitment to politics: "I was 'political' not just because I was involved, but in feeling I must choose to defend a good cause against a bad one."[22] Although Spender took on an active political role, traveling around England representing the anti-fascist position, in a letter to Isherwood he admits "I still secretly and perhaps exaggeratedly believe that a very good book about things one cares for is a potent instrument. And imaginative work is more important than one more voice added to a controversial babel."[23] While Spender's "imaginative work" would not be overtly, or even subtly, political, Cecil Day-Lewis, who, like Spender, joined the Communist Party at this time, believes that a "proletarian poet" can play a direct role in politics: "To speak to the workers and for the workers he does not need, as bourgeois poets do, to learn a new tongue: he has only to make poetry of what is his native language."[24]

Of course, simply writing politically engaged work is one thing; putting oneself in danger is another. As the drama of the Spanish Civil War was playing out, some of Isherwood's friends and fellow writers of the post-World War I generation made their way to Spain. In early 1937, Spender, together with the writer, Cuthbert Worsley, traveled on a dangerous mission to Spain for the *Daily Worker*, to investigate the fate of a crew of Russian seamen whose ship had been sunk in the Mediterranean. It was believed that the men were being held prisoners by the (Fascist) rebels in Spain. A less dangerous but nevertheless risky mission presented itself in late 1937 when a delegation of writers were invited to Spain to declare their support for the beleaguered Spanish republic. Isherwood and Auden were among those scheduled to attend. Isherwood later recalls enjoying the drama of preparing to embark on a potentially dangerous trip to Spain, even making out a will. At a farewell party for Isherwood that Forster attended, when asked why he was not planning to go, Forster replied simply, "Afraid to." Forster's simple honesty deflated Isherwood.[25] As it turned out, because the delegation's trip was repeatedly delayed, Isherwood and Auden decided to go ahead with their planned journey to China.

From his vantage point in England, Forster was becoming increasingly alarmed by developments in Germany and Spain. In 1934, Forster consented to be the first president of the newly formed National Council for Civil Liberties whose purpose was to protect individual rights against what was viewed as increasingly totalitarian policies in England. In June of the next year, Forster was invited to lead the British delegation at an International Congress of Writers held in Paris. The congress was organized by French communist writers, and the attendees included notable writers who were dedicated anti-Fascists, such as André Malraux, André Gide, Louis Aragon, Maxim Gorki, Bertold Brecht, and Heinrich Mann.[26] In his speech to the audience mainly consisting of young Communists, Forster explained that he was neither Fascist nor Communist and drew attention to the current danger in Britain of "Fabio-fascism . . . working quietly away behind the façade of constitutional forms, passing a little law (like the Sedition Act) here, endorsing a departmental tyranny there, emphasizing the national need of secrecy everywhere . . . until opposition is tamed and gulled." He also acknowledged that his old-fashioned liberal idealism was out of step with younger members of the British delegation who "may say that if there is another war writers of the individualistic and liberalizing type, like myself and Mr. Aldous Huxley, will be swept away."[27]

Forster's most eloquent statement of his beliefs is found in his celebrated pamphlet, *What I Believe*, published in 1939. Forster maintains that "Tolerance, good temper and sympathy—they are what matter really, and if the human race is not to collapse they must come to the front before long." Yet he acknowledges that "for the moment they are not enough, their action is no stronger than a flower, battered beneath a military jack-boot. They want stiffening, even if the process coarsens them."[28] The strength and flexibility of Forster's idealism in these lines are in keeping with his attitude during the unfolding crisis. Equally illuminating is his position on personal ties: "I hate the idea of causes, and if I had to choose between betraying my country and betraying my friend, I hope I should have the guts to betray my country."[29] Forster also strongly believes in the indefatigable strength of artistic creativity for the good of all: "though Violence remains and is, indeed, the major partner in this muddled establishment, I believe that creativeness remains too, and will always assume direction when violence sleeps."[30] These views come across either overtly or subtly in Forster's letters to Isherwood as the threat from Germany becomes ever more real—and relevant—to England.

Although Forster periodically reveals his fear of the coming disaster in his letters to Isherwood during the mid and late 1930s, Isherwood sees Forster as someone whose values render him impervious to the pressure of outside events. He records in his journal during the Munich crisis of September 1938, "Lunch with Morgan. It pulled me together, a lot. I don't feel I want to see any weaklings, nowadays: they are like sufferers from a dangerously infectious disease. Morgan says he's afraid of going mad—he might suddenly turn and run away from people in the street. But he isn't weak. He's immensely, superhumanly strong."[31] Twenty years later, in his novel, *Down There on a Visit*, Isherwood expresses his love and admiration for his mentor-friend on the eve of the war:

> Well, *my* England is E. M. [Forster]; the antiheroic hero, with his straggly straw mustache, his light, gay blue baby eyes and his elderly stoop. Instead of a folded umbrella or a brown uniform, his emblems are his tweed cap (which is too small for him) and the odd-shaped brown paper parcels in which he carries his belongings from country to town and back again. While the others tell their followers to be ready to die, he advises us to live as if we were immortal. And he really does this himself, although he is as anxious and afraid as any of us, and never for an instant pretends not to be. He and his books and what they stand for are all that is truly worth saving from Hitler. . . . [32]

In January 1939, Isherwood and Auden boarded a ship bound for America, where both would remain during the war.

It was while crossing the Atlantic that Isherwood records making an important realization: "I turned to Auden and said: 'You know, I just don't believe in any of it any more—the united front, the party line, the antifascist struggle. I suppose they're okay, but something's wrong with me. I simply can't swallow another mouthful.' And Auden answered: 'No, neither can I.'"[33] What fueled this realization was Isherwood's discovery that he was a pacifist. He asks himself: "How could I have ever imagined I was anything else? . . . My father taught me, by his life and death, to hate the profession of soldiering."[34] Isherwood also realized that his pacifism derived from his relationship with Heinz. He acknowledged that he would never be able to shoot Heinz or his Nazi companions because "every man in that Army could be somebody's Heinz."[35] Isherwood articulates his position to Forster. In July 1939, he writes: "Force is no good—even to achieve the grandest objectives. One's enemies can only be won over by active goodwill. If you exterminate them, like bugs, the poison only enters into yourself, so you are defeated anyway." Forster does not question Isherwood's pacifism and, in fact, during the same month, writes: "I very much hope that you and everyone will try to keep away—it is clearly your job to see us sink from a distance, if sink we do." Once the war began, however, some writers in England spoke out against Isherwood and Auden's emigration to America.

In a letter to John Lehmann in July 1939, Isherwood confesses his fears that his pacifism will cause him to lose some of his friends: "I am sure this is how I will feel for the rest of my life. I'm afraid this will mean that I shall lose a lot of friends but, I hope, none of the real ones."[36] It was, however, not his pacifism per se that elicited the first published criticism. In the February 1940 issue of the new literary magazine, *Horizon*, the editor, Cyril Connolly offers this commentary on Isherwood and Auden's emigration to America: "Auden is our best poet, Isherwood our most promising novelist. They did not suffer from lack of recognition in England . . . nor have they gone to America to animate the masses, for Auden has been teaching in a New England school and Isherwood writing dialogue in a Hollywood studio. They are far-sighted and ambitious young men with a strong instinct of self-preservation, and an eye on the main chance, who have abandoned what they consider to be the sinking ship of European democracy. . . . "[37]

Isherwood incorrectly attributed the commentary directly or indirectly to Stephen Spender and in a letter to him, defends himself against what he sees as an unjustified attack. Isherwood maintains that his relocation to American was not a sudden flight but rather something he had considered doing for several years. He explains: "I am quite aware, of course, that it seems unpardonable, nowadays, that anybody should be living in safety, in a beautiful climate, earning money. And I often feel guilty about this."[38] This admission of guilt is absent in his letters to Forster—but undoubtedly felt particularly during the height of the bombings—possibly because Forster assured Isherwood that he was doing the right thing by staying out of England. Lehmann attempts to mollify the attack by telling Isherwood that his critics could be divided into two groups: "those who were jealous all along (like [J. B.] Priestley), and those who can't forgive themselves for not having got across in time (like Cyril [Connolly]?)."[39]

The attacks on Isherwood and Auden did not end with the *Horizon* commentary. In an article appearing in the *Spectator* in April 1940, Harold Nicolson chastises not only Isherwood and Auden but also Huxley and Heard for distancing themselves from the war: "How can we proclaim over there [i.e. in America] that we are fighting for the liberated mind, when four of our most liberated intellectuals refuse to identify themselves either with those who fight or with those who oppose the battle?"[40] In June of that same year the following epigram appeared in the *Spectator*:

> 'This Europe stinks', you cried—swift to desert
> Your stricken country in her sore distress.
> You may not care, but still I will assert,
> Since you have left us, here the stink is less.[41]

Forster responded on behalf of his absent friends in a sharp letter of approach published in the *Spectator* on July 5, 1940. He reprimands not only the writer of the epigram but also those who have been "snarling at absent intellectuals." Forster suspects that the motivation for these attacks are not only patriotism and moral outrage but rather "unconscious envy," like that of a schoolboy being punished when all his classmates are out playing. He goes on to warn that such attacks divert attention from those wealthy, influential Englishmen who from their position within "the City and the aristocracy" pose a greater threat to the country.[42]

Forster's wartime letters to Isherwood are an invaluable record of a sensitive yet indefatigable writer's survival during unnerving, exasperating, and dangerous times. In January 1940, Forster confides in Isherwood: "I don't expect to behave well when the trouble starts, shall be offended and maybe go mad, running slowly in large circles with my head down is the way I see myself." Yet when the "trouble" does begin, he holds up quite well, maintaining his accustomed life of social engagements and beginning a regular stint for the B.B.C., broadcasting weekly or bi-weekly talks about literature to India. As bombings continue and restrictions on travel take effect, Forster bemoans to Isherwood about being isolated from the rest of the world: "We get very provincial. Since the war started, I have not even seen the sea. Our lives are interned without being spiritual." There are poignant moments as well. In the midst of the Blitzkrieg, Forster lists a dinner menu cooked by Bob in order to reassure Isherwood that they do in fact have enough to eat; at an another time, he sends Isherwood a postcard signed by Isherwood's friends who had gathered together for Christmas dinner.

Forster's guarded optimism comes across in his failure to give in to doomsday scenarios, even when the windows in his West Hackhurst home are rattling from bombs dropping nearby. In the darkest days of the war, he expresses his hopes for the future in a letter to Cecil Day-Lewis: "Well, let's hope something acceptable will come along—not that Better England which can only last ten minutes, but the better world which will make our lanes and fields again habitable."[43] Forster sees his role as a writer unchanged by the war. He writes in his *Commonplace Book* in 1942:

"Function of the writer in wartime? Same as in peace time." He goes on to note that "We are fighting for self-preservation and can't know what we shall be like until we have won. When we have won we shall arrange this planet in accordance with our characters. Planning now is merely a game."[44] Forster appraises societies of the past and visualizes a better future in an eloquent essay, "The New Disorder": "Viewed realistically, the past is merely a series of messes. . . . And what I hope for and work for to-day is for a mess more favourable to artists than is the present one, for a muddle which will provide them with fuller inspirations and better material conditions."[45] Forster maintains that artistic creativity can survive the dark, horrific times they presently live in: "even when we are universally hurt and frightened, even when the cause of humanity is lost, the possibility of aesthetic order will remain and it seems well to assert it at this moment and to emphasize the one aspect in which the artist is unique."[46]

Meanwhile, Isherwood was coming to terms with his self-imposed exile in California, as a writer and declared pacifist. In a letter to Lehmann in the fall of 1941, Isherwood writes "It's no use—I shall never write anything till this war's over. My voice is changing, like a choirboy's, and I can't find the new notes. But I am more certain than ever that something is happening inside . . . and there will be something to show for this exile."[47] He also attempts to articulate his understanding of pacifism. In another letter, he tells Lehmann, "I am not, and never shall be, a pacifist in the militant, political sense. . . . Pacifism, as I see it, is only helpful when it is part of something much bigger—a whole philosophy of life and a technique of behaviour, and a belief—otherwise it's just tiresome obstructionism."[48] Isherwood's declared pacifism led him, via Gerald Heard and Aldous Huxley, to study and practice Hinduism under the tutelage of Swami Prabhavananda at the Vedanta Society in Los Angeles. In 1943, with the end of the war nowhere in sight, Isherwood informs his agnostic friend, Forster: "I honestly believe that I now believe in 'God'"—although he admits that he cannot actually define what he means by "God." He does, however, "rely on Him, and will turn to Him next time things get tough." Forster replies, "I do not understand your feeling that God will help you—i.e. I don't ever feel that I shall ever be thus helped myself." He claims that he gets through his emotional difficulties on his own. Each one, nevertheless, respects the other's position and the wartime letters focus more on the pleasures, fears, and anxieties of their markedly different daily lives rather than differences in their religious beliefs.

In the 1940s and 1950s, Forster and Isherwood continued to discuss ways to change the ending of *Maurice* into a happy, optimistic one. Since Forster insists that the last chapter as written must remain, Isherwood proposes inserting a new penultimate chapter that brings Maurice and Alec together.[49] Forster, who is insecure about the relevancy of his pre-World War I story, is touched that Isherwood still likes it and cares about it. In response to Isherwood's suggestions, Forster writes in 1952, "I was not at all sure that you would still like M[aurice] and feel very happy." He begins drafting a new chapter that is eventually inserted. In gratitude for Isherwood's help and no doubt also an acknowledgment of Isherwood's faithful encouragement over the years, Forster assigned Isherwood the rights to publish *Maurice* in the United States after Forster's death.

When viewed together the letters describe an evolving friendship. Despite the fact that Forster and Isherwood hit it off well immediately, they develop intimacy gradually. In his first letter to Isherwood, Forster begins: "Dear Isherwood—we do drop 'Mr', don't we?" Forster's dropping of "Mr" and use of the last name alone (which Isherwood does as well in his letters) is in keeping with the familiar yet formal style of address male students usually adopted at elite universities such as Oxford and Cambridge at this time. After addressing one another in their letters as "Isherwood" and "Forster" and closing with "yours" followed by signatures of their complete names for several years, they begin to close with "love," and shortly thereafter address and sign off to one another by first name. One can trace this growing familiarity and affection in the changing content and tone of the letters themselves. Isherwood reveals more and more information about his relationship with Heinz, Forster freely mentions Bob, and as the political climate in Europe becomes more dire, they both let down their guard, expressing their fears and anxieties.

In 1935, Forster and Bob traveled to Amsterdam to visit Isherwood and Heinz and spent several days together as two "couples." In that milieu Isherwood and Forster would relate to one another not merely as disciple and mentor but also as friends having a good time with their respective partners. Isherwood later recalls that visit: "Forster, beaming through his spectacles, was probably enjoying himself most, since Bob Buckingham was with him. They kept exchanging glances full of fun and affection."[50] Although Forster writes upon his return to England that he enjoyed himself but regretted that they had little time to spend alone with one another (and presumably talk about their writing), the visit drew him closer to Isherwood; for it is in this letter that Forster first addresses him as "Christopher" and closes with "love, Morgan." In subsequent letters, Forster closes with "much love" and "very much love." In the postwar years, one can read Forster's continued affection for Isherwood in his excited anticipation of Isherwood's visits to England. Isherwood's letters reveal that he considers Forster much more than a mentor. In the mid-1930s he writes with concern and worry about Forster's health following a series of operations Forster underwent. Fearing that Forster is suffering from food shortages during the war, he sends him food packages. When at the height of the bombings too much time elapses without word from Forster, Isherwood sends a telegram begging him for reassurance that he is safe.

Although there are very few letters after 1952, Forster and Isherwood maintained their friendship. Isherwood regularly paid visits to Forster in England. Their last written correspondence dates from 1966 (four years before Forster' death at the age of 91). Suffering the effects of several strokes, Forster dictates a brief letter to Isherwood: "Much love to you, naturally & to your work though I am sorry it is not bringing you to England." P. N. Furbank, Forster's biographer, remarks that "[t]he central preoccupation of his life, it was plain to see, was friendship, and he had a rather special attitude towards friendship. He never casually dropped friends, as most people do, out of forgetfulness or through change of circumstance. . . . [I]f someone became a friend of his, he might expect to remain so for life."[51] This observation is echoed by Don Bachardy, Isherwood's companion for more than thirty years and who had visited Forster together with Isherwood in the 1950s and 1960s. Bachardy remarked that when Forster admitted someone into his inner circle, he was a friend for life.[52] Obviously, Isherwood was one such intimate friend. The letters reproduced here trace this mutually intimate, long-lasting friendship within the contexts of the extraordinary—and everyday—social, cultural, and political events of the mid-twentieth century.

E. M. Forster
Drawing from life by
Don Bachardy,
September 1961

**Christopher
Isherwood**
Drawing from life by
Don Bachardy,
November 1, 1976

I

The 1930s

12-10-32

West Hackhurst,
Abinger Hammer,
Dorking.

Dear Isherwood—we do drop "Mr," don't we?—

I was very glad to have "All the Conspirators." I don't like it as much as "The Memorial,"[1] but that is not the point, and there are things in it I do like very much. Thank you for sending it, and for the letter in it, and for "The Seven Pillars,"[2] which I found at the club, packed with incredible care.

I hope you found your friend better than the news suggested. It is an awful worry, that illness at this time of the year. I'm very sorry you've got this on you, and annoyed with life generally for being so often *just* wrong. Again and again the wonderful chariot seems ready to move.

I have read The Orators[3] and liked what I understood of it and what I couldn't too. There's a very impressive voice at it, and an active eye. Only, I had a queer feeling that everything might suddenly stop, and the lights of common day be switched on. This may merely be because I know Auden is a schoolmaster: it is the profession which, after hospital-nurses, disquiets me most, and renders all my judgments hysterical.—I think that last ode is very agitating and marvellous: I get from it all sorts of sounds and sights outside the ones he actually provides.

I hope you'll write again and let me know when you are back in England, and I'll let you know if I ever come to Berlin. I hope your novel is going well. I am broadcasting, worse than schoolmastering [*sic*] it might be argued, still I do get anonymous letters signed "a disgusted listener" or "the old ladies who remember you 20 years ago at Perugia and can't help feeling sorry."

Yours
EM Forster

* * *

[October 1932]   Berlin W. 30
                                                          Nollendorfstrasse 17
                                                                  Bei Thurau

Tuesday.
Dear Forster,

Thank you for your letter. I didn't send you my novel so much because I thought it has any particular merit as because I once refused to show it you, and this seemed to me afterwards silly.

I'm glad you like the Orators. Auden isn't by any means what one expects from a schoolmaster. Perhaps he more resembles a hospital nurse—a comic one in a film. He is coming out here at Christmas. I suppose there is no chance of your joining us?

Thank you for asking after my friend. We went to the doctor the other day, and I'm afraid there's no doubt that one of the lungs is already affected. This weather doesn't help much, either.

I feel as if I am shortly going to enter upon a period of travelling, half against my will. I don't want to start shifting about, and yet I know I shall never be happy till I've visited the places one sees on cigarette cards. Did you go to India for any special reason, or just because it's such a long way off?

I am writing an indecent bumptious stupid sort of novel about Berlin which I fear you won't like.[4] It's strange, I long to do very moving Dickensy scenes with tears, and when it comes to the point I dry up like a stone and write something venomous. It's as if I had some nasty green poison in my system.

My mother heard you over the wireless and said: what a charming voice.

There was a cabinet meeting here the other day to discuss the permissible limits of bathing dresses. Prussia seems to be in the hands of the Roman Catholics.

                                                                     Yours
                                                       Christopher Isherwood

                                *   *   *

As From: 4-1-33
                                                      West Hackhurst,
                                                      Abinger Hammer,
                                                             Dorking.

Dear Isherwood,

I was so glad to hear form [sic] you—have been meaning to write—and so glad you saw I'd had the pleasure of mentioning *The Memorial*. (Your mother thought my voice sweeter than ever, I hope!)

It's exciting about Manchuria, but I won't mention it even very definitely to myself, for it would certainly be annoying to come to Berlin and find you weren't there. I've several times dallied with the thought of coming. But my voice incommoded me, and though it is now happily silenced I am [taught?] up in the memoir of a friend—Lowes Dickinson. It's so long since I've written a book that it feels like opening a tomb.

If there's no news your end there must be less here—except that between the last paragraph of this letter and the present paragraph I went to bed and dreamt that, although still writing to you, I had been to Russia. What can this mean? No doubt someone can tell one. But I reflected in my dream that I should be able to continue this letter in a more interesting way, and I felt complacent.

I will write again, so will you, and specially you, for I want to hear about the Manchurian plan when it develops. You did not mention (in this letter) about your friend. I was very sorry indeed about the bad news which you gave me previously. It is such a wretched time of year too. I do hope things are going rather better. And good wishes for 1933.

                                                           Yours ever
                                                          EM Forster

*   *   *

[Postmark: Abinger Hammer, Surrey, April 13, 1933]

Dear Isherwood,

I was very pleased to get your card on my return from Ireland. I wish you would be so kind as to ring me up on Saturday morning before 10.0 if you are in town, so that we may see when we can meet. It is Terminus 5804. I am not there for the moment but in bed in the country and feeling rather muddled. However I shall be there, if somewhat complicated by an Indian. I do hope we shall meet soon.

Yours ever
EM Forster
Thursday

*   *   *

Monday [April 1933?]   West Hackhurst,
Abinger Hammer,
Dorking.

Dear Isherwood,

Symbolically enough[,] the roof of this house is falling off. I have to put it on again and I can't be sure of doing so before Tuesday evening. I must therefore take back the suggestion I made to you, much to my regret. I do hope I haven't put you out. I hope to get up Wednesday. If you could send me a p[ost] c[ard] (here) as to your movements this week[,] I should be grateful.

Yours ever,
EM Forster

*   *   *

[April 27, 1933]   West Hackhurst,
Abinger Hammer,
Dorking.

Dear Isherwood,

I am very sorry not to see you again. I count on your letting me know when next you are in England. I don't suppose I shall get to Germany. Bob and I did talk of it for his holidays in the latter half of June, but no doubt we shan't get further than England. I was very glad you liked Maurice, especially the part about Alec, which I have just read again. An example of domesticity, such as you were asking for, is presumably to be found at "Tisselcot"[?] but I daren't thus instal them, no, nor even under a hay-stack. I think what might happen is a permanent relationship, but with all sorts of vagaries, fears, illnesses, distractions, fraying out at its edges, and this would take a long time to represent. One might shorten it, perhaps, if one made them take a vow, and Maurice could take it, but I doubt about Alec, as about myself. We are, both of us, more likely to look back and realise that we have, after all, sacrificed enough to bring the thing off.— I've some other stuff to show you some time, thought it better than *Maurice* until recently, but begin to have my doubts; as you say, why shouldn't one date? [i.e., be dated]—William [Plomer] will have given you my message, that the MS [manuscript]. is to be left at the Reform Club. I don't come up till Monday. I wanted to hear more about the German with whom you might be going to Brazil.

Yours ever
EM Forster

* * *

[1933?]　　　　　　　　　　　　　　　　　　　　　　Reform Club,
　　　　　　　　　　　　　　　　　　　　　　　　Pall Mall. S.W.1.

Dear Isherwood,

Your address is pleasantly reassuring. However, look at mine. Do send me your promised letter, in fact it is to secure it that I write, for I have not much in the way of news. Who's the friend with you? The one who was ill? I do hope he's on the mend. Also have you seen Gerald Heard whom I have just heard as being in Greece too.

God, this is going to be a dull letter. Still, why not? I have just come from a committee meeting of the London Library, which was presided over by Sir Arnold Wilson, victor in the Hitchin bye[-]election with an immensely reduced majority, and sister to Mona Wilson, my friend. A shit of a man. And last month, our chairman was Lord Riddell. I had just finished, unknown to my fellow members, a dialogue between a porter and a passenger, which is not publishable nor indeed very amusing. Sir Arnold looked as if he had just finished with Lady Wilson, and Lord Riddell was not there at all. We discussed Stephen Graham, who at the last annual meeting had been the sole dissentient to our application for a Royal Charter. We had got our Charter, and the question was whether our report should be sullied with the mention of Graham's name. Not a name I want to see in other places, but here. . . . It was finally decided that his name should be omitted but his protest recorded, and we parted fairly pleased.

[no closing or signature]

*   *   *

July 8 [1933]

L'ILE ST NICHOLAS
CHALIA
BEOETIA
GREECE

Dear Forster,

I wonder where you are and what you are doing? If you happen to be in Greece, please come and call. All you have to do is to get to Chalkis by train, then persuade some farmer to bring you as far as Chalia with his cart, from whence half an hour's brisk donkey ride will bring you to the shore. From the shore you must shout very loud, and I will come over in a boat and fetch you.

It is not really very nice here. The landscape is superb but it is far too hot. And there are too many insects and body vermin. Also we have a permanent water shortage as water has to be brought from the mainland in cans. We live in tents and await the building of the house. It is promised to be ready by the middle of August.

You know Greece well, of course. What do you make of it? Can you fit Plato and Sophocles on to these mountains covered with spiky bushes and these vallies [sic] like ovens, full of sand, inhabited by goats and vultures? I can't, but I expect that is because I had the wrong sort of classical education, designed to make the classical Greeks as much as possible like Varsity rowing blues. The Greeks nowadays seem so strident and cunning and picturesque. The Spartan toughness remains—I see that. But I simply can't picture even remotely any of them caring about the Golden Mean or the Good Life.

How are things with you? I see your Irish autobiographer was duly translated[,] published and praised.[5] I wish I could read him, but I shall do so as soon as I'm back in England. I would leave this place tomorrow but have spent so much money getting here that retreat is not easy. I believe I really shall settle down in England this time. China reappears on the horizon, however.

I think very often about you and our day in the country at Charlton's.[6] Also about that manuscript.[7] How I wish you'd publish it. I think it would do good. I am so utterly weary of these *impure* books. They are like the salt mixed with sugar which we've unfortunately had to eat for the last week, owing to a slight mistake on the part of the cook.

I stopped this letter for five minutes in order to torture two blood sucking flies to death. Living here has made me fiendishly cruel. We are always murdering some insect or animal. I feel like Macbeth. This—by the way— is another thing I can't quite reconcile with the classics. The Greeks simply revel in and feast on cruelty. Or is this a mere tourist's impression?

Please write to me. Nobody ever does, it seems. I need a letter a day to keep the horrors away.

Yours ever
Christopher Isherwood

* * *

16-7-33

West Hackhurst,
Abinger Hammer,
Dorking.

Dear Isherwood

I am so very pleased to get your letter and reply at once. I did reply at once to your post-card too, as you will see from the enclosed, but you will also see why it was never finished. And perhaps this letter will be as dull. Yet I have a feeling to the contrary and will at all events not wait until tomorrow to make sure.

Do I know Greece well? I should hope so. I was there in 1903 and have not been there since. I got tuned[?] up [boarding school slang] by a modern Greek who stole another archeologist's coat before we landed and said I had given it to him. For I was an archeologist in 1903, just as I was a surgeon from 1915–19 in Egypt, and a physiologist in 1924 at Stockholm and an ethnologist for 1927 in Africa. What remains, however, to our present purpose is a remark made to the surgeon by Cavafy, who was himself an official in the Third Irrigation Circle and a great poet. Cavafy said "Never forget about the Greeks that we are bankrupt. That is the difference between us and the ancient Greeks and, my dear Forster, between us and yourselves. Pray, my dear Forster, that you—you English with your capacity for adventure—never lose your capital, otherwise you will resemble us, restless, shifty, liars . . ." Which is an answer of a sort to your question. And I think that both the cruelty and the exaltation of cunning could be paralleled in the 5th century B.C.

My own questions are of a different type and vary in vulgarity from "Who are you with?" to "Where does the money come from to build a house?" You need not answer any of them when you write but I do hope you will write. I am still in England and still unable to decide whether she is good or evil, but at the moment of writing occupied in loving her and in wondering how you could have left the zinnias and the gooseberries, which I have just gathered, for your goats and their flesh. The bother of talking and of moving increases as I get older, so I would rather talk English to Bob even though my mother does think his voice common, and he drives round the western counties by him in a car, advancing to be sure into Wales, but retreating from it on the grounds that it was un-homey, and that the Welsh did not wash. We were away for a fortnight, and how, life being like this, any of these questions ever will be decided I can't see. I mean I look back in my own case on a constant alternation of emotions about England. Europe and anti-Europe. I wish I felt that "old experience might attain to something like prophetic strain." Then one could know whether to live here or abroad in time.

Of the people you met that day at Esher,[8] our hosts are much as usual. Joe Ackerley is back for a holiday in France, and Dawkins is taking one in Greece at the beginning of August. I don't know whether you wish him to be given your address. I shall give it him if you say, but not otherwise. Bob I have mentioned and also myself. I have just been to Cambridge but find it rather queer. I can't tell you how glad I am you liked my book [*Maurice*]. Yes, if the pendulum keeps swinging in its present direction it might get published in time. But the more one meets decent and sensible people, of whom there are now a good few, the more does one forget the millions of beasts and idiots who still prowl in the darkness, ready to gibber and devour. I think I had a truer view of civilisation thirty years ago, when I regarded myself as hiding a fatal secret. Though I am of course much more civilised myself now than I was then, and so are we all, those good few of us who count.— What do you mean by "impure books"? I daresay I agree, but don't just know what you mean.

I anticipate to be here or in my flat till the end of the year. Now do please write. I will send you Twenty Years a growing[9] tomorrow.

Yours ever
EM Forster

＊   ＊   ＊

July 22 [1933]

L'ILE ST NICHOLAS
CHALIA
BEOETIA
GREECE

Dear Forster,

Thank you very much for your letter, which came as a consolation this morning after three postless days—the village shop keeper had gone away to a feast in another village, so we couldn't get at our mail. Thank you also in advance for Twenty Years A Growing. It will probably arrive soon. I am longing to read something other than detective stories. Why are detective stories almost always so badly written? I suppose because they're mostly by maths masters at Public Schools. I am making a collection of phrases from them. The best so far is: "He bestowed upon her what was intended as a confidential embrace." Pleasing also, because utterly cryptic, is: "He was a decent clean living type of young chap, though his behaviour at times left something to be desired."

The island is leased by a friend of mine named Turville Petre. His is the money which will pay for the house. He knows P[ro]f[essor] Dawkins and extends a hearty invitation. The best way to reach us—as I think I told you—is to take the train to Chalkis. Other inhabitants of the island include a German Communist named Erwin Hansen, who cooks. He has known Turville P for a long time, and took this opportunity of escaping from the Nazis. There is also a German working boy of eighteen named Heinz Neddermeyer. He is not the one who was ill. The one who was ill came to an end. It had never really been a success. He is now in happier financial circumstances and, seemingly, much better. If you wade through my next novel, you will gather a good deal of information about him and our relationship. As for Heinz, I hope you will see him, because I plan to come with him to England in the Autumn. The obstacles to my doing so are purely external—I don't know how easy or difficult it is to get permission for a German to land, or how long he would be allowed to stay. Do you happen to know anything about this? My great problem at the moment is where to live. I ask nothing better, temporarily, than to stay in England, if we're both allowed to.

The days here are all alike. They are remarkable to me only for my failure or non-failure to work at my novel. We live on microscopic scraps of gossip. Everybody exhaustively discusses every remark made or alleged to have been made by every body else. Favourite topics are: The erotic performances of the poultry and their results. The Price of Food. Action of the Bowels. There used to be several Greek boys here, as sort of servants, but they mostly stole or developed venereal diseases, and now there is only one. The nights are quiet but the days are deafening—the hack-saw rasping of the cicades [sic], the quacking of the ducks and the demoniac yelling of the Greek masons, who yell louder and louder as the sun gets hotter. The house really is nearly finished at least.

Do write again soon. God knows, my letters aren't worth answering, but write in human charity.

By "impure" books I meant adulterated books—just as jam is adulterated or milk. A good example which I read the other day is Susan Glaspell's "Ambrose Holt & Family."[10] Have you read it? It all starts off so genuine. And then, suddenly, half way through, one gets a curious whiff. Only a whiff. And yet, all the time, Miss Glaspell is being so charming, so entertaining, that one hardly likes to say anything and at length can only very diffidently suggest: I say, do you think—er, I mean, is this *quite* all right . . . ? But the whiff gets stronger and stronger, until, at last, the whole fraud is exposed, and one sees as plain as daylight that the book isn't what it's pretending to be, or what the publisher says it is inside the cover—Albatross Edition—but merely a *description* of some of the effects which the authoress would like to produce, and can't.

Heinz has begun to sing: "Good bye, my Bluebell"—all the English he knows—so, I must stop.

Can't you send me the dialogue between the porter and the passenger?[11]

Yours ever
Christopher Isherwood

*   *   *

[September 22, 1933]

West Hackhurst,
Abinger Hammer,
Dorking.

Dear Isherwood,

You did give me a turn over the German book you so kindly lent me. I sprang out of bed, certain I had lost it, but a book which had been called overnight "Toadstools of the British Country Side" turned back into it as I touched it, so I live. Another cause for my optimism—more solid than my great thought of the week which you saw in the Observer and which must have come out of a rather bitter article I wrote against the public schools, attacking General[?] Sir Archibald Montgomery Massingberd, Lord Goschen, the Rev. F. C. Day and others by name.[12] At least I can think of no other source.

[typed addendum on back side]

22/9/33

Exactly. Have let this lie about for weeks[,] only just returned your book, done nothing about seeing whether your German friend can stop in England. I'm very sorry. I want to see you as soon as you can manage it. I am just going to the Woolfs for the week end (Monks House, Rodnell, Lewes), and a line there at once would catch me. I expect to be in London Monday evening. Could we meet then, or could we lunch Tuesday? Please communicate if this reaches you, and when I get your communication I'll wire definitely. You know my London address—26 Brunswick Square, W.C., telephone Terminus 5804.

EM Forster [signed]

*   *   *

17-2-34
West Hackhurst,
Abinger Hammer,
Dorking.

Dear Isherwood,
I am coming up Tuesday evening. Could you come round to 26 Brunswick Square at about 9.0? Or I could meet you elsewhere. Send me a line here and if Tuesday does not suit you please make some alternative suggestion.

I shall like seeing you, and I like calling you Isherwood. This cataract of Christian names—Tombobblewalterall—too often disappears into the abyss.

I am trying to read "Behind the Smoke Screen" for review purposes[13], but simply haven't the pluck. It is rather humiliating. I don't think any one could possess social nerves today, unless he was a fool or a communist, and I am too intelligent to be the first, and too old to be the second. All that I can do is to work out a new private ethic which, in the outbreak of a war, might be helpful to me. The individual is more than ever the goods.

Yours ever,
EM Forster

I am O.K. personally, as we call it.

*   *   *

S.S. Zeelandia
April 5 [1934]

Dear Forster,

This is just to let you know where I am. In a fog, as a matter of fact, hooting somewhere off the Isle of Wight. We are trying to get near Southampton, to take on board a Mr. Abercromby, about whom Heinz and I indulge in the liveliest speculations, as he is also (as the neat little card on his cabin door, next to ours, informs us) going to Las Palmas. We arrive there on the 12th. Not very thrilling, but it ought to be warm and nice, and all the really interesting places are so expensive. As for Tahiti, there was no time to catch the boat. It left on Monday from Marseilles, and the French authorities demand the most complicated formalities. Our address will be:

c/o Banco Hispano Americano
Las Palmas
Canary Islands

Do send me a line. I have just read The Passage to India again, in the Albatross Edition. If I were a parish lady I should say: "I want to thank you for writing it"—because I really feel just like that. I hadn't read it for ten years, nearly—when it first came out—and I see how it has influenced everything I feel about novel writing. That picnic. I could hardly go on reading. It was like the most delicious sweets. I was afraid that one of them *must* be nasty, because the others were so succulent. But they weren't, and I finished the box.

Well, if I go on like this, I shall make you blush.

Anyhow, do write soon. I feel as if you were with us on this ship.

I hope you've been seeing Viertel.[14] I've never known him to be so excited about meeting anyone. "He has wonderful eyes," said V.—and added anxiously: "He is not living like a monk, I hope?" No, I answered, I believed not.

Yours ever
Christopher Isherwood

*   *   *

The Woolf's. Rodnell. 7-4-34

Dear Isherwood,

I was very glad to hear from you and learn that you are both in the same boat. It all sounds nice. Grand Canary will be warm if clear, and I wish I was in Mr Abercrombie's pyjamas. Here the cold is incessant and I am irritated at being left so much "to myself" in the various short visits I have been paying. First there was a preparatory school in Dorsetshire for Easter where my host was either fomenting the toes of the little boys, or at Church, or thinking about Rudolf Steiner while he put all the wrong letters into the wrong envelopes and had to write them all again. Then, near Salisbury, was Stephen Tennant, sick and unable to be in the room with his guest for more than 20 minutes twice a day, and covering his eyes with a bandage when he drove to town, in case the scenery made him giddy. And here, with less excuse, I think, are the W[oolf]s, who read, Leonard the Observer and Virginia the Sunday Times, and then retired to literary shanties to write till lunch. At least L. has just come out, but I, piqued, continue my letter to you, and he, not displeased, cuts the dead wood out of a Buddleia with a small rusty saw. No doubt I am exacting or deficient in resources, but I am fed up with these two-day visits where I am left to myself. It's a bit of sham modernity, like the silent greeting. When I entertain—but I get out of that by never being able to entertain. When you entertain—but you can get round that by suggesting I "join" you somewhere sometime. That's quite different, and possibly always better. Hospitality, where art thou? Gone down the general drain, perhaps, with free hold estates and pairs of bays.

But Viertel—after what you say I really shall invite him to the Reform Club. The fact that he praised my eyes is very reassuring, because one's eyes are always with one, they do not vary from day to day like the complexion or the intelligence. Let him gaze his fill. I shall certainly like to see him again and to thank him—which will probably be a mistake—for a most remarkable and enjoyable evening. I have often thought about it and described it to other people without interesting them. It *is* a milieu—so energetic[,] friendly & horrible. I can't believe everything isn't going to crash when such a waggon [*sic*] gets so many stars hitched behind. Every film I ever see will now appear incredibly good, also I shall suppose that it has allowed people like you and Heintz to escape for a bit into the sun. Virginia has now come out, aprony[?] from some article or passage, and has suggested a photograph should be taken of me. L. thinks it is a good idea, and continues to saw the buddleias. It is 5 minutes to one—no, one, the bell rings, and I must jolly well lock this letter up during lunch, or it'll get read. I know these particular ethics. This evening we go to a meeting of the Memoir Club, at Maynard Keynes, and if this letter were read there, and aloud by me, it might be the star turn.[15]

12-4-34

Memoir Club and much else over. I am back at home, quarrelling with my ground landlord through our respective solicitors. He lives 100 yards from me, but before we can exchange a reply there is

letter from self to sol[icitor]
letter from self's sol[icitor] to his
letter from his sol[icitor] to him [entire list is enclosed in a bracket on the left]
letter from him to his sol[icitor]side, [and written next to it:"one week, with luck"]
letter from his sol[icitor] to mine
letter from my sol[icitor] to me

17-4-34

Still waiting for the reply, and think I shall go to the South of France. Bob is ill, or rather laid up, and I can only see him in his own home. I must send this letter at once, or it will never go. Please write and tell me the colour of Mr Abercrombie's pyjamas. I do hope you will have a good time. Please give my regards to Heintz.

Yours ever,
EM Forster

[Postscript:] My blow for British freedom is struck on Thursday.

*   *   *

c/o Banco Hispano Americano
Las Palmas
Canary Isles
April 30 [1934]

Dear Forster,

Thank you for your letter. Mr. Abercromby was a distinct disappointment—an elderly man with a military moustache and dishonest blue eyes, he approved of Dollfuss because he had never seen a word written against him in the Times. He was very informative about how to avoid tipping hotel attendants in the [. . . ?]evant[?] or the best way of getting a good cabin on a liner. Other key-phrases included: "My friends tell me I ought to work with a camera." "It's what I call a potty little island." "He's a strong-looking devil" (We were in Madiera harbour and watching a boy diving for coins). "They kept the two of us waiting—just like servants." "She was a very smart girl—I'm not speaking immorally." "The German is no good; he goes to pieces at thirty." "One of these tripper hotels where you see young chits stripped to the belly-button."

Here there are black volcanic hills and white flat-topped houses; an African town, with palms. A sand beach protected by a reef from sharks. The inhabitants are beautiful; quite a lot of them fair-haired, the remnants of an earlier race, the Guanchos, who worshipped one God, had blue eyes and imprisoned anyone who spoke to a woman without being introduced. Why don't you come here, instead of France? It would be much cheaper. Up in the mountains, the peasants live in caves and mix poison for their relatives. There are banana groves and cathedrals and extinct craters and no snakes. We have a lovely room on the roof of the hotel, looking across the bay to the peak of Tenerife. We like it so much here that we're staying another month. It isn't in the least a fashion resort, like Funchal. Some of the characters from a Passage to India are staying here, but they don't bother us. They go to some mysterious club and play golf and come home too tired to be aggressive. There are also Germans who bow from the waist and say: Permit. My name is Schenck. The Canary Islanders themselves are gay and handsome and are just discovering, with enormous excitement, the Cocteau decadence cult of 1925. The only statue in the Public Gardens is [dedicated] to a poet. There is a Carlos Marx Street. Real live canaries fly about from palm tree to palm tree like sparrows.

I have ordered your blow for British Freedom and await it eagerly. At present I am reading "Great British Modern Plays." Well, at any rate, I suppose they're British.

Do write again soon, and consider seriously if you couldn't come. It such a simple journey; and no customs examination when you arrive.

Best love
Christopher Isherwood

Goodness knows what happened to Mr. A. He disappeared as we landed.

*   *   *

15-5-34   [St. Rémy-en-Provence]

Dear Isherwood,

I was getting on all right here until your letter arrived when I wished I wasn't here but with you. I enjoy myself here as much as usual and always wonder why the usual isn't a little more. My friend and his wife are of peasant stock; intelligent, affectionate, gay. Provençal cookery[,] which I like, all natural good sense and natural good taste. [C]omfortable rough little house without taint of artiness and bang against that rough little range of hills which runs from Tarascon to Cavaillon, peasants coming in and so on. Why isn't it acute pleasure here? I think I don't ever get more intimate with my friends or with the scenery, it must be that, and I know that the peasants are always women or old men. So I am wanting to come to the Canary Island and since I can't do that [I want] to go home. It's too quiet. Amusement or work can alone stop one from brooding on the coming smash. My particular impasse for the moment is: (i) Nothing can be done/ (ii) yet the people I admire most try to do something—and character is *the thing I care about*, both in myself and others,/ (iii) but if one has realised (i) then any attempt to avert disaster is only an attempt to show how admirable one is/ (iv) which isn't admirable.

I think the explanation of the impasse is that the human race has never before been faced with a world wide dilemma, and the individual has the right to be staggered at it and to pity himself at having been born just now: a right he is still too shy to exercise.

At this point we went in the bus to Avignon and I tried to buy you a tie, like the one Bob bought his brother the railway porter three years ago. But I couldn't see one.

I ought perhaps to make clear that the friends I am stopping with are called Charles and Marie Mauron, that he translated A Passage to India into French, that their house is called Mas d'Angiranz, and that it is close to "Les Monuments" of St Rémy-de-Provence. They pay for everything (which they cannot afford) so my holiday will only cost me £10. Still I do wish I was[*sic*] on the Canaries.

If Mr Abercromby had disappointed you less he might have me more. I can't tell you how glad I am to know about him, nor how lightly I condole with you for a companionship which produced so many memorable phrases. I do not mind his having disappeared. I hope that my Blow for British Freedom has reached you by now. I struck a puff for property too before leaving England: I arranged that the lease of the house where I live should be extended to cover my mother's lifetime and I refused to sell a freehold wood adjoining it, which the landlord, Lord Farrer, tried to make me do. Instead I devised a compromise which has been very well thought of, but I have not the patience to write it out for you. Indeed I will stop for Charles Mauron is taking this to the post. Please write home. I really have no reason for not coming, but I am unequipped and slightly imbecile. I am *determined*—and few things stop one when one's determined—to spend next January out of England, and if you are within reach and sitting anyth[?] still I should like to join you. Bob has been ill—I forget whether I told you that—but now he is better. It's partly he who keeps me hanging about near home. My remembrance of the past and my sense of the future have made these present years and days seem very exceptional.

I am reading J. Romains Hommes [de] Bonne Volonté[16] which I meant to quote somewhere in this letter, but [the] letter has to go as I've already told you once.

Best love,
EM Forster

*   *   *

c/o Banco Hispano Americano
Las Palmas
Canary Islands.
May 28 [1934]

Dear Forster,

Thank you for your letter. I am very sorry you aren't coming, though I hardly expected you would. Certainly let us be together next January, if we are both alive and at liberty. This is a time when I want to see as much as possible of all my few real friends. We must get together more, prepare some kind of defences, consolidate. At least disaster isn't coming upon us suddenly this time, as in 1914. We all expect it, so we ought to behave better. I doubt if we shall.

I have just finished your book. It moved me very much. You make me see him, or imagine I see him, very vividly.[17] Today we have been in the mountains and I have thought about you and Dickinson all day. I feel I understand your books so much better now. There is so much in your generation which my generation just dismisses stupidly and hastily, because it seems quiet and dull and we are all, or most of us, little Macbeths who have killed Duncan and have to go on murdering and murdering. And when one of us does turn academic, he is usually so shallow and tidy and anxious. I wish there was more of your own life in the book, and I suppose you wanted deliberately to keep it out.

My own novel doesn't get finished and changes its form daily. I read chiefly books about what is going to happen in Europe and study maps. Then, when I have supped full with horrors, I terrify the unfortunate Heinz. Still, there are brighter moments. It is sometimes so beautiful here. It would be strange, but not inconceivable, to live in Las Palmas always. A few of the inhabitants are charming civilised human beings. They sit out under the palm trees until two o'clock in the morning talking about painting, or meet in each others' rooms to listen to the Kreutzer Sonata, like undergraduates. And they are gay and gentle. There is one boy of eighteen, a sculptor, who is a genius, I think. I have photographed two of his figures and will send them to you if they come out well. He is very quiet and shy and has epileptic fits.

Please write again soon. I like getting your letters. Let me close with a fashion note from the Daily Palma Post (Palma in Mallorca; *no* connection with us)[:]

"Anne's beach wear hinges on shorts, which are shown for use in the sea or on the promenade back of the water's edge. The close-fitting bathing-suits are also shown for the benefit of those who feel the need of the most revealing attire."

Best love,
Christopher Isherwood

[handwritten addition]

I quite forgot to tell you about our only female friend. Her name is Leonora Pohly. We met her a month ago, wandering about the mountains at sunrise with her arms full of flowers. She has red poodle hair and a blunt nose like a dog, and is covered with freckles. She comes to see us every day and we have got quite fond of her. During the war and the revolution, she was one of the imperial gardeners at Potsdam. All the proper gardeners had gone to the front, and a most weird collection of cranks, cissies [sic] and mental deficients were wandering about the greenhouses, composing poems on the plants. One of them said to Pohly, speaking of an unusual wallflower: "It is dark as the ebony writing-table of a misunderstood woman."

Pohly rendered us one signal service: she got the German Consul here to change the profession in Heinz' passport. Up to now it has been: manservant—a fatal word largely instrumental in all the trouble we have had. Now it is: Language Student—the Consul's own, extraordinary choice. He might as well have written: Archdeacon. However, now that Heinz is a language student, he has decided to learn languages—any languages; the more the better. He stops guests in the corridor and says, beaming all over his face, in Spanish: my friend is very ill. This is so far his only Spanish sentence. It gives rise to misunderstandings, as you can imagine.

*   *   *

9-8-34

West Hackhurst,
Abinger Hammer,
Dorking.

Dear Isherwood,

I was very glad to get your letter and feel that there is a sort of alliance between us. Let me know when you get to England—you may even be there already. Some of your news was good. I do hope that Heintz will have no further trouble with the customs. Yes—let's hope that if there's a crash we shall all behave well, but I do not even know yet what "well" will be. It is all so inconceivable. I work up into a fuss about it for a little, and then calm down, write the Book of the Abinger Pageant,[18] go in a char[-]à[-]banc to Oxford with eighteen policemen on Bank Holiday, prepare to entertain Mrs Myslakowska, who tried to seduce me in Cracow two years ago in order to get rid of her husband, and is now in England.[19] Then I get fussed, and contribute Notes on Passing Events to the newspapers, which you would easily follow if I sent them to you, or go on a deputation to the Attorney General in connection with the Sedition Bill.[20] I think it is sensible and suitable, this alternation between fuss and calm, and I gather you are practicing it yourself. It is the right conduct for our time—better than all calm, and far[,] far better than all fuss. But if the war started, I don't know what would be right. The very meaning of words would change, and "war" [would] be the most meaningless of them all.

I meant to write you a letter full of news, as you might like some, but it all boils down to my having a certain amount of trouble at home, and very little elsewhere. Next week I shall go to town to see Bob. The week after he will stop with me at my flat. The day after that (Aug. 22nd) I go to Falmouth and pay a visit to the Hilton Youngs. I have known H.Y. a great many years and am fond of him, and I get on with her. Her son, Peter Scott, is rather an enigma, a toad without a jewel perhaps, though a pleasant toad. He paints pictures of geese, pictures of geese, pictures of geese, pictures of geese, and no sooner has Sir Philip Sassoon or Mr Amery[21] opened them than he has painted still more pictures of geese. He has also written a short story about a crane, which is rather on my mind, as I have lost it. However, that is surely enough about Peter Scott. I expect to be quite comfortable down there, but not to stop very long. I would rather like to start some more writing for one thing. I am very glad to have done that Lowes Dickinson book.

We will talk about January when you return. Have you been reading anything to speak of? I am just finishing Anna Karenina, which I never got through before. I do not think it is very good—except for the balancing of the two couples, which is certainly marvellous. Any other writer would have had to tether them into their position with a few strings, but Tolstoy leaves them to float naturally in his air. I can't think of any other novelist, dramatist, etc. who could do this. It's neither a plan, nor is it a happy chance. It's something for which there's no word in criticism. I didn't even know Tolstoy could do it—I don't remember anything of the type in War and Peace—and in this respect A.K. has been a great pleasure. But the characters are not really masterpieces, Anna has been much overpraised and Kitty's nothing at all. And what's still more disappointing and surprising to me, the sense of family groups—so overwhelming in W. & P. and so desirable here—never gets conveyed. Perhaps all the characters ought to have been introduced as children.

However, that's enough for Anna. She has taken even more room than Peter Scott's geese geese geese, and I don't know whether you've read her or want to.

What I did mean to say, when I asked you whether you were reading, was to ask you whether you were writing. I was looking forward to your novel so much.[22] However, if you can't get it down it can't be helped. I don't suppose it matters. It's much better not to write under the tyranny of time. "This, this, have I achieved before civilisation crashes"? No, no—I feel advancing at this point to some Grand Pronouncement. However, it will not come. I must knock off and write a line to Bob, who is at this moment—which is midnight—driving about a mystery car with a wireless set inside it to detect "crime."

Please give kind greetings to Heintz if you are with him. I shall send this to Wm. Plomer. He may know your whereabouts.

Yours ever
EM Forster

*   *   *

From next week:

Tenerife. August 26 [1934]   c/o Banco Hispano Americano
                                                                    Las Palmas
                                                            Canary Islands.

Dear Forster,

We arrived back yesterday from a tour of the smaller islands to find a stack of post, including your letter. I was most interested in the pamphlet you sent. I knew about the Sedition Bill, of course. And had heard a good deal about the Council for Civil Liberties[23] from the *Week*. What I didn't know was that you were at the head of the troops. May you lead them to victory. How entirely I understand what you say about the alternations between fuss and calm. Alas, with me, it's nearly all futile fuss. My conscience pricks me, and I feel like leaving for England by the next boat: To do . . . what? And, if so, what is to become of Heinz, whose relations now more or less openly beg me to keep him out of Germany? We think his father must be in some kind of political trouble. Probably, I shall compromise by settling in Copenhagen, fairly soon. Meanwhile, I have finished my novel; which is less a blow for anybody's freedom than a home-made jam-pot grenade flung rather wildly in the direction of Berlin. I can't even throw straight; and am lost in admiration of your marksmanship in the G.L.D. book,[24] which I have now read four or five times, and like better and better. Do you know, I have never read a word he wrote, apart from your quotations? When I'm in civilisation again, I shall try to get the International Anarchy. I think that's what I should best like of his, just now.

Can one help your Council with money? If so, I'll send some.

What is your next book going to be? I'm starting on a write-up of my Berlin diaries. They ought, at least, to form quite an interesting set of illustrations to a serious work on Fascism. I have learnt far more about what "educated" Nazis think since I have been here, than I ever did in Germany. Most of them are school-teachers who have never read any history.

The trip to the smaller islands was enjoyable as far as we two were concerned, but it filled me with despair. There they are, in the middle of the sea, with their wonderful ravines, full of palms and muscatel grapes. And on them are thousands of inhabitants of both sexes; the younger ones with very beautiful eyes. And it is all dead, dead, dead. It is how our civilisation may be after the next war. On Gomera, the night before we arrived, five young men had gone into the church, collected armfuls of those stiff gorgeous little dolls, Christ, Maria and St Cristobal, and burnt them on the beach. They were now in the lock-up, but to be released [the] next day.

Nobody seemed to care much, either for or against. The young men belonged to a club which calls itself Socialist. It was all rather depressing and a bit pathetic. Comic relief was provided by two of our fellow-travellers. We met them first on the boat going across to Hierro. The more conspicuous wore a khaki uniform, puttees down to his bare ankles and sandals. When the boat started, he exchanged his solar topee for a smart felt hat. We hadn't left the harbour many minutes when he handed us his card. It was headed: The Spanish Explorer-Captain, Don Ramiro Sanz. Who has travelled for eighteen years on foot from Alaska to Cape Horn. Beneath was a picture of the Captain, in white uniform and Nazi boots, armed with a rifle, a cutlass and a revolver. On the other side of the card, was a posed picture against a studio background of two fat girls, obviously whores, dressed in the alleged costume of the Andes Indians. We were requested to contribute a trifle to the Captain's travelling expenses. Presently another traveller appeared; a young Hungarian in a very smart flannel suit. It appeared that he also was in the same business, and that, by an unfortunate chance, both explorers were now headed for the same island, which could hardly be expected to provide funds for more than one of them. The Hungarian told us a good deal about his profession. He wasn't exactly a beggar; in that he didn't, for a moment, pretend that he was starving, or even short of money. It appears that, especially in Spanish peasant districts, this attitude is quite fatal. You must be boastful, affluent and aggressive. "Look what they gave me in El Pinar" is the right note to strike. If they are very stingy, you say: "This village is full of Arabs." On arrival in a village, the Hungarian would go straight to the mayor and demand five pesetas. He almost invariably got it; indeed, he looked upon the money as his absolute right and perquisite. "I've got three mayors to go and collect from this morning," he remarked, as though he were the gas-man. When I asked where the money came from, he replied vaguely that he supposed it was taken out of the taxes. The Spanish Explorer-Captain collected not only money but rubber-stamp-marks, in his autograph album. Anybody who had a stamp would do; most of them were from grocers and chemists. On Hierro, he got a poem as well, dictated by a village poet, who was blind, to his "secretary." From the very little I could understand of Spanish, it seemed remarkably good satire: "Oh thou," it began, "who hast travelled the Earth from the burning Equator to the freezing Pole, and art come at last to the door of our insignificant hovel . . . " The Captain had to admit, however, that business on the island had been comparatively poor. The Hungarian cleaned up the chief village and then left for the next island, to pick that bare before he arrived. Apparently, there are dozens of these people in Spain, most of them foreigners. The most successful is an Englishman, who travels with a very large dog.

Yes, I've read Anna Karenina. Twice. I don't like it as much as War and Peace; though I can't judge it as severely as you do. I feel a strong personal affection for Tolstoy (which few people seem to share) and enjoy him even at his silliest; as in The Kreutzer Sonata and the notes to What is Art? Certainly, Anna is a failure: Partly, I think, because Tolstoy tried, consciously or unconsciously, to write a "great" novel in the French manner which he pretended to detest. And so there has to be a "great" tragic theme. The moment he had written "Vengeance is mine, saith the Lord," on the flyleaf, he had doomed the whole book to disaster; though the heaviness is eased off a bit by the confused ending, floating the reader back into life again, after the suicide. Any of the French masters would have closed on Anna's death, I believe; and left one feeling as though one had swallowed a plum-stone. Nevertheless I am very fond of it, it patches. The row at the opening and the horserace and the haymaking and Anna's thoughts as she is driving to the railway station for the last time (one of the earliest examples, perhaps, of the modern technique of reported thought?) And Vronsky nearly comes off as a great comic character. There is a scene when he's already had Anna once or twice and is being very polite about it: "For an instant of this bliss . . . " which makes me smile whenever I think of it. Of course all this retribution stuff is nonsense. Tolstoy can't seriously have believed in it, himself. There is a bit where Dolly comes to visit the guilty pair when Tolstoy makes obvious, brilliant efforts to save the book by proving that the liaison was bound to be unhappy in the long run. But he doesn't prove it, because it wasn't.

Today, I am thirty. Did Villon say that, at thirty, he had drunk all his "hontes"?[25] Or was it thirty-three? I feel as if I still had some pretty unappetizing ones in store. Like you, I am aware that this is the moment for a pronouncement. Like you, I fail to make it. I have no message whatever to the British Public or the boys of the old school. At forty, if spared, I'll try again.

[handwritten postscript:] Heinz returns the greetings. Please remember me to Bob.

Yours ever,
Christopher Isherwood

*   *   *

16-1-35   West Hackhurst,
                                                          Abinger Hammer,
                                                               Dorking.

Dear Isherwood,

Dr Norman Haire[26] has lettered to William [Plomer] that if my novels were analysed they would reveal a pretty mess, and that the works of H. Walpole and S. Maugham would be even prettier. So I thought I would set to myself, and began last night in a lockable book. There are things in my earlier stuff which are obvious enough to me now, though less so when I wrote them—e.g. the rescue of Eustace by Gennaro in the Story of a Panic, and Gino's savaging of Philip in Where Angels—, and there is one curious episode: the sacrificial burning of a number of short stories in 1922 in order that a Passage to India might get finished. So I thought I would put all this down, but soon got tired and am unlocking myself to you instead. I wish you were in England for several reasons. For one thing we always agreed to spend January together—do you remember—and it's already half gone. For another thing[,] I would very much have liked your advice over the Council for Civil Liberties. Can I work with people like Claud Cockburn or not?[27] You could have told me. I can't be a communist because I can't apply my mind to communism. There may be other reasons: you could have told me. And oh my god tomorrow evening we are to consider what my committee calls a "Charter," and to specify what blessings in the way of free speech[,] free thought and free assemblage we propose to confer not only on Great Britain but on North Ireland, India, and West Africa. Substitute "f" for "ch" is my own thought, but even thus emended the charter will not carry far, for it has no guts behind it. We have not money, or if we have immediately spend it. The evening after that will be better—a play by Virginia [Woolf] called "Freshwater" (or "an evening at the bay"), and the evening after that will be best, for Bob comes.

Dr Norman Haire, about whom William has already made numerous puns, leads one a circuitous course I must say. To start again at my own writings, I am trying to put together a volume of reprints. There is plenty of stuff and much of it quite good in patches, but slight terrors steal over me. It's been so ineffective, when one considers the course of affairs, and it's so imperfect when compared with real writing. I was very pleased to hear from you. I "owed" you a letter as a matter of fact, and had it been written at the proper time should have told you how much I liked Little Friend. It was wonderfully little spoilt. I went three times. I wish that Len would act again. I hardly ever see anyone whom I care to look at on the films. My other news would have been that, last November, I went for a day to the Saar. It was more like some one else's expedition than my own, but a great success. Thence I proceeded for a week to St Remy de Provence, where I often go. This was a great success too, but sunshine and calm instead of fog and romance.

Well it is 1.0 A.M. and I seem to have written nothing at all. Day after day goes by in a muddle. We had curried eggs for supper, I have read half a letter of Horace Walpole's, Mrs O'Brien and Miss Pollak think Mrs Morgan is going to be married, the wireless is less good for regional, Sir Akbar Hydari writes on gold-speckled paper which was used for ancient Moghul documents. What is one to do with all that? I will go to bed. I am at last getting a few dreams again about lovely landscapes and trying to remain very quiet when I wake up so that I may remember them.

Please give my remembrances to Paul Kryger[28] and my regards to Heintz. I do hope you will both get to England sometime soon. I don't suppose I shall get to Denmark unless I can do so with or without Bob—i.e. during his holidays, which again I have not much chance of spending with him.

With love,
E.M. Forster

17-1-35

The Danes, always thoughtful, have decided this morning to translate A Passage to India and I am signing the contract. Or was it that you gingered them? They are Berlingske Forlag, 34 Pilestraede, Copenhagen K.

*   *   *

Classensgade 65
Copenhagen
February 7 [1935]

Dear Forster,

Thank you for your letter. I have been a long time answering it because I had to finish typing the play Auden and I have written together.[29] Also I have been to the dentist.

First, I must warn you that you will shortly receive a review copy of my novel.[30] Please don't misunderstand this. It is in no sense a hint that you shall "do anything" about it. But merely a device for saving money at the Woolfes' expense; I am sending review copies to all my friends who can be classed as "literary": as the six copies I get free don't go far, and, this time, there is a more than usually large number of libelled persons to be propitiated with suitably inscribed volumes.

How like Dr Haire to "titter" to William abut the unconscious content of your novels. I met him once in Berlin. Really, these sexologists are hardly adult. As if all of us hadn't made these momentous "discoveries" while still at school! However, it's an amusing game. The Gino-Philip savaging is perhaps your classic instance, but I can think of two others: The death on the football field in "The Longest Journey" (very fishy) and the moment when Rikky (spelling, or am I mixing it up with the mongoose in Kipling?) faints on hearing that he has an illegitimate brother (obviously because he was in love with the young man all the time and was horrified to discover that his passion was incestuous). So, you see, Dr Haire is not the only smut-hound on the beach.

Of course the Council for Civil Liberties is *some* good; the question is, how much? And the answer to that is, how far are they prepared to go when it comes to the point. Utopian charters are irritating, of course; but, on the other hand, it isn't a bad thing to get one's i[. . . ?] clear while there's still time. Later, events may move so fast and ti[. . . ?] may be need for such rapid action that unless you know exactly what yo[u] mean to do[,] you won't do it.[31]

Meanwhile, I sit here, waver and am in a mess. On the one side, there is the logical course of duty to what I believe: come to England and do my bit, however small. On the other side, there is Heinz. But I've told you this before.

There remain, as you say, the curried eggs (which I don't even know how to make)[,] the letters on coloured paper (but only yellow from the Hogarth Press and dark blue from John Lehmann) and the landscape dreams (which I can only get if I take aspirin).

I am glad the Danes are translating the Passage to India. Rather late in the day, isn't it? No, I wasn't responsible, I'm afraid.

Heinz and Paul Kryger send regards.

If only we could meet. It's marvelous weather here, now.

Best love and write again soon,
Christopher Isherwood

[handwritten postscript:] Please remember me to Bob.

∗   ∗   ∗

[11-5-35]

Dear Isherwood,

Have now read Mr. Norris twice and have much admiration and enjoyment. I liked it less the first time because it is not altogether my sort of book—dwells on the contradictions rather than the complexities of character, and

THE 1930s **43**

seems to reveal people facet by facet whereas the Memorial if my memory serves tackled strata. However I get over that and managed to read what you've written, I think. The construction is fine and Margot was a complete surprise to me. It's marvellous too the way you've maintained standards of right and wrong and yet left Norris an endearing person. And you've made him both silly and witty, like a character in Congreve.[32] He's awfully good. The necessity of combining knowingness and honesty in William render him more of a problem, for in art these are uneasy bedfellows. However you bring him through pretty well. I was a little worried in Switzerland to what extent he was paying his employer's way with the Baron. Did he go the whole hog or turn a pig-skin cheek? I don't the least mind, but feel that in the first case he would violate the fastidiousness and in the second the integrity of his character. Still perhaps I needn't worry, for he was only hired to make the Baron move, not to make him happy.

Do give me an address to write to. I suppose you are in Brussels by now and do hope all's well. It was a great pleasure seeing you.

With love,
EM Forster

Otto for my island! Oh I do hope he got to the Saar!

* * *

1-6-35
West Hackhurst,
Abinger Hammer,
Dorking.

Dear Isherwood,

I didn't mind what you said about T. E. [Lawrence] either at the time or afterwards, and it helped me towards sizing him up. The circumstances have been very distracting. I ought to have arrived there the day he was buried, and I did go there last Tuesday with the Sassoons. Pat Knowles, the bat-youth, received us and showed me all the preparations they were making for my visit. Everything very grey and quiet and touching in that rhododendron dell, but outside I know Lord Lloyd was waiting. S. said he looked absolutely foul at the funeral. Well he must vomit for someone else now.

On the top of this worry has been another one connected with property—our "family friends" the Farrens have been trying to close our thirty-year old path to the village and to take away our field: for announcing this iniquity by a "humourous" poem professing to come from a mare and actually written by a bitch. The disorders of life are much confused: in my half-waking worries I scarcely know whether I am thinking of the lost path or the lost friend.

Well Bob's there anyhow, and I got him down on the Sassoons my last day there. It is a gigantic plain country house in Wiltshire, lawns and woods rising to the sky, no gardens or trimmings, very attractive and grand. Sassoon's wife sweet, S. I have always been charmed by. I have come away thinking what a gap there is between war writers, especially poets (S.S., Blunden, etc.)[33] and post-war writers. The pre war writers (self) seem actually nearer to the war than what is being produced at the present time. I don't mean that I follow it but anyhow I'm not affronted or scared by it. Any liaison work to be done here? And by Day Lewis? I don't know him but feel he might connect groups who are rather regrettably out of touch. There are such shits of every age now about and they are so powerful that some secret groping in decent quarters seems desirable.

This has led me I don't know how far from Bob. He was delighted with Heytesbury House,[34] and drove me up to the flat after tea. How I do wish we could come to Holland, but expense will be one thing, dates another. He hasn't yet fixed his lease. His wife is "ever so much better," whatever that means. She has come out well and people have been nice to her. I should have gone with him today to see her if he could have got the car but he couldn't. We will think about Holland. All else failing, I might run over alone. Did you know I am going to Paris to this freedom-congress for writers on June 21st?[35]

Well this is a letter of sorts. I am writing in the garden which has suffered more from the frost of 10 days back than any other place in England: not only wisteria, azaleas, tulip tree, tree of heaven, weigelia, ci . . . tus[?] gone, but even beeches and oaks. You will have gathered that if not a lovely it is anyhow a fluffy garden: planned by one old lady—my aunt—conserved by another—my mother—, and only ennobled by my own excessively moderate austerity. It is quite ridiculous to reflect how seldom I have felt happy here.

I am getting Lowes Dickinson's autobiography typed. It is a remarkable work. It makes me sad and a little irritable.

With best love and also love to Heintz.

E. M. F.

I am very sorry about the passport.

* * *

28-7-35

From this place (Edinburgh) and its tedious wind I send a line about our visit. We shall certainly come if you are still there. Will you send me a line as soon as it is certain about Heintz's Passport. We shouldn't come if you're not there. The notion is to arrive about Aug. 25th for four or five days, and be with you and go around with you as far as your plans allow. I presume your address isn't a hotel. I was told that the Y.M.C.A. is good but noisy.

I seem to have quantities of letters to write to people who are ill, so must stop—not to write them, but to remind myself that I am doing nothing pleasant. Down below, three agreeable and enlightened women discuss the affairs of the University, and the Professor, who has been inoculated against Russia, sits apart with a gloomy arm. Edinburgh is a strange place. Last night was Saturday night—all the gardens closed, the castle illuminated, Princes Street deserted, an enormous crowd circulating inside the Railway Station and nowhere else. It might be such a fun-city. There was a man here called Raffalovitch who was said to have a salon. I went to a depressing lunch party with him once. Now he is dead.

Well I will finish up now and write again soon. The fact is I am sleepy and cold and haven't been out all day, but wanted to write definitely about our holiday. The news of Bob's wife is good and his child continues to get larger and to recognise him.

With best love,
EM Forster

*   *   *

as from

9-9-35   West Hackhurst,
                                                     Abinger Hammer,
                                                     Dorking.

Dear Christopher,

Perhaps I rather overdid ignorance and vagueness when ringing up your mother, still I think she was glad to hear.[36] Then we went to Birmingham, but very indignant as the promised car had not been insured and Bob dare not handle it. By the Monday—that is to say last Monday—the insurance had been fixed up and we motored off to Devonshire, that doubtful county. I enjoyed myself there as much as I have ever, and took my part in outdoor sports. The red sandstone, the abundance of characters and absence of character, displeased Keats and never please me, still the place was as good as possible, and the drive through Dorsetshire superb. I saw the Cerne Giant for the first time. *What* an affair! The very reverse of that deplorable photo. Heinz could find nothing to complain of and Bob was reduced to a series of reverent exclamations. It's on such a lovely hillside too. From Sidmouth (to complete this pointilliste rendering) we returned to London. Today Bob has gone to see his wife. I am stopping with him for a couple of nights more, since my flat is lent. He was very pleased to receive Heinz's letter. How very well it is written[;] he is making grand progress. I think you did realise how very much we both like Heinz.

As for Amsterdam, my only objection to it is that I had no time there whatever alone with you. There was nothing I wanted to imbibe or impart, still it would have been an additional enjoyment. After all, we are both of us writers, and good ones.

I will write again. This is really to thank you for all your kindness—you did do no end, courier, etc. and manoeuvring lady over [our?] room. I want to hear your plans. If you go to Belgium I might go that way into France at the end of the year and see you both again.

With love to you, also to Heinz,
Morgan

Stephen [Spender] has been seen by Wm Plomer, not by me so far.

*   *   *

Villa Alecrim do Norte, San Pedro, Sintra, Portugal.
21st Dec. 1935.

Dear Morgan,

I have been meaning to write to you ever since I left London because Bob, who very kindly put in an appearance at the station, told me that you weren't well and I have been worried, wondering if perhaps it wasn't something serious. I do hope you are better now. As you see, we have arrived here. We have taken quite a nice little house on the hill above the town on a three months lease. Could you possibly come and visit us, do you think? The voyage might do you good and the weather here is said to be lovely in January. You would like this place very much indeed I am sure. There are all kinds of old palaces and ruins to be seen and dozens of excursions to make. I think we might quite possibly settle in this country if we can find the right house and if Heinz can get a reasonable assurance that he will be allowed to stop here indefinitely. In many ways it seems quite ideal.

I hope you have a nice Christmas. Please give my love to Bob.

Best love,
Christopher

[handwritten postscripts:]

Got a nice letter from Bob[,] will write him later.
Many greetings to you both [from] Heinz
Greetings & love to yourself, Bob, and all—Tony
Love and best wishes for Christmas and the New Year from Stephen

*   *   *

Villa Alecrim do Norte
January 15. [1936]   Sao Pedro
Sintra.

Dear Morgan,

I was so sorry to hear from Bob about your operation and that the trouble isn't cleared up yet.[37] It is so tiresome and miserable for you and I expect you haven't been feeling well for ages, although, typically, you never said anything about it when I saw you last. But now I do hope they will be able to deal with it once and for all and that, by the Spring, you'll be well on the way to recovery. I have been thinking a great deal about you lately—we all have—and the others all send their best wishes.

The weather here is obscene, but we enjoy ourselves, as there is lots to do. The animals in our household multiply daily. We have now Teddy, the dog and the fowls (six hens and a cock) and two white rabbits and today a kitten has arrived. It is very savage and we are all afraid of it. Whenever any of us goes near it[,] it makes a curious booming noise like a foghorn. Heinz has just clipped its claws.

Stephen and I write a good deal; Tony keeps the household accounts.[38] He also deals with the two servants, as he is the only one of us who speaks Portuguese—that hideous language: (No More, for instance, is "Naow Mash": "Naow" should be pronounced with the maximum cockney accent.) Like all Latin households, the kitchen is a club-room, always crammed with people who chatter and laugh until far into the night. The meals are quite good, however. Stephen's brother, Humphrey is here. Heinz has just persuaded him to shave off all his hair (to make it grow better) and today the act has been performed. Humphrey is now ashamed to appear in public without a beret.

There are some very peculiar neighbours here. One lady believes in fairies and has prepared an authentic map of fairy-land. Another has had a lot of reincarnations. Her first was as a Syrian lad who fell in with some Roman soldiers who, believe it or not, behaved no better than other soldiers. She is said to have described all her misadventures in a book which she shows to very intimate friends. I have wasted a great deal of time trying to become intimate—so far without success. Tomorrow, we are to be received by one of the leaders of Sintra fashion, a woman named Lady Carrick: we are a little nervous, as usually at Lady Carrick's house they have charades and Stephen is afraid that Tony may be asked to take a female role and give a too convincing performance.

You would love the palace of Pena, which is right on the top of the hill: it is built in all possible styles and on the opposite hill is a statue of the nineteenth century architect in full mediaeval costume. There is a view over half Portugal when the weather is fine. But as soon as you're better you must certainly come here and see it all for yourself.

I wonder how soon your book is coming out. I am longing for that. William may have told you that he and I are making an appearance in a magazine-book edited by John Lehmann called New Writing. It is said to be going to be published at the end of March by John Lane.

Don't answer this, of course: just tell Bob to send me a card some time. I was so grateful to him for sending news. And get better soon.

Best love,
Christopher

*   *   *

23-2-36

West Hackhurst,
Abinger Hammer,
Dorking.

Dear Christopher,

I think I had better answer your letter, as it increases my chance of getting another one. It was collected with a letter which William had received from Stephen, and the standard of accuracy in Portugal proved surprisingly high. I hope that the reincarnations proceed apace and that the animals also breed nicely. How is the clipped kitten? Micky, one of the pair here, had just killed an elderly pigeon named Mr Pompous, and public feeling ran so high that it was thought he too ought to be clipped. But no one knew how to do it. Heinz couldn't be got at, and public feeling has died down.

Yes, I never told you I wasn't well when we parted. There seemed so much to say and I was so happy seeing you. I am to go back into the Nursing Home on Wednesday, when I hope they may think me fit enough to have the main operation. I haven't had any pain or even been much bored or depressed. I have wondered why. Sometimes I decide it is because I have a great mind and have Won Through, at others "No, merely idle." My book, Abinger Harvest, comes out next month. It is dedicated to the people who helped me to put it together—to William chiefly, but to you too. So you'll get a copy! I've just got a copy of John Simpson's Family Curse. I think well of it. Shall I send you my extra copy? I have one.

I'm in bed with two cats on it, waiting for the local doctor. The weather is vile, but there is a very pretty woolly Surrey view out of the window, a charming old-fashioned Morris frieze, a general sense of security and comfort. Letters have been received from Joe [Ackerley], William, Bob and Lord Kennet of the Dene.

The dog got bitched by a guardsman—that is to say I thought we had better go to a newsie[?] instead. I shall have another try tomorrow (Monday) when I go up in a car, drop my mother at her sister's, and pick Bob out of his family. He is very anxious to go, too. The press was surprisingly civil, and septuagenarians such as Miss May Lowes Dickinson write with pleasure.

I am full of plans as to what I will do when I get well—e.g. attend every dog that runs, visit the English Lakes, Portugal and Dorsetshire, reform the Police Courts, read all Milton, not lift a finger to hinder the next world-war, be very kind, very selfish, and incidentally write masterpieces. I wonder whether you are on one of the latter yourself. I do hope so.

Please write me your news. I hope Heinz is well and that the particular anxiety you mentioned to me is nothing.

Give Heinz my love.

With love from
Morgan

* * *

March 31. [1936] Villa Alecrim do Norte.
Sao Pedro. Sintra. Portugal.

Dear Morgan,

Thank you so much for sending me the signed copy of Abinger Harvest. I am so pleased to have it and so glad to hear from Bob that you are really better now. If I haven't written for so long it certainly hasn't been because I have not been thinking about you and wondering how this beastly operation had gone off. But I thought that you probably wouldn't be allowed to read letters anyhow and I suppose this is why I haven't written. I think Abinger Harvest is fascinating: there are parts of it I read again and again: and how amazingly it hangs together. I tried to say this, and other things, in an exceedingly stupid review I did for the Listener. But it all came out wrong and sounded stiff and chilly or else just the reviewer's usual soft soap. The trouble was, I kept wanting all the time to explain something by referring to your visit to Amsterdam or to something I remembered you saying: and then didn't, because I think that kind of thing doesn't do, at least, not when I try it.

Auden, who is here now, is also very admiring. He likes particularly the T.S. Eliot essay and, of course, the speech. Also your own centenary. We are writing a play together, much better, I hope, than Dogskin.[39] It is chiefly about our conception of T.E. Shaw.[40] It will be finished in a couple of weeks. Stephen and Tony have gone. They are in Barcelona and will soon be in Greece. They like Barcelona very much: it seems to offer a happy blend of night-life, concerts and the feeling of something about to happen without which neither of them are ever really at home.

Here, on the contrary, it is quiet as the grave, which, for the moment, I prefer. We have had awful weather, but I still hope that it will turn fine very soon. At any rate, it is quite warm. Any hope of your coming to convalesce? You should have every comfort, including a hot water bottle and a room with a view. Perhaps you would take to gambling, as a recreation: the noblest spirits seem to succumb—yesterday evening, after keeping away for nearly a month, I lost three pounds. Heinz saved us by winning heavily. Auden won a pound and then firmly and wisely refused to continue. My other amusements include walking and taking French lessons from a young poet whom you would like, I think: but I believe I told you that before. The white rabbit ate all her young except one, whom she seems, for some reason of her own, to find indigestible or sympathetic. The hens are reduced to eight. Incidentally, if you come, you may well be the first major English novelist ever to have been killed in an earthquake: one is expected very shortly now. An earthquake, I mean.

Auden and I are deeply involved in the occult sciences. We go to Rudolph Steiner readings at the house of the ladies I told you about. The readings are boring and we argue, which delights the ladies; but what we are vulgarly after is the Tarot Pack, which is produced on special occasions. Also the cakes are excellent.

At a place not far from here, nineteen years ago, there was miracle. A shepherd boy and three girls saw the Virgin who promised them to do a very good deed for Portugal on that spot on the 13th of May, at 12 noon. So thousands of Lisbonese, including journalists and atheists, went out to the place to see. At a quarter to twelve, the clouds began opening and shutting like doors and at twelve sharp, the sun revolved on its own axis and shone so brightly that ladies fainted. Later showers of white petals descended on the heads of the crowd and a spring of water leapt out of the earth and has been running ever since. It cures all diseases. I got this from my landlady, whose cook was present. They are going this year to see what they can see. We may go too.

I have decided to say nothing about Hitler in this letter, so shan't.

Goodbye, best love from us both, greetings from Auden and do get better and come here soon.

Christopher

* * *

May 12 [1936]

Villa Alecrim do Norte
São Pedro. Sintra

Dear Morgan,

No news of you for ages and ages. And yet I feel sure you must be getting along all right, or Bob or Joe would have let me hear. Perhaps you have gone off somewhere for a rest? If so, don't of course bother to answer this, but ask your host or whoever is with you to send me a post-card saying: "Forster well" or "Morgan middling" or some such bulletin.

As for us, it is quite as if we had lived here all our lives. Really, the perverseness of exiles knows no bounds. Having removed myself all these hundreds of miles from England, I am now seated in front of an English fireplace in an English armchair in a cottage of English design, sipping English tea. It is true that the cottage has been designed by an English lady, our landlady, so we can't be held responsible for that—but I have seldom behaved in so English a manner as I do here, ringing the bell for the maids, instead of bawling down stairs, and teaching Anna to serve us from the left hand side.

I love Portugal. The people are charming. They lean over the wall when we are having meals in the garden and wish us a good appetite. But how they do sing! The two maids sing in harmony, very old folk songs with hundreds of verses, until I have to ask them to stop, as I can't hear myself write. And the farmer, ploughing with oxen just beyond the garden wall sings a song to the oxen which lasts all day. Sintra is a queer place. On one of the hills, a man and a boy (now no longer) are building a luxury hotel. They have been on the job, all by themselves, for ten years, and they reckon that another ten will see them though [sic]. Then they will sell it to a combine—but not in our time.

I am slowly learning Portuguese. It is hideous but rather amusing to see how indistinctly one *can* talk. You must never, whatever you do, open your mouth at all.

Heinz is very happy here, with his ducks, hens and rabbits. He does a lot of carpentry, making hutches, nesting boxes, etc. And it always seems to be time to feed the animals. We have one "treasure" of a maid, named Anna. The other is nice but has been sacked because she utterly refuses to get up till 10 or 11 in the morning, and she is the cook. Anna is learning to read and write, in her spare time. As far as I can make out, she believes that all foreign languages are simply "writing," and that, when she learns to read she will immediately understand English, French and German as well.

As I think I told you in my last letter, Stephen went off, more than two months go, with Tony, to Spain and Greece. Then Wystan came and we wrote another play together, called: "The Ascent of F.6." It is about an expedition up a mountain and attempts to explain why people climb them. It will be published soon, I hope, and perhaps produced this autumn. I wonder how you will like it. It is far better than old Dogskin, anyhow.

Am also at work on my new novel. Part of it is a most disgusting crib on The Longest Journey. By the way, I must get hold of that book on the great novelists. I want to see what Mrs Alphabet Jones writes about you. I always feel slightly aggressive when people write about you, and promptly add a few mental pages to that classic Essay on Forster which I like to pretend I shall one day produce.

As I have said before and shall say again—I do wish you'd come out here. Sea-air. 900 feet. Every comfort. Private sitting room provided. I suppose it's too much to hope you really *will* come; but you once trifled with the idea of the Canaries, which are three days further on.

Anyhow, do get well, and write me a letter.

Best love
Christopher

My best love to Bob. How is he?

[postscript in different handwriting] Hoping that you are well again. How is Bob? Best love to both of you. Heinz

*   *   *

[May 20, 1936]   [West Hackhurst]

Dear Christopher,
    Morgan middling.
    (i) Legal. Sir Murdoch MacDonald, M. P., a wealthy & elderly consultant
engineer is bringing a libel action against Arnolds & myself in respect of
the article *A Flood in the Office* in Abinger Harvest. Article (written 1919)
reviews a pamphlet (written 1918), which, though none of us knew, was
condemned as libelous [Br] in a consular court in Egypt in 1921.
Consequently republishing of review in 1936 is libelous [Br]. We have no
case, and that Sir M.M. should demand withdrawal of book, public apol-
ogy in court or elsewhere, payment of costs, and possibly a small sum for
charity did not seem to us unreasonable. We staged him as a nice cross old
gentleman. He has however tried to get £1000 damages out of us, and we
shall certainly have to pay £500, which he will spend on himself.[41]
    (ii) *Medical (a)* bladder. This, though it does not hurt, remains infected
and I swallow some rather terrifying medicine four times a day, tastes like
something off another planet, followed by cachets which after dissolution
"repeat" like decayed sweetbread. (*b*) feet. These, though they do not hurt
except when I walk, have dropped their arches owing to the carelessness of
the Nursing Home when I was in bed. Altered shoes arrived by the
Portuguese post this morning. (*c*) teeth. These though they do not hurt are
said to have to come out. (*d*) rash on chest and back may have been
measles, but I dared not say so in case my lawyers were afraid to see me. It
did not hurt.
    So it would be idle to pretend I'm not depressed and scared, and I've
found I difficult to write to friends because the whole thing's a bore and all
they can do is to write back and say they are sorry. I have often thought of
you though and am very glad you wrote again, as it has got me over the
edge. As to the international situation[,] I am terrified like every one else,
nothing original.
    Oh well, to have lived to have loved etc., and I am glad to have done
both, yet it isn't a comfort to say so as it seems to have been to the
Victorians. Too like the Great Tune at the end of an Elgar Symphony.
    Am now out of bed, and my mother in very good spirits and a black
dress which arrived too late for King George's funeral, is preparing for a
long drive to Uncle Philip near Orpington, having hired a comfortable car
for that purpose. What do I want to write about though? You knew that it
is fixed up that I edit a selection from T. E. [Lawrence]'s letters for his
trustees, and as they are practically his brother, whom I like, it will be [a]
suitable full-time job. I have already read several 100 letters, more keep

coming in, and in the flat, unread, are hundreds of letters to him, and many documents. Brother well says the shorter book the better, but how is it to be done? A difficult job for which I am as well suited as anyone. Dear me what an odd chap. I want more than ever to read your and Auden's play. I don't really get behind him. I think he felt [more] the acuteness of his separation from the ordinary man than I do mine. When the o[rdinary] m[an] is nicely encased I can usually make some sort of contact with him. T. E. was always apart, straining or striving. A sad fun.

Bob was bounding when I saw him last week, but in trouble since, as his wife has gone pregnant, neither knows how. I had letters from both of them this morning, and she is to have an operation, apparently super rosam[?], presumably because she is tuberculous. She has turned out into a very decent sort. I go up about once a week to Bob or business, otherwise lie about here in the sun. Also by Portuguese post, I receive the unpublished parts of De Profundis, sent me with much empressement [french, meaning display of cordiality] by Leo Charlton.[42] They are from shorthand notes illegally taken down at the Ross-Douglas trial, and it seems that everyone except myself & Leo knows of them. Forrest Reid, now here, says that they have been published in America.

Now here, indeed! This letter is hamstrung. I am trying to maintain it— is all written at a go. Whereas somewhere after the ink begins[,] Monday passes into Tuesday. I have not seen your story yet, but have reread the Memorial. News of a new novel from you makes me very happy, and the Longest Journey is far from incapable of improvement. I have just written a bawdy short story—I do them sometimes when feeling upset, they tend more and more to occur in heaven of course. Joe and Jack Sprott like them but they don't quite tickle William's bell. I didn't ever write to you about the Dog—I have read it twice and seen it once. I enjoyed it, and more than the Dance of Death. Bob let a shout of "that's Christopher" when we heard the Virgin Policeman, but it seems it wasn't.

I'll lead this letter to a close, anyhow I'll send my love to Heinz and much love to you and sign it

Morgan

Will write again soon. Much love again. It is a great pleasure to hear from you and about the Portuguese.

*   *   *

Villa Alecrim do Norte
Sao Pedro. Sintra.

May 23 [1936]

Dear Morgan,

I am sorry to have to write and say I am sorry, but your letter leaves me no choice. What ailments! What accidents! I am torn with indignation, against the idiotic nursing-home, for failing to prop up arches of your feet, and the unspeakable MacDonald. The mentality of these libel-bandits leaves me simply speechless. You'd think that a man like that would have his share of vanity; yet, when he is advertised from one end of the English speaking world to the other, put on the literary map in block capitals and assured of a footnote in all your biographies—he resents it! But let us be charitable: perhaps he is being blackmailed by a Piccadilly poof and is at his wit's end for cash. William, in a letter also received today, refers to the case but remarks "it seems that the business will be settled fairly soon and satisfactorily." Does this mean that he doesn't yet know the worst, or have there been stop-press developments? I should have thought that if anything in Abinger Harvest really was libellous, it was the reference to Churchill in the Gallipoli Graves dialogue. Has nothing been heard of that? Churchill is pretty snappy at actions, as a rule.

Condolences also to Bob. I do hope that will pan out all right. I suppose there's no danger if it's done properly. But it's very depressing and unpleasant.

Do you really suppose that it was a comfort to the Victorians to think that they'd lived and loved? Personally, I should have thought that if you'd really done either it would only make it worse: but maybe they hadn't. What is meant by living, anyhow? Most people, nowadays, seem to long for the cloister or the brothel in one form or another. Which brings me to T.E. Lawrence. I am awfully glad you are doing the letters and hope you'll write a long introduction. Please don't expect our "F.6." to cast a dazzling light on the subject. I only say the play's about him for shorthand-descriptive purposes. Actually, the main character is all tied up in his Mater Imago: also, his brother is a knighted politician. In fact, the whole conflict is entirely different and much clumsier, as it seems to have to be on the stage. It's only in so far about Lawrence as the problem of personal ambition v. the contemplative life is concerned. And there's a lot of high-hat talk about the significance of power, which ought to go down well if the actors declaim it in sufficiently woozy voices and the stage is suitably lit.

I knew of, but have never read, the unpublished parts of De Pro[fundis]. I should much prefer your short story: haven't you a copy? When I was in Greece, I began a novelette called: "Werner and Fritz," but it became more an more positional and less psychologic, and at last even the positions were exhausted, and I threw it away. It is comforting to know that private pornography is one of the few handicrafts you are still legally allowed to practise, as long as you don't require any audience. To quote the classic review of Lady Chatterley in John Bull (which I think I once showed you?): "There is, unhappily, nothing to prevent a man sitting down in an English home to create a literary cesspool with an English pen on English paper."[43]

Heinz is very well. Having finished the big house for the ducks and chickens, he is now building a skyscraper for rabbits. It is very high indeed and we fear it may fall over in a gale. Meanwhile, I study the Portuguese irregular verbs and occasionally go over and take a peep into the wardrobe, groan and hastily shut the door again. The reason I groan is because there are thirteen books in there waiting to be reviewed for the Listener. (You needn't tell Joe [Ackerley] this). Did you read Stephen's "Burning Cactus"? I must say, I thought the reviewers were very unjust to it. "The Burning Cactus" itself is a masterpiece, I think: it is the whole history of post-war Germany turned into a kind of fable. I don't think any [of] the other stories are quite as interesting or successful: but they are all well worth reading. And, in comparison with that frigid arty H.E. Bates,[44] they are marvels.

The neighbours we don't see much of, lately. But we have a new friend, a very nice Lisbon advocate named Dr Olavo. We visit him on Sundays. Scrambling into his chair, he rests his chins on his chest, his chest on his stomach and his stomach on his thighs; then he dangles his little legs high above the ground, orders whiskey and soda, and regards me with anticipation, hoping I shall say something very intelligent, because I am an English writer. We sit like this for hours, waiting for me to compose a sentence in French about Liberty, of which we both approve. The sentence is never forthcoming, but it doesn't matter much. The whiskey is followed by tea, which is followed by Madeira cognac and light port. The French poet arrives and talks about Verlaine. The ladies come in. We now begin another game, which is to create situations in which I shall be able to let off my two French expressions: C'est quelquechose de formidable and O, en effet! Alfred, the French poet, helps me here, as he knows what I want to say, having taught me them himself. Then suddenly Heinz, whom everybody has forgotten, says very carefully and slowly: Voulez-vous une cigarette, Monsieur? And we all laugh and applaud for several minutes.

Or I go across to my landlady, Mrs Mitchell, to listen to the wireless news, and we talk dogs with a deaf neighbour from over the way. Naturally, the great dog-topic for English residents here is the English quarantine. They discuss the relative merits of the various quarantine homes for hours on end. The manager of one home where the dogs are not well treated is spoken of as if he were Hitler at least. It is a milieu, I say to myself, but I get rather impatient when they can't stop talking while the news is going on. Europe interests them about as much as the works of Chaucer.

[Handwritten:] This letter now comes abruptly to an end. There are too many domestic disturbances. I have to keep stopping to throw my shoes out of the window at the ducks, who are not allowed into the lower garden: and each time I do this, the cook very politely brings them back. Then the cat keeps attacking the chickens and Heinz hammers loudly: he has just discovered that the rabbits' skyscraper is so big that he can't get it out of the carpentry room—so they will presumably have to live there. I will write again soon, and hope you do the same. And don't forget Portugal as a possible holiday.

Best love from us both to you and Bob—

Christopher

* * *

[July 30, 1936]   [West Hackhurst]

Dear Christopher,

I am rattled by the news from Spain this evening and feel I am saying farewell to you and Heinz. You know those feelings and can discount them; the last parting is never when or as one supposes. I had been planning to come to Portugal in the autumn. Now all seems impossible—there's Spain; there's my libel case still unsettled and stirring slightly when all seemed dead; there's the rumour that you have had renewed passport difficulties. I am writing most particularly about this last. I want first hand news— please give it me. I stayed last weekend with Rosamond & Wogan [Lehmann]—they are gossips I hope. This shall go to the London address.

What next for one who is proper worried and scared? A little news, I suppose. William at Dover. Joe at Dover. I at Dover—as I shall be tomorrow, and Bob with me. This may be very pleasant. I have taken a shave in Joe's flat there.

This nightmare that everything almost went right! I know that you have it over the Communist failure in Germany. As a matter of fact one's activities (and inactivities) must have been doomed for many years. I'd throw in my hand if all these metaphors weren't nonsense; there's nowhere to throw one's hand to.

This great podge [variation of pudge] of T. E. letters is often a comfort. They contain nothing which can help the world (unless the example of courage helps). I should have been flustered if it had been Lowes Dickinson [i.e., his Dickinson project], and feared I shouldn't finish before the bombs fell. Such an interruption on T. E. would be appropriate. The book leisurely takes form—it is mostly a question of arrangement. Desmond MacCarthy came over the other day and was very helpful.

Bob's wife is all right—aborted and sterilised—so they can go ahead as much as they like whenever they want to. This brings me to my shameful stories. I too have had difficulties with the positional. Implications and innuendo are now basic necessities with me. Someday, or, to put it less primly, when we meet, I will show you one. And since I began this letter by saying farewell I have surely described a perfect parabola.

Dear me, Amsterdam was good. We often talk of it. I can't believe it was only last year—two big wars since, two operations on myself, and so on, place it on another planet. Heavens what a queer age! Sexually, I'm lucky to have been born into it, but in most other ways unlucky.

I will now conclude with no apologies. I have enjoyed writing to you very much, Christopher. I send my love to you and to Heinz.

How does the novel go? I am glad it imitates the Longest Journey. Heavens what a queer book!

Morgan

*   *   *

August 8 [1936]

Villa Alecrim do Norte.
Sao Pedro. Sintra.

Dear Morgan,

Thank you for writing again. During the last month, I've been sunk in sloth and now this Spanish business has cut off all overland post and letters sometimes take as much as nine days, if one can't manage to catch a boat.

Otherwise, the situation here is quite normal. Everybody follows the civil war with the wildest interest, of course; because most people think that, if the Spanish Govt wins, the Red Plague will spread to Portugal. The newspapers are quite openly on the side of the rebels and so it is utterly impossible to gather what is really happening. I manage to hear the English wireless news now and then; that's all. My own feeling is that this struggle is the most important thing which has happened since Hitler, for all Europe; but out of touch as we are with things here, it's difficult to judge.

On June 25, H[einz] got a letter from the German consulate in Lisbon telling him to report there in connection with his military service. He didn't. Since then, no word. Immediately, I set all possible wheels in motion to get his nationality changed, legally and definitely. Everything is still hanging fire. There are various possibilities, including South American. All of them are quite astronomically expensive. My mother, who's been here, was very decent and helpful about this. Meanwhile, we are at the mercy of the authorities. I am told that they are quite capable of extraditing H. on to a German boat. Every time the door-bell rings, we jump out of our skins and the postman is awaited daily like an executioner. Still, one gets used to anything, and my nerves are better now than they were four weeks ago. The only motto for these days is "You're not dead yet." This business has rather disinclined me to write letters, hence my failure to communicate with William, please tell him, and to write reviews, please tell Joe. But I am more sensible now. Only yesterday I did Elinor Glyn's Autobiography for the Listener.[45] No other work as yet. The novel is postponed. I must finish living it first. Meanwhile I am doing a book of short things, sort of autobiographical sketches, including The Nowaks from New Writing.[46] Chiefly to keep Methuen quiet.

We have got some nice people in the house at present, James Stern and his wife. Do you know his short stories? I didn't, but they are good, I think. He has only published one actual volume, called "The Heartless Land," all of them abut Rhodesia. He is a great admirer of William's African work. His wife is German and the sister of two communists, who escaped by less than half the skin of their teeth from Germany. She is one of the most human women I have ever met. It is a real support having them with us just at this time.

Is your visit really hopelessly off? Even if things clear up, as they still might, for a little? Yes, Amsterdam does seem very far off. Your time there was much the best part of it: for a few days I emerged from the dreary dishonourable trance of funk which I seem to have lived in for the past three years. But I refuse to say farewell to all that. No, never. As long as there's a kick left in me I shall secretly go on hoping. The only thing you can hope for nowadays is a miracle. Very well, I hope for a miracle. I demand a miracle. Have you ever read [D. H.] Lawrence's preface to Magnus' Memoirs of the Foreign Legion?[47] I just have. He used to say it was the best thing he ever wrote. It's certainly very funny and spiteful and in a curious way very inspiring. It also deals, once and for all, with the subject of crooks. If I'd read it earlier I'd never have written Mr Norris. This is so much more comprehensive.

I look forward to T.E. [Lawrence']s letters, but chiefly to your introduction. What an opportunity! I'm sure it will be in your best manner. I hope your feet are better. About this libel, have you already paid, or what? Does he want more? I wonder who'll be the next victim. Is there no possibility, after all these scandals, of the law being altered?

Heinz sends his best love to you and Bob. I'll write again soon, as soon as there is any news at all to give you.

Best love,
Christopher

*   *   *

[The following is a handwritten postcard.]

23 Avenue Michel Ange
Brussels
Sept. 15 [1936]

Just got your letter. Alas, it isn't possible for us to return to Ostende. We have booked our room here for a month.

But can't you really come here? With the trains connecting up as they do, you can be in Brussels within 1 1/2 hours of landing. Think it over. You'd both enjoy Brussels—at this time of year—far more than Ostende, which is getting very windswept.

Best love from both to both
Christopher

*   *   *

23-9-36

West Hackhurst,
Abinger Hammer,
Dorking.

Dear Christopher,

I have just reviewed F.6. for the Listener: to my own satisfaction, and I'd like to think to yours, but whether to the Listener's remains to be heard. I don't consider it ought to have had a review copy at all, poor thing. I read the play 2 1/2 times, and enjoyed it very much. It is far better than Dogskin [Dog Beneath the Skin], as you say.

We considered Brussels again, but a 10.0. P.M. arrival makes it so late. We might have been tired next day, and then the holiday would be over. I shall come myself in the New Year. We are going to Dover on Friday, and Joe, Jo-jo, Leo, Tom, and Sandy are coming too. Counting William, and not counting Sandy since he is a dog, we shall be seven. Would that you and Heinz could make nine!

I hope you are all right. I have had war-gloom, consequent on a lunch with Aldous Huxley. I believe he likes upsetting one. He is also very nice, and as long as one has trifles to do[,] the gloom's kept at bay. This T. E. stuff is a great convenience, and not feeling ill another. Indeed my illness, hygienic and expensive, has got me all wrong on the subject of pain, and because I nearly died without having any I've got the notion that vesicant spray etc. won't hurt. We shall see—or perhaps a lot of us *will* manage to die without suffering. I hope so. Mr Wells can keep his limelight. Like Gunn, I'm afraid of being killed.[48] The combined toughness and complexity of the body makes it so awful.

Monday, Aldous H., Professor Bernd[?], Miss Gardrin[?] and myself sat in my rooms for 3 hours, discussing whether intellectuals ought to say that there ought to be a Popular Front in this country. We decided that they ought to say it but not too loudly.

With love to Heinz and yourself

Morgan

* * *

11-10-36

West Hackhurst,
Abinger Hammer,
Dorking.

Dear Christopher,

Thanks for your card. Was it your Belgian[,] your Mexican or your Equadorian friend who accompanied you to England? One of them, I do hope. Sorry about the tonsils.

I think I have no news of the sort called real. My visit to Oxford, to the university of the Lawrence plaque, was curious. One ought to unveil more. Lunch afterwards at All Souls. Lindemann, who makes bombs, to my left. Sir Arthur Salter, who hopes they won't go off, to my left.[49] Winston Churchill opposite, saying there won't be no war—just yet, so *that* was no news, and deploring the turning of human beings into white ants, which wasn't news, even at the time. His neighbour, and on-hanger, turned towards him the whole time, and never looked at Captain Liddell Hart once.[50] But the Warden had the instincts of a gentleman. Mr Lionel Curtis, our host[,] spared me a moment on a sofa.[51] Sitting down as if we should chat for hours, he said that the most terrible calumnies had been spread about [T. E.] Lawrence, and that what was so dreadful was that people who were like that themselves tried to make out all others were the same—for instance[,] a man who had been in prison had come with an incredible tale to Sir Herbert Baker. Then he sprang up and was gone. I know, from papers which oughtn't to have come into my hands, that they are worried about me. I was worried too, but the evidence does point to asceticism.

With love—which Bob too will send when I see him.

Morgan

* * *

October 25 [1936]   70 Square Marie Louise
                                                                                    Bruxelles.

Dear Morgan,

Thank you for your letter, not to mention them kind words in the Listener. I felt very honoured: I'm sure Wystan did too. Actually, we're neither of us satisfied with the play as it's printed, and have been trying to alter it; or, to use your phrase, to discover a kind of spectacles through which the whole subject could be seen at once. We are doing this partly by attempting to show more clearly how Ransom was, at the critical moment in the Monastery, forced into going up the mountain by his followers, like every dictator. And we're also making Mrs Ransom more like a dictator's public; submitting to him and yet preying on him. I don't know quite how this will work out. In the last resort, of course, every play is a kind of mad rugby scrum, out of which the players fish balls of various colours and sizes and rush off with them in all directions.

We are back from Spa, where the enormous hotels—some of which have existed since 1780 and housed Tsars, Kaisers and notorious novelists—are empty and the leaves are falling and there is a non-stop casino which nobody visits. We had a very nice room, with the kind of stove in it which killed Zola. I returned with a few pages of a new book; very defeatist, because it is all about the twenties. I am writing it in the spirit of the shipwrecked sailor who puts an M.S. into a bottle. Getting back, I found Stephen's book waiting in proof, and felt inwardly rebuked, because, instead of putting things into bottles, he is doing something which may really be some use and help to clear peoples' ideas. It is awfully good, I think. There is no index, but don't worry: you are mentioned all right. On page 173, you are "a defender of freedom and a great writer" and you express "a real and important doubt" about communism.

To return to the ignoble trivialities of my life, I recently spent a night in quite the most unpleasant pension I have visited in all my long and terrible travels. A Scottish lady, speaking French with a Scottish accent, argued with a young Persian student, speaking French with a Persian accent, throughout supper about why Persia (pardon, Iran) had a French superscription [on] its stamps and not an English one. She then went upstairs into the room next ours and began feeding her canary, which sang till 2a.m. From 2 to 3, the cats obliged with rapes. At 3, the Scottish lady got up and performed an intimate function, no nuance of which was lost on us: a peculiarly irritation sharp high note was given off by the utensil. At 3.15, a special all-night service of trams came into being. At 6:30, the landlady's family started to get up and immediately turned on the wireless. At 8, we gave notice. We are now at another pension, called La Source, but of what we do not yet know. So, I prefer to give Hamilton's address for post. Heinz, poor dear, is to be operated in a fortnight: the chief operation, this time, on the nose. He is scared; but I suppose we shall have to go through with it. Meanwhile, Mexico proceeds satisfactorily and may be settled, barring accidents, in about a month. Please don't mention this however, as far too many people are talking about it already.

How are you? How are your feet? How are Lawrence's letters? Have you read Auden's new book of poems? If so, do you like them? I have just got a copy, but maybe they aren't out yet.

You have probably seen in the papers about the Rexist demonstration which was to have taken place here today and how the Govt has forbidden it.[52] Until this evening, we shan't know what's going to happen; but I'm afraid that Rex is very strong here. Everywhere you go, you see their filthy paper in people's hands.

Tomorrow, we are going to see a play about a boy of fourteen who has a baby. I mean, he becomes a father. It is called "Dame Nature" or rather Darm Nattyour (I never knew you could say that in French). It was a great success in Paris, it seems, and the juvenile lead is said to be brilliant.

We think and talk chiefly about Spain.

How is Bob and how are [sic] his family? Well, I hope?

Best love from us both to you both

(did I tell you that my Mother understood his name as Robert Button on the telephone?)

Christopher

* * *

29-12-36

West Hackhurst,
Abinger Hammer,
Dorking.

Dear Christopher,

In the first place thank you for the sweet Christmas card, both. I had no idea there were snow and robins on the continent, only imagine, though I don't think the breasts are quite as red as those of our dear English "robins"—"robin-redbreast."

Then I get your letter. I will get forward with Bob. If he can't come that weekend, I think I shan't come either—aha! not come *then* but a little later in the month. This is so that I may have a visit from him in London instead, which I have not had for a very long time, owing to Christmas, etc. However we'll see and I'll write again in a few days' time.

I had not known about Auden or even about Tony. W[illia]m [Plomer] certainly has been worrying, says he knows he's not a pacifist, but with both parents ill & dependent on seeing him is not likely to enlist. He is very irritated and wretched about everything, and has not the comfort of being satisfied with his work—the prose has certainly gone downhill for the last few years, though I think he does poetry as well as ever.

This letter is rather "robin" style all through, but I am engaged in starting with my mother for London, she is sewing on a button, reading [a] letter from housemaid's sister aloud, dealing with cat which now will now won't sit on her lap, etc. and so on.

I want to get off something to you. I may finish in the flat. I have had rather a tiresome Christmas.

Flat

Bob has rung up—*yes* the 16th does look all right—that's to say the 15th, we would hope to arrive that evening[;] he would have to return Sunday evening unless he flew Monday morning. I would stop till Monday or Tuesday.

I shall want to talk over your plans. Would Heinz go too if you did? Feel muddled too. I am sure you *oughtn't* to go, but these matters are seldom decided by one's sense of duty.

Flat full of relatives. Trying time continues. Joe—trying Christmas. We go to the Witch of Edmonton this evening.[53]

Love to Heinz & yourself,
Morgan

*   *   *

5-1-37   West Hackhurst,
Abinger Hammer,
Dorking.

Dear Christopher,

The Spain news is terrifying this evening. I assume that we shall find you both at Brussels unless I hear to the contrary, and you will assume we can come unless you hear we can't, but I feel the world is close to the edge. The passage in literature which suits me best is War & Peace pp. 1184–1185 (Mrs Garnett's translation).[54] There is another passage which I cannot locate to the effect that people when war approaches them sometimes take every precaution and sometimes are utterly reckless; they tend to the first course when they are alone and to the second when they are with their friends, and both courses are equally sound.

We had better eat in the train on the 15th. It arrives nearer 10.0 than 9.0. I think.

I hope that you are getting on with the book which is a letter to me.

I hope that Heinz is all right and not worrying too much. Oh that we all had the wings of one dove.

With love,
Morgan

I see Bob in London tomorrow—he stops at the flat. J. B. Priestley may ring up to suggest that I go with him and Miss Margaret Kennedy to complain to Mr Bildurn about the libel laws.[55]

* * *

12-1-37

West Hackhurst,
Abinger Hammer,
Dorking.

Dear Christopher,

Our obstacles have increased to three. Bob thinks he may be able to wangle to catch the 2.0. on Friday. On the other hand, his father is having a sudden operation and if things went wrong he wouldn't be able to leave. (I should in that case probably come alone on the Saturday). Thirdly, the European Unrest—this morning more composed. His leave might be cancelled if things turn worse, and in that case I should probably be too frightened to come myself.

It stands that if you hear nothing, we shall arrive by the train reaching Brussels at 9.0. (Even if we do get it, we shall still wire if we can). We shall probably leave together—1.0. train on Sunday or early plane Monday.

With love to you both
Morgan

I go on Thursday for the night to 26 Brunswick Sq. W.C.1

* * *

28-1-37
West Hackhurst,
Abinger Hammer,
Dorking.

Dear Christopher,

I have several scraps to impart. Firstly, I heard from the solicitors, and sent a suitable reply. Then I do hope you won't forget to let me have two seats for the opening night of F.6. I heard something about Feb. 19th for the date. I do hope Bob will be able to get leave.

Then, to complete business, Peter Burra drove me from Reading to Oxford and I talked to him for his safety. Not with conspicuous success. I will tell you details when I see you, as I hope I may soon. He admits close touch with the Embassy—but clings to the numerous friendly references to yourself and G. H. which are made.[56] He is in the position of a host, not of an employer, and wishes, he says, to terminate the visit, but knows not how, and he says he is bored; but it may be boredom with ecstatic interruptions.

Heavens, how queer one's English gets. English, the language of the Free!

Thank you for what you said of my Will. I will speak to you again if I ever decide to trouble you again.

The Lawrence MSSS have been returned.[57] *Now* what? Our maid has partly answered this question by breaking my typewriter. And Johnny Fisher seems to have broken the washing basin in my flat. Smashes & bills everywhere—new clothes wanted. I ought to have at least 3 suits.

Love to you & Heinz. It was a glorious holiday, I loved Brussels and all we saw there, and the Royalty bedroom. Thank you both so much for all your kindness,

Morgan

Shall be glad to be put wise over F.6. as soon as it's convenient.

* * *

27-2-37
West Hackhurst,
Abinger Hammer,
Dorking.

Dear Christopher,

I will put down some impressions in case they are useful towards alterations in the acting version.[58]

Act I—splendid. My only query was Mrs R's circumambulation, the discussion about the two sons, and the slinking away of Levantine James: "but this will come clear later on."

Act II—kept me more critical. The *monk*—not good nor good to look at. Presages are not interesting in themselves, and Ransom's, which is interesting, comes out well enough in his ensuing talk with the Abbott, John S[impson] and I felt the monk could be cut.

The *Abbott*—the finest scene in the whole play. Quite marvellous. Then troubles gather, for which the meagre scenery isn't wholly responsible. The elimination of Lamp made me wonder "How will they get rid of the other two?" Ian's was good—jealousy does carry one along. David's too slow. Then Ransom—falling into the audience almost, realistic, panting: "I will kill the demon"—it wouldn't live in that theatrical bleakness, nor would Mrs R's rocking chair. I'm sure the changes here are all for the worse: the summit ought to seethe with visions as soon as R. goes wampy; and why not? You couldn't, even with expensive settings, carry out this losing of comrades in the course of a long crawl, unless you thickened the climax with reminiscences. James *must* be put back—besides, the preparation with him in Act I is left hanging in the air. And I should have thought the Abbott back too.

Then we thought the farce of the final scene quite wrong. The villainy is much more telling if the villains are left to speak it with dignity. To show them up by making them squabble and giving them ridiculous flags is a great mistake, and I don't think it was made in the text. When they've intoned their faiths, I'd have the Announcer: "Dance music will now follow —" and curtain to a strain from those amazing singers.

The A's—v[ery] good. Their dash off to Hove shouldn't have been cut. The other two tragedies I saw in the play were the temptation to exercise power, good too, and the mother-business which doesn't work out as it should dramatically.

How good the music is—and the acting. Play didn't seem the least long, and if you remove the monk there should be time to restore some essentials.

Veiled figure—not demon. Mother on ice-throne, not rocking chair. The rocking chair is the sounder, but it won't come across. It's a moment when you *must* sacrifice psychological propriety to poetry.

Will be up Thursday and will ring you.

With love,
Morgan

* * *

2-3-37

West Hackhurst,
Abinger Hammer,
Dorking.

Dear Christopher,

Could you have tea with me on Thursday at 4.30? I would come up and go straight to my flat and meet you. I dine out at 8.0—Or I could go to the Club.

Yes, I see the Visions will tear holes in that stage.[59] So does a rocking chair. You want something easy for the spectators, and the easiest is mother in white on ice-throne. I am annoyed that the success of the play has been risked by such narrow circumstances. I shall not feel happy until it has been transferred.

The final scene (microphone) is excellent, and there is a grand addition (Lady Isabel's) to the text. My only complaint is that it was all guyed and consequently rogered. I wouldn't end with mother's paw-paw.— Her acting wasn't up to the standard by the way.

Dukes must have wanted to keep the party to those concerned in the play, so I'm glad we didn't stay on.

Hoping you can manage Thursday.

With love from Morgan

*　*　*

Luxembourg, le 27th April. 1937
Hôtel Gaisser
Luxembourg
30, rue Beaumont et rue de la Porte-Neuve

Dearest Morgan,

Here I am, in this last resort of the police-chivvied. I arrived here on Sunday night, after the worst crossing of my life, and a very dazing non-stop-talking dinner with Mr Norris: "Here you are, my dear boy, to the minute, I must really apologize that everything isn't quite ready, but this is the very best duck obtainable, tell me honestly, don't you think it's decidedly on the cold side, well well I must apologize, but don't let's waste our time we must really talk about your affairs, yes, yes, actually, I've not been feeling very well all day, what sort of journey did you have, I wonder where that boy's got to, but do start, now let me see, as I was saying, my goodness, there isn't any mustard." etc. I caught the train on to Luxembourg from Brussels by the skin of my teeth.

Heinz I found a little crushed, after a week in the Grand Duchy. He firmly denies most of the charges made against him in the French police report. (They include seduction of a deaf and dumb chambermaid, aggressive behaviour to the authorities and male prostitution!) Personally, I am convinced that he is the victim of a really swinish frame-up on the part of two prostitutes who inhabit the hotel Savoie. The trouble is that all this is now engraved in bronze in French archives and no power on earth can erase it. Kind friends have been spending their time trying to persuade me that it would be better if H. were packed off to the Fatherland or Mexico for good, and altogether I have been in a terrible state of bother and nerves. I am now feeling rather ashamed of myself for having listened to everybody except Heinz himself, who, even under English law, had the right to be heard in his own defence. And I feel correspondingly grateful to the very few, chief among them yourself, who did *not* offer advice, interested or otherwise.

Anyhow, everything is now cleared up between us, and the mere difficulty remains that he mayn't go back to France or enter Belgium, at any rate for more than a few days. This ban, it seems, may be lifted by the Belgians after the Mexican business has been put through, which ought to be the end of this week. Meanwhile, we wait here, under the sulky pout of the Grand Duchess and the charming grin of her fourteen-year-old son. If only it would stop raining, I should feel quite gay.

Do send us a line to the above address. Love to Bob and his family. Enclosed with many thanks for all your kindness is the cheque for five pounds.

Best love from us both,
Christopher

* * *

30-4-37   West Hackhurst,
Abinger Hammer,
Dorking.

Dear Christopher,

Thank you for the cheque, £5 in repayment for 500 francs. I never tire of helping people in such ways as these. I was also glad to get your letter, though how are you? I don't suppose you are very well, what an endless run round. When we meet I have much to ask—partly about the inadequacy of Mr Norris.

Now there is Peter Burra, killed while flying, and I keep thinking about death. The worst thing in it is that people seem different as soon as it has

happened, and one will seem different oneself. The word "loss" is inadequate. I have lost my fountain pen, but it does not alter.

No doubt everything in human beings is changing all the time; and so,
under the surface, is one's feelings for them—indeed here there are two fac-
tors for self's human too. O see Proust! But it's so difficult to remember the
change is going on, especially when one establishes what are called "permanent" relationships in daily life. Death turns the dead person into something worse than nothing—something deflecting—where all one's
affection for him or criticism of him becomes false. The most satisfactory
dead are those who have published books.

With best love to Heinz and to you. I am hoping for news about the
Mexican passport.[60]

Bob will be spending the weekend of the 8th–10th with me—I suppose
in the flat.

Morgan

* * *

Brussels

Tuesday [June 15, 1937]   Sq. Marie Louise 70

Do forgive my not writing. Have been expecting to return to England
very soon and do the film: may still do so—they haven't yet decided if they
want me. No news from Germany, except a nice letter from H[einz], who
has had rheumatism and a cold but now feels better.[61] If only they'd settle
things one way or the other. These postponements are getting me down.
Bob wrote such a charming letter, which I didn't get till after my return. I
can't help feeling that you and he are the only people who really care—for
H[einz']s sake, not merely for mine. I must see you again soon. Jean is very
lively and sends his love. He has visions of popping over to Dover—for a
Belgian it's hideously easy. Oh dear, how complicated everything is. Thank
you so much for sending the book. It's waiting for me at home.

Christopher

* * *

4-7-37

West Hackhurst,
Abinger Hammer,
Dorking.

Dear Christopher,

I think the date is the 7th; please send my love and Bob's also as soon as it is possible to do so.

Meanwhile I hope you will not find it too dreary in England. I have found it drearier myself since you have been here.—Of course you know what I mean, as they invariably add in England.

I will come up on Tuesday, will bring 2 or 3 of those stories with me, and will ring you up. I hope that your foot is better.

I have written a very emotional poem, and cannot make out whether it is good or not. The title is:

Landor at Sea

I strove with none for none was worth my strife:
Reason I loved, and, next to reason, doubt:
I warmed both hands before the fire of life
And put it out. [62]

*　*　*

I have also been considering what has been most satisfactory in my own life, and ruling out Bob on the ground that he is not in a cheap edition. I have come to the conclusion that it is the *Passage to India*. It's amazing luck that one's best book should be the widest read one, and the one most likely to do good, as well. When writing the *Passage* I thought it a failure, and it was only owing to Leonard [Woolf] that I was encouraged to finish it. [B]ut ever since publication I have felt satisfied, and find very little in it that nauseates or irritates me.

So I shall ring up—probably about 5.0. on Tuesday, or perhaps you might then ring the flat. Bob will be with me and we might meet you later if all are free.

With best love,
Morgan

*　*　*

[postcard]   17-7-37
West Hackhurst,
Abinger Hammer,
Dorking.

And you shall have one too. I may ring you up Sunday evening for news, or on Monday morning if not too rushed. I leave for Paris at 10.0. I remarked during a performance of Uday Shankar's that you were intending to address the Cambridge Majlis.[63] It would seem prematurely, for the Indian to whom the remark was addressed simpered that you had not so far replied to him.

Popped over to Brighton last night in a car and gave a certain William there quite a surprise. Wish I was more often surprising, but cannot design the suitable machinery. Am delighted this morning by notices from the "Right" Book Club[,] so called it says because it gives people the right opinions. P.T.O. Can we not form the "Wrong" book club now, and if so what shaped note paper will it require?

M.

*   *   *

17-2-38   West Hackhurst,
Abinger Hammer,
Dorking.

My dearest Christopher,

I do wish I'd written before. I didn't want to write, which was anyhow something to write about, and now your letter posted at Columbo arrives. When I get to London on Saturday I may send you a cable. Bob and I enjoyed that party, though I believe it wasn't the general verdict and the wine-cup vile and Rupert Doone an obvious crook. Since then a good deal has happened as good deals go. I have taken my Northern Lecture Tour, and stopped for three days with the Lord Lieutenant of Northumberland and walked for once upon the Roman Wall. I liked all this. Today mother and I and Aunt Rosalie have been cutting up oranges for marmalade, and I have—at last—finished Guy Mannering.[64] Tomorrow I must start tearing up family letters—there are about 200 years of them in this house, all insipid, and like most people I am the last of my race, but calmer than most, since I accept the theories of Mendel. I'm glad that you came to this place, and think of it as sane: glad that I am [of] any use to you whatsoever. I always thought you were right to take this outing.—Bother the Test—am so certain I shall fail in mine that I can't think about it.[65] Now and then I get towards facing facts, but get too tired and bored to keep on at it. I only hope I shan't let any one down badly: *that* thought does precise itself [i.e., make itself precise] rather alarmingly.

Bob seems older. I think it is stirring him to do something about his painting, though. May is like all women here; no respect for art when it is practiced by her man. I have never seen friction between them, but have the impression that when he wants to win he does and that he will get the oil-paints which will make the front parlour smell and might have been a great coat. His intelligence is so great that it makes up for his inferiority to her in will—if there is such a thing as will. I am going to supper there on Sunday, and he to me on Monday. I could go on writing bout him at length, and I know you would read all I say. He is doing very well at school—*this* sentence refers to *Robin*—and can already read and write a little and tell his parents about Jesus.

I hope I'll get to Berlin, Christopher. My mother is the difficulty, as she thinks Hitler will cut my head off. I will see if Mr Bennett of Caius [College] can't again be helpful, and quiet her. Anyhow I will write to Heinz. And when I go up to Caius again I will be seeing Ian. By the way, I liked Oliver Low at your party extremely.[66]—What a paragraph is this! all the big bits seem to have got together. Like when one cuts up for marmalade. Bob wanted to come to Berlin with me, an April weekend, but it doesn't look possible.—Well, writing this letter makes me rather sad, perhaps [that is] why I didn't write it before. I wish we could be talking and I wonder why and how it is that we help one another, for we do. I'll go to bed now and have some of my extraordinary dreams. These are *either* sentences which I sometimes write down as I waken, and are I believe proofs that, as a novelist, I have gone underground. *Or* they are about war, aerial bombardment, gas, marshalled by me without any appropriate emotion.

I know that sort of voyage and am very sorry about it. Well it's over now. I love you, and Bob and I love you,

Morgan

* * *

[handwritten postcard]
Hankow. [China] March 16 [1938]

Thank you so much for cable and letter. Off tomorrow to look for the moon in the Yellow River. Wystan says may he print your Landor parody "I strove with none," in Oxford Book of Light Verse? Fine weather here, snow all gone, but full moon, so the raids have started. Best love to you and Bob. Thinking of you so much.

Christopher

*   *   *

Friday. [August 1938]

My dearest Morgan,

Have just spoken to Oliver Low. He will send you his address. He was enchanted at the prospect of seeing you again.

Have finished "Maurice," and am in a state of reverence which even my most irreverent moments of you do nothing to dispel. What a book! In some ways, your very best. In those scenes with Alec, you are positively clairvoyant—nothing like them has even been written about the class war, by anybody. And Maurice himself is a masterpiece—one of the few truly noble characters of fiction. It seems odd, and pompous, after all these years, to be paying you compliments, in words which we both feel are rotted through and through with misuse. But I can't help it. You are a very great writer. And I am more proud than I can say to be your friend.

I have nothing, really, to criticize about the ending—except that you shouldn't stop there. Or there should be a sequel. Alec and Maurice have all their troubles before them. Maybe, it'll be all right—but one wants to know. I suppose Maurice threw up the office? I suppose they both went out to the 1914 war? I should love to know what they're doing now.

Thank you for my visit to West Hackhurst. I hope there will be others.

Your loving
C.

*   *   *

28-8-38

Fritton Hithe,[67]
Nr. Gt. Yarmouth.

Dearest Christopher,

There was and perhaps somewhere is an Epilogue chapter to Maurice but everyone thought it a mistake. Kitty, on an old-maidish weekend in Yorkshire, comes across them both as wood cutters. This seemed both too short and too long. Yes, Maurice chucked his office, and—though the tale is set pre-war—they went to the war, I suppose. That would now make them, if alive, now about 50 each. I can only still see them together if they have passed a life of adventures together.—I have sometimes thought of Alec marrying.

The third section of the book was once much the weakest. I have worked on it cautiously as I gained new experience being very careful not to make it my experience. I was in 1914 ignorant in this way of class—it stimulated my imagination, that was all. About ten years later I met old Reg Palmer, (and about seventeen years later Bob) which gave me knowledge, and stuffed the frame of Alec out in places suitable to his physique. But I tried to keep him as the dream which turned into the scare and then into the mate. I was always determined not to end sadly—as we were saying, it is not worthwhile.

Yes, Maurice is a good man I think and so a nice one.—I think, to run back in this letter, that part III should have been more gradual and longer, more social wrenchings shown or heard "off" [*sic*].I wish it could be published, especially after getting your letter. But it isn't so much my mother now—it's Bob. Everyone connects him with me, and this Dover muddle showed me how careful I must be not to bring bother or harm his way. My "*Life*" if briefly and blazingly written, might be worth doing after my death, but that's ruled out too while he lives.

Your letter firmed me up a lot. It certainly is a comfort to know that my work is respected by someone whom I respect and are [*sic*] as fond of as you. It confirms my belief that life is not all nonsense and cruelty—the inversion of Victorian complacency—but has hard spots of sense and love bobbing about in it here and there. The people here, in this Hithe, seem grimly chaotic, just holding on to the wharves till they slip off, the news gets worse and worse, and they don't seem able to feel—still less are they able to *do*, none of us can do that. I warrant you, I silence them all at the breakfast table.

However, my visit is in no sense a failure. We bathe, go to Lowestoft Regatta, sit in the lake-ward sloping garden. On Tuesday I go to c/o J. [Icelandic] Sprott, Magavelda, Blakeney, Norfolk, and to the flat for a night on Friday, where [I] will ring you up.

My mother much enjoyed your visit, she writes. I specially liked the talk about China, or rather the Atlas. I think a good deal about the book. It's a major technical problem.[68] Howsoever that's solved, the book will come easily, but unless the solution is the correct one, the book won't be good. And I cannot think what the correct solution is. Perhaps Wystan divinely distrait, will hit on it, but I am more disposed to rely on you.

Well I must conclude, hoping that you will like this letter and your household its envelope. Coronets seen everywhere, on the little boats, on the bigger boats, on the bath towels. I cannot make it out. Host and hostess are out calling on some Colmans ("we're all mustered here"). Weyland[69] and his cousin—15 o[r] 16, pleasant—have gone out in a pram, which is a little boat, to visit boys across the lake, and I have been walking round the estate with Lady K.'s slightly critical elder sister.

With much love & great gratitude from

M.

* * *

[October 1938?]   Sunday

Dear Christopher,

I find that M. M. Gabet and Huc had exactly your and W[ystan]'s problem to solve, and the result of it was "Huc's Travels." H. writes sometimes "I," sometimes "M. Huc" and of course sometimes "M. Gabet." The result is very readable.[70]

It is 10.0. P.M. and I have only just found or indeed looked for my pen. I am really very depressed and perhaps shall join the Labour Party. Communists, cut off from the one practical experiment in their creed, will become even more flimsy and irresponsible than they are now. The alternative to the Labour Party is to find some ballast in my own past.

Nothing seems right—the table is too high, the bed packety [sic], and all because four people who could under no circumstances have been my friends have met at Munich.

I come to town Monday and go to Scotland on Tuesday.—I was very pleased to hear that the Chinese book is to be dedicated to me.

With love,
Morgan

* * *

14-11-38

Dear Christopher,

I am "thinking of you": a nice evening for the elderly lovers, no rain and not much wind. I shall see it in London.—I come up on Wednesday, at least I suppose so, but have mild influenza or a bad cold. Under their stress, I have signed Toller's letter to Roosevelt, sent Richard Acland money for Mr. V.[?] Bartlett,[71] favour the arrival of Czech refugees at Hollingbury, recommended copulation to Zukunft, and asked my M. P. to support the Abolition of Capital Punishment. But I have refused to ask New Zealand to send mutton & butter to Spain. One must show a little proper pride.

Perhaps I shall see Jackie some time.[72] I can't feel that Guy Burgess matters. I used to take him seriously, but he used "a priori" where it made no sense, which I found disconcerting. The si*tua*tion, the taking away someone from someone, is more serious I agree, but if J. is a strong character this won't matter either.

May ring you up Thursday morning if only to ask you Gerald Heard's address.

M

*   *   *

W[est] H[ackhurst]   23-12-38

My Dearest Christopher,

I have had your card, and—today—your letter. I rang your mother up the day before yesterday, having forgotten your dates. She told me in brief a story which you will now have heard at length from her—namely that Heinz had rung up the house, under the impression that you were leaving almost at once for America. This suggests that letters between him and you have been miscarrying. She gave me an address to which I sent a card and to which I had better write, I think, after I have had a reply from you, and learnt your latest news or absence of news.

My life is a water-colour rendering of yours: a burst water-pipe instead of a frozen radiator, cough and cold instead of clap, failure to start an article on "How I listen to Music" instead of a novel, and a £50 loan to poor Mrs Morgan at the garage instead of an American debt. I will not mention to anyone what you have told me. I don't wonder you feel a bit down. When I see you again I shall like an account of the illness, about which I am vague, I've had catheters, and if they are the painfulness to which you refer, it gets less and less each time. Is the doctor good as well as sensible? (The Englishman always assumes that every continental doctor is sensible).

I shall see Bob, May, Robin, Mum, Dad, Ted, Vi, Con, Les, Else, Monday if I'm well enough to go to them; then I have to broadcast twice in that same evening. I have been away (Nott[ingham]s[hire] & elsewhere) for about a week.

You don't mention Wystan's operation. Please send all news, particularly about Heinz. I was very glad to hear about Jackie.

We are almost snowed up here—primitive and comfortable, plenty of coal, food, and wine, and the gardener can flounder as far as the accumulation and the postman as far as the back door.

Love to Wystan. Very very much love to you, and thank you for your letter.

Morgan

* * *

237 East 81st Street.
April 29. [1939]   New York City.

My Dearest Morgan,

I am so sorry to hear that you have been ill. I do hope it wasn't very serious? Wystan has written to you, and you'll have got his letter by this time; but I don't know if he told you any of our news?

Barring accidents, I am leaving New York on Saturday next, en route for Hollywood, travelling by bus, with my American friend, Harvey Young, whom I think I told you about. We plan to make a big loop to the south, taking in New Orleans, then up through Texas. The whole journey might take three weeks.

I certainly shan't be sorry to leave this city. It's really not New York's fault, but mine, that I've got so little out of being here, except the feeling of pure despair, values dissolving, everything uncertain. The war-scares, the central heating and the publishers' cocktail-parties have combined to create an atmosphere which I can only compare to the wood at the beginning of the Inferno. Perhaps, too, it has to do with the approach of my thirty-fifth birthday, which is a key-birthday, I believe. But where is Vergil? The only one I can espy on this continent is Gerald Heard, so I must go out west to talk to him. Particularly, I want to talk about pacifism, for I know now (it's about the only thing I do know) that I'm a pacifist: or, as Wystan defines it, I won't kill people I don't know personally. And certainly I wouldn't kill even my dearest friends to save the imperial trade-routes. So what is to be done? Gerald thinks the Red Cross. I agree. But it's more than that. You have to get into a state of mind. You have to stop hating. I mean, *I* have to stop hating. You, I know, never have: that is why you and people like you are the only visible towers of strength in this awful time. I suppose, if I knew definitely in advance that the English authorities were going to shut all conscientious objectors up in prison, without the option of doing medical or other work, I wouldn't return to England at all. There is no sense in being a muzzled martyr; unless, of course, you're so famous that [your marty]rdom makes an impression on other people. Or what do you think? [Wyst]an, provisionally, is staying here. He has been more or less definitely [off]ered a teaching job next month, at a public school upstate. We both plan, if war doesn't break out, to get on the quota, which will enable us to take any kind of employment here. That doesn't commit us to becoming American citizens. In fact, you have to have been on the quota two years before you can even make your first application. And, in the meantime, you can return to England if you wish. So nothing irrevocable has happened.

Do write soon, to say how you are and what you have been doing. We entirely lack any reliable news about England. One day the newspapers tell us everybody is in a panic, the next day they are calm. How has conscription been received? What do the Left say? Are they simply preparing to kill the entire German nation in order to free it from Hitler? Or have they thought up something else?

I have written nothing, and shan't do so, until I'm free of my present mood, which is worse than useless. I seem to have lost what little courage I ever possessed; but it will come back, no doubt. Perhaps I've simply been eating too many oysters, or drinking too much milk.

How are Bob, May, Robin? How is your Mother? My greetings to her. I suppose you never ran across Jacky Hewit again? He's another problem. A very big one. I heard something from Heinz, the other day. He's just had an operation for hernia. I only hope it exempts him from active military service. Oh dear . . . it's all very well for Gerald to talk about non-attachment! Which reminds me that the other, all-too-attached Gerald tells me he's been seeing you. I'm afraid that Satan has been deserting His own, recently. Poor Gerald seemed in a very bad way.

My address in Hollywood will be c/o Christopher Wood. 8766 Arlene Terrace. Hollywood. Cal. Hope to hear form [*sic*] you there.

Love, as always,
Christopher

* * *

W[est] H[ackhurst]   14-5-39

Dearest Christopher,

I don't seem to want to write letters to you. An unfinished one lies somewhere, saying how wonderful I thought Wystan's poems in the China book, and how I found the prose a very good account, but not as good quite as your talking. I meant too to write to you after I saw On the Frontier in London.[73] Meant & meant. You ask how things here are, whether people are upset or not. It's very difficult to describe. I have not been upset myself for nearly a month. I don't think my conduct out (as Bob has his), but I try, by shirking the wireless news and most of the newspapers, to keep calm and cheerful, and often succeed. It's a choice, for me, between (i) "facing reality" and feeling and acting poisonously in consequence, and (ii) being amusing and helpful and carrying on a few private dreams. The trouble is the awakening, which might make me go crackers (certifiably insane); "yah—you haven't hardened yourself—BLOP." But I'm fumbling after the belief that *one ought not to mind before hand being caught out*, one *ought not to insure*, and that's all that the hardening process is.

The above state, and other people's proceeds from the extreme singularity of the social scene; the crisis has gone on for a year now: unheard of: and it's impossible to echo its crescendo with a personal one. In that sense the individual has already given up, thrown in his hand, failed. If you don't play the crisis' game though—and Gerald Heard will teach you how to do that—failure will seem less certain. I wonder that I should have taught you anything, but it is quite true that I don't hate a lot, if that is at all exemplary. It is partly idleness, partly an attempt to avoid being hated, but partly an impulse towards love. I have had a very lucky life—my best book (Passage to India) has been translated into many languages and become a Penguin, and my heart has been given Bob. This is out of the way luck.

But what are you to do dear Christopher. I don't see, after what happened to Heinz that you can help hating, and I hope G. Heard won't try to persuade you out of it. If you can come to love in your own way that's all right of course. But don't feel worried at being bitter.

I have still not told dear Christopher what he is to do. Well *I* in your shoes would not return to England unless the social scene normalises. Your mother can go to Cheshire if there is a bust up, and those of your friends who are caught in London—you couldn't save them by getting caught too. Don't complain[,] I'm talking common-sense. I know I am.

Your account of America is depressing, especially the letter in which you referred to Lincoln Kirstein. My heart lept up at his name—I thought him so nice when I met him in London a few years back. I thought you were going to say that lots of Americans were like him. Instead of which you say none of them are like him. I look forward though to see[ing] this film maker (name forgotten).

I have done nothing about Jackie. I wish I had seen more of him before you left. I don't know how to talk to him, though when we have run into each other he has been very nice.

G. Hamilton has not told me of his troubles. He introduced me to the purlieus of the Wine & Food Society, and I have written an article for their magazine called "Porridge or Prunes Sir?" but am not sure what J . . . Symonds[74] will think of it. We lunched at the Ecun[?] de France—silly and bad, I thought. [A]nd how sillily and badly the Hogarth Press have brought out my Pamphlet by the way. I told John Lehmann too, I did. Give me back the Woolens if 6d cannot buy a better clothing than that. Now I must go to bed.

15-5-39

I do not seem to have answered your questions, but here is the backside of a calendar.[75] I don't know how conscription is taken. There was an enormous procession against it the other day but my taxi driver was in favour. I may send you Liddell Hart's pamphlet against it. I see rather less of the Left or of the poor. Must counteract these omissions. My health is all right again. I have two major works in progress—the editing of A Modern Symposium for schools, and the sending of England's Pleasant Land to a publisher. I have just been reading an article by Priestley who rightly prefers genius to wealth, and wants genius to be boosted as wealth is. I don't know what will happen to Conscientious Objectors. Nothing in the present mood. It entirely depends on the Axis. I go to the Libel Committee twice a week and like the Chairman (Lord Porter).[76] It is soothing, with the Thames flowing under the gothic windows, but it is fatal for a writer to know so much about the Law. Even if the Law is improved, things must get worse & worse for literature and all forms of public expression, it seems to me. Everything will have to be considered and vetted.

Bob, May & Robin are well—if there's war May, Robin, Vi (Ted's wife) and Shirley May and Bob's mother & father will all get to Berkshire I hope. We expect Cousin Percy and (ugh) his wife, also two schoolchildren (little boys).

Had such an affectionate letter from Wystan.

Bob and I hope to go walking in Dorset soon (Cloud Hill).

With very much love,
Morgan

* * *

W[est] H[ackhurst]   17-6-39

Dearest Christopher,

At a Cambridge commemoration dinner this week, Guy Burgess, supported by Anthony Blunt, came fussing me because you had behaved so badly to Jackie.[77] As I daresay you have, and they then wanted me to read a letter from you to him which they had brought to the banquet. This I declined to do, to their umbrage. I could not see why I had to, when neither you nor J. had requested me to do so. G. B. [Guy Burgess] was insistent I should write to you, which I should have done in any case. He is [a] most cerebral gangster.

I wrote not long ago to J. suggesting a meeting, but had no answer, and now understand why, and am glad he did not answer. I guess the situation, and feel very sorry for the boy. This much I will say, that now you know you can miscalculate you will be more careful another time. Have you to provide for him at all?

G. H. [Gerald Hamilton] whom I saw lately, spoke guardedly, that it to say, god how he chattered.

I am well, and until recently stable or impervious. But a couple of letters of George Thomsom have joggled me a bit—he hates my "What I Believe."

Previous to that I had 3 lovely days walking in Dorset—all bread and cheese and beer and Bob. We went over Portland, then along the cliffs to Lakeworth and Cloud Hill and Wareham. We were both very happy. I have some other pleasures ahead if the weather holds. On Tuesday I go to Geneva to see the Prado pictures, on July 3rd to Glyndebourne to hear Cosi fan tutte and on Sept. 4th to Stockholm, to represent the P. E. N. Club. The Libel Committee continues to make progress.

I never travel, and am rather in a flutter over Tuesday. I would have come with you to America, I think, but was not sure it suited you and Wystan, and I have been too afraid to come since.

Am anxious for further news. Do hope you feel richer and happier. How did the bus tour go off?

With love from
Morgan

Do you know anything of an American dramatiser called Jo Eisinger?[78] He has done A Room with a View, without permission. It does not look good and I am turning it down, but wish you were here to advise. Thornton Wilder is brought here by Lady Colifax to tea tomorrow.

*   *   *

[The following is typed at the top of the page:]
No, never heard of Jo Eisinger. Usually, these people turn out to be ambitious university students. But, for all I know, he may be the flower of the U.S. stage.

7136 Sycamore Trail.
Hollywood. California.

July 3 [1939]

My Dearest Morgan,

I was so glad to get your letter. Yes, of course I have behaved badly. Very badly indeed, but, I hope, quite straightforwardly—if breaking promises can ever be called straightforward. How like you to refuse to read my letter:

I am very grateful for that. Really, if I'd known that it was going to be bandied round Cambridge, I'd have drawn up a proper document, headed: To Whom This May Not Concern. I would be angry with Burgess, but I am not in a position to be angry with anybody. It's no more than I deserve.

Why didn't I tell you all about it? Because I felt ashamed of myself. I am still ashamed; but don't see that I could have acted differently, having got things into such a mess. The whole business was a problem of distance and money. I couldn't afford to fly to England and speak to J[acky] personally, which would have straightened everything out, and left no hard feelings. So, I wrote. And all letters of that sort, however well expressed, sound brutal.

You are right to warn me to be careful in future; but don't worry, I shall be. This time, I really have learnt my lesson.

The papers say there really will be war, this time: and here I sit, waiting for it to start. I still feel as I did when I wrote to you last, and as I shall continue to feel, I believe, for the rest of my life: that I have been absolutely wrong. Force is no good—even to achieve the grandest objectives. One's enemies can only be won over [by] active goodwill. If you exterminate them, like bugs, the poison only enters into yourself, so you are defeated anyway. And a semi-victory is even worse. At a reptile show here the other day, I saw an elderly, dowdy spinster (of the type which usually fusses over dogs) stroking the heads of two big Indian cobras. She has kept poisonous snakes for twenty years, and never once been bitten. She can tame any snake in a fortnight. "You see," she explained, "they know I won't hurt them. So they aren't frightened of me."

Gerald Heard, our master and guide, is away just now. Huxley impresses me much less. He is a big aimiable [sic] cyclops, but he learnt everything out of a book. He just cannot stop quoting, comparing, annotating. And he has a rather sinister underlife of smart luncheons. Harvey goes to art-school five days a week, and is out all day. I take and fetch him in a very wobbly Ford. Our little house would amaze you. It is really beautiful—high up the hill, among woods. There is great deal of work connected with it, which keeps us both busy; and I am trying to write something about Ernst Toller. I have hardly any money left, and no job yet; though Mrs Viertel promises something as soon as Viertel arrives. He is in the train now. I am quite happy on the surface, or perhaps I should say under the surface: there is a layer of gloom about Europe which is likely to thicken. I still don't really know what I shall do if war comes. Return, Wystan says, and nurse the wounded. But should we be allowed to? If only I hadn't wasted all this time with the hate-brigade. When you start trying to think for yourself, every step is so painfully slow. I miss you dreadfully. More than anybody in England. And you would love it here. The country is so beautiful. And that great garden-suburb down in the valley doesn't matter at all. It's even convenient, for they have very good bookshops. The studios and their life is as remote as it is in London. If you're not in it you never see it at all.

Wystan, in the midst of the greatest love of his life, is careering about the New Mexican desert. I think he is growing up very fast. Anyhow, his work gets better and better—really classic. In my little way, I think I am imitating your curve. The war-silence is setting in, before, I hardly dare to hope, The Passage to India. But, alas, I'm not writing a Maurice.

All my love to you, and to Bob, and respects to your Mother.

Your erring
Christopher

I find I've said nothing about J[acky]. I wish I could do something to help. I paid, of course, for the Pittman School, which he should have finished by now. But the money was going through John Lehmann, and I gather that J. and John had had some kind of coolness or quarrel—anyway on J's side. I wrote to John when I wrote to J. and asked him to stand by and help. Of course, I was and am terribly worried about how J. would take my letter. He seems to have run to Gerald [Hamilton] (Gerald wrote me) and told him everything. Gerald, no doubt, provided some worldly-wise comfort. But what is he going to do now? He has, or had, his old job at the hotel Goring. (This I heard before he got my letter). He had no need to take the job back, because I had asked John to provide adequate money for him to live on, as long as he was at the school. But maybe, owing to this friction with John, he didn't go and collect it. There's a great deal I shall never know.

I do think that, if you feel strong enough, it would be a very good thing if you talked to Jacky yourself.

Needless to say—if you ever do read that notorious letter—I wasn't quite exact in what I wrote about my reasons for not wanting him to join me out here. I had to express things in Jacky's terms. What I couldn't explain to him—perhaps not entirely to anybody—was a feeling of utter spiritual impotence. I just suddenly knew that I couldn't cope. I knew that, however much I dread loneliness, there is something inside me which has to be alone, and which wasn't alone when J. was around. Heinz was different. So is Harvey. Perhaps because they are foreigners. I don't know. Anyhow, this all sounds rather tiresome when I write it down, like the sensations of a character in D.H. Lawrence.

The only thing that matters, of course, is that J. shall emerge from this business with the minimum amount of mistrust in the human race. That's where you could help him, if you would. Most of the people he has known seem to have been such utter skunks.

If you get this letter in the middle of an air-raid, just burn it. I suppose 1914 cut short a lot of similar tangles. Please write again soon.

* * *

10-7-39

Dearest Christopher,

Do not forget me. We are getting rather dim over here I think. I mean I rather think that there is going to be "a war," and that a sort of veil must be descending. I very much hope that you and everyone will try to keep away—it is clearly your job to see us sink from a distance, if sink we do.

Now what have I done today, previous to writing the above thoughtful paragraph?

Picked some raspberries and helped to bottle them, and finished writing an unpublishable though not indecent comedy-story.

I have, however, become worried by aeroplanes—the stunting overhead has got on my nerves and I cannot find out how to ignore it and keep on regretting Abinger Hammer's lost peace—it only lost it early this year, after having had it for thousands of years. I used to get round this sort of discomfort by self-pity, but partly owing to Bob I have given that up and have to remain uncomfortable.

I go to London tomorrow, lunch with Ian! who has kindly invited me, and not to dinner with Nik what's his name!! and Sandy something!!! who have by a coincidence also invited me. (I cannot go, because George Thomson is coming.) I enjoyed Geneva—or have I written since?

Best love from
Morgan

* * *

W[est] H[ackhurst]   23-8-39

Dearest Christopher,

Yes the news certainly is unpleasing and I feel in a farewell-letter mood. One or two people I am very fond of will get envelopes posted to them today. I hope the same idea has occurred to you. I had intended to go to Sweden next week but England is the best address. This evening I meet Joe with perhaps a Jamaican Blackamoor[79] at Piccadilly Circus. Blackamoors are a distant mystery to me. I am very busy and rather resolutely happy and cheerful. Bob is on holiday with May in Devonshire, but the wretched woman on a farm where they once stayed is ill, and May who doesn't like her has gone to nurse her and run the place, while Bob remains in Sidmouth with Robin who makes too much noise. My mother is well, but somewhat shattered this morning by the German-Soviet non-aggression pact. I took her for a few days to London last week, various relatives and refugees were seen, also a play of moderate merit entitled "Alien Corn." Post Card from Ian, investigating social conditions in Greece. Met Max Beerbohm on Sunday. Oh yes and by God a Mr Wheeler or Wheler called last week, and said he was a friend of yours and you were so happy in the States. He is what Catullus would call a "salaputium dissertum."[80]

Can you or any one else in the happy States translate that?

Mr W. also delivered a homage speech which left me dumb.

Morgan's best love.

Bob, I, Oliver Low and his wife spent a most pleasant evening together lately and went to a play of moderate merit entitled "The Women."

2

The War Years: 1939–45

W[est] H[ackhurst]   1-9-39

Dearest Christopher,

Sergt Button [i.e., Bob] and self rang your mother up on the 29th and urged her and Richard to get off at once. So I feel and indeed think I was useful. We didn't write to Heinz as B. thought that even if the p[ost]c[ard] got through to him it would do him no good.

I know you want to know how I feel. Well I cried a bit when my mother paid her usual morning call to my bedroom, and I'm a little irritable and hysterical but not at all bad. I am going to write some notes on Beethoven's Sonatas, and have bought a 2/- book rather than a 4/6 one to write about the war in. Sweden cancelled. I am rather at a loose end. Poor Mrs Barger is here, wearing herself and others out, about her tiresome neurotic daughter who, against her orders, has been dumped by her bossy son in a mental retreat.

It is going to be awful here I expect. *Whatever one does is wrong,*[1] so do not come back here, that is the wrongest.

Love,
Morgan

*   *   *

September 27, 1939
303 South Amalfi Drive
Santa Monica. California

My dearest Morgan,

Thank you so much for your 2 letters. I only got them yesterday, as Gerald Heard is quite a long way from us now we've moved to above address. Please write here. It will be forwarded, if I suddenly leave.

This place is in the same road as Aldous Huxley, whom I scarcely ever see—and Viertel, whom I see all day: we are doing a film together, in the intervals of listening to the radio. I believe we are both already crazy—but it's so hard to tell. Anyhow, one lives in a dull, stolid ache of misery, illuminated by hysterical laughter, and alleviated by chain-smoking. I think, at intervals: "Of course, it's quite ridiculous—I can't possibly go on like this." But I do. Everyone does.

The outside world—which could hardly be less real to the most enlightened yogi—is a thin noisy tone film of fast cars, the Pacific, bathers of superb physique, palm trees, filling stations, mountains, advertisements. Garbo comes to lunch, and one is not surprised. She has very long eyelashes. There are heat waves, quite big floods. One eats meals. But you, and Stephen and Heinz, and several other of my friends are every bit as solid as the people I talk to in the so-called flesh. I talk to you, too, and have horrible nightmares.

You were only too right in your prophecy that the war, when it came, would be crazy. Just how crazy it is, we have yet to find out. Even as I write, there is an Alice in Wonderland rumour that Germany and Russia will form a new League of Nations.

What shall I do? Stay here for the present. I am half an American citizen, anyway. Later, perhaps, an ambulance corps. Wystan is in New York. Whatever we do will probably be together.

Give my love to everybody—especially Bob—and write again soon.

As ever,
your loving
C.

*   *   *

W[est] H[ackhurst]   8-9-39

Dearest Christopher,

Bob writes "I hadn't the heart to write to Christopher. I feel he must be so upset that I am afraid of making things worse." As for me, I write, but shan't do so again until you write to me. (Not huff, Blackmail).

We are comfortably, all too comfortably, settled in—mother, self, cousins Percy & Dutchie, Agnes (servant), and Mrs Jeffrey, former servant, comes and helps. No evacuees so far, on account of my mother's age. There is no reason I should go to London and danger, since Bob is working or confined to his house when he isn't. I feel unhappy of course, sometimes very so, but not afraid. I found Gerald's book most interesting—have reviewed it for Joe.[2] My "plans"(!) are (i) to live by journalism rather than by govt subsidy for propaganda work[;] (ii) to give up the B[runswick] Square flat, and take a cheaper and safer one near Bob[;] (iii) to play and make notes on Beethoven's Sonatas. I bought a large note book to write in about the War, something was wrong with it, couldn't think what. Then in a few days I realised what I wanted to do. I have been lent Tovey's edition of the Sonatas.

Well, this is the very last letter you ever get from me, unless—

Love to all, as per usual.

My ex[ecut]ors are (i) Williams Deacon's Bank, 20 Birchin Lane, E.C.4 (ii) a personal ex[ecut]or.—J. Sprott, failing him, you, failing you, John Simpson. If Sprott shouldn't act and it comes to you and you are still as I hope you will be in the U. S. A., you should pass on the job to Simpson.

Morgan's love.

* * *

W[est] H[ackhurst]   31-10-39

My dearest Christopher,

So you have been naughty, not religious. I had all sorts of theories as to why you would not write to me, and had made up an amazing sentence about looking at one's navel and seeing something like a fountain pen. But you have merely been naughty and idle. My chief extra news is that Bob has portated me into a flat near him at Chiswick—same accommodation as B[runswick] Sq. at 1/2 the price and a lovely view over Turnham Green which reminds me of Harrogate.[3] I don't much like it, but I came not much to like B. Square. Bob arranged the move, took up and put down the lino, called in his helmet on the electricity and gas, fixed the black-outs up, and May stitched, lengthened and stretched.

I seem to have mislaid your letter. I am very glad you and Viertel are doing a new film. As you know, I want you to stop where you are. I don't know what I feel about the State of Emergency prevalent this side. I seem to get used up trying to be in good spirits and pick up scraps of art. One has slightly smiling confessions with the most unlikely people: "Well, as a matter of fact I feel all right."—"Well, why, fancy! so do I." The country looks sweet, there are no aeroplanes. London looks lovely when it is moonlight, and has a charming ultra-violet lamp at the bottom of the Haymarket, which looks like a fuchsia and lights up the luminous paint upon the sand bags. There are good lunch hour concerts at the National Gallery, at one of which I sat close to the Queen. It feels like the end of an age, and I can picture a new

London which other people will consider sensible and civilised. Of course, when I *think*, all seems raving nonsense, as it does to you—except that I'm sure it's it, not we, who are mad. I wouldn't smoke so much. Foolish. Nicotine. And if I *look forward* I'm sure we are all in for a bad time during the next six months, perhaps for being killed. That's one of my reasons for not wanting you and Wystan back here. Another is that you both must and can carry on civilisation. I have had some praise for being civilised lately, from John Simpson, Michael Roberts, etc., and lap it all up. You must take care not to get so desperate and hysterical lest there is, in this pompous word, something worth carrying on.

> With love, as always,
> Morgan.

Will write again soon. Many messages from Bob.
[written along the margin of the first page of this two-sided letter:] Will you send me a newspaper now and then—not the New York Times, which I see. Something of Hearst's? Or are they too silly?

*   *   *

31-1-40   West Hackhurst,
                                           Abinger Hammer,
                                           Dorking.

Dearest Christopher,

I got your letter yesterday. I have told Bumpus[4] to send you most of my non-fictional work, also *Where Angels [Fear to Tread]* and *The Longest Journey*. My books can't all be out of print in the U.S.A., though, as I keep getting cheques form [sic] Harcourt Brace for them. As for the newspapers, I didn't *know* I had got any from you, but perhaps I have mistaken yours, for Harold Barger's. He sends us a good many *New York Times*, and has presented me with a subscription to *Time*. Now and then a *Life* arrives. Would that be from you? I have had no Pacific-side papers.

I am very glad you are making money, as some day you may have to give us some. I have had good luck financially though, as an investment which I thought was a goner has paid up in full plus arrears of interest. And my new flat is half the rent of the old one. Bob has got it very nice. I like the bedroom, tolerate the sitting room, but hate the pokey passage, kitchen and W.C. On this last I have seldom sat, as the pipes have been frozen for weeks. I suppose it is the war that makes me not happy there. It would be difficult to say when I was happy, but it would be untrue to say I was unhappy.

Though we have had a good deal of trouble here with my cousins, domestic misery indeed, they came here for the duration and left at Christmas in a huff. I think they behaved very badly. The other protagonist was my mother. My nice aunt Rosalie is here for the present, and we are snowed up. I meant to go and see Bob tomorrow. Do you get news of H. N. [Heinz Nedermeyer] by the way? If you do I should like to know. We had a Christmas dinner at Bob's—he, May, Robin from the country, Ted & Vi & Shirley May, Mum & Dad, Les & Con, not Else, not Sid who had made her great with child, me, and Joe came in with a blackamoor. May is nursing, but because she wants to and has nothing to do: private patients at the West London Hospital.

My life isn't socially rich, though. I have this home stuff and the Bob-stuff, and a good many cheap invitations from exactly the same people I've known all my life, though some of them get younger. No Charlie Chaplin, no Krishnamurti. "Oh but you could see them if you liked." Yes—and more easily than I think, I do think. I asked, very hesitatingly, Norman Birhelt to dinner. He didn't come for weeks so I thought he didn't want to. No—merely busy, and now he writes me a friendly almost raving letter out of the blue, proud to know such a person as myself. Sometimes I regret my long mouse-tunnel and shake my head at all the mice I have met at the cross-ways—I must poke my head out and roar before it is too late. I must ask the French Ambassador to lunch and not have J. B. Priestly to meet him. I must remind Sir Edmund Ironside that Tonbridge, where we were both at school, might well be forgotten. Over all this, I suppose, or upon it, sits Gerald (Heard).[5] Is it true that he is fat and has a beard and likes robes? I do not mind, but has he? I myself am much fatter than you remember me—the result of the operation, it's thought. I am certainly more cushiony and courageous than I was, but more irritable and with fears of hysteria. I don't expect to behave well when the trouble starts, shall be offended and maybe go mad, running slowly in large circles with my head down is the way I see myself—I think I once told you. Oh this believing! As soon as you believe a thing it goes dead in your hands, and you have to begin again, and on the same thing. It makes being a prophet or a teacher so impossible, and *for* the life of a mouse. All the splendour and solidity I encounter now is in books written in the past, the shut-away, unnibbled past of Madame de Sévigné.[6] I wish I could write one more book myself, and may still be young enough to have it forced out of me by suffering. Wisdom is not a sufficient impetus by itself. I will shirk suffering if I can, don't worry about me, but if it catches me I would like to make something of it.

Love as always, and Bob will join.

Yours affectionately,
Morgan.

Write a bit about Harvey—don't know him.[7] Send his photograph? Love again, M.

P.S.   11-2-40

This has laid about as your address was at Bob's and now I open it to mention our call upon Mr. Norris. We found him in his cul-de-sackery, and he read us your letter to him about the Tom Driberg quotation—I think because he guessed I should have heard the more lurid version, according to which he sold it. His explanation is that T. D. scribbled it down without his knowledge.[8] Passing thence to the cellar, his stock did not rise, for there were a quantity of bottles of 1921 Château d'Ygnem and he had much the most persistent efforts to drink the 3 bottles which I had been given for an article in this Food & Wine Magazine. I had only saved them by lying to him, and saying they were drunk. Returning to the drawing room, my stock fell, as I made a festive reference to that day we (though particularly he) were tracked at the Hague. Vagueness and surprise were registered—the chief point though is that you did write him a very nice letter, I thought.

Much has happened in a twiddley way since I began this. Speech to Paul Morand at a P.E.N. luncheon.[9] Deputation to Mr Allen [?] about the Defence Regulations. Lunch with H. G. Wells—but not till next Tuesday.

                                                                M

*   *   *

London The Olde Worlde   21-4-40

Dearest Christopher,

I must start a letter to you. I have been feeling depressed and scared and meaning to write in that mood. But the feeling seems to have passed. Though there is no reason it should have. I have thought a good deal about the comments on you in Horizon which you mention, and with indignation, as you surmise.[10] I think Connolly is just an opportunist, who saw good material for journalism—I have no opinion of him, although many of his attitudes are acceptable and cleverly put. Stephen (whom I have gently ticket off) is another case, of course. I think he gets hypnotised by the notion of being sincere. Once when I was a child, eating rice and sweet sauce alone in a room with my great-aunt Monie's picture, I got up and smeared some of the sweet sauce upon the gilt picture frame. I did this not because I wanted to but because I had the *idea* of doing it and felt that I should be more straightforward if I put the idea into practice. This is the explanation of much of Stephen's conduct, I think. Afterwards, as I did, he tries to rub the sweet sauce out, and, as I did not, he probably succeeds. But to go on a bit, how very odd people are. I am thankful you are out of Europe at the present time, and wish nearly everyone else I loved was too. If you could save us, even at the cost of your own life, I might beckon you back, but such a notion is utter balls. You could do nothing. Where you are you can do something: manipulate the civilisation of the U.S.A. You will smile thinking that I know nothing of the hardness, the hurry, the shoddiness and the salads in which your public life is spent. I think I do know. And I think they constitute *something* to get hold of, whereas Europe, having missed its beat at the moment of the Spanish War, provides nothing. We may—having reached exhaustion point—start again, and have enough good books unburnt and good buildings standing to make the start a successful one. But that is mere speculation. Your immediate job is to stop and work where you are.

I have been reading old books too, and older than yours, I bet: Locke and Bacon. I have been ill with pleurisy, which by the way accounts for my moods. First you lie in bed swallowing these dreadful new tablets which make you sick, and despairful [*sic*] of civilisation. Then you get better and read Locke and Bacon. Then you get all right and come up to London as I did yesterday, and are reunited to Bob. I am at present lying in bed in the bedroom of my Chiswick flat. I mention the bedroom because it is a very nice little shaped room. The hour is 9.30. I shall go to lunch with Joe [Ackerley], and William [Plomer] will bring a friend to tea. Next week-end I hope to stop with John Simpson at Birmingham and to see Johnny Fisher and George Thomson who both live there now. You will gather from these names that a good deal of water has passed to and fro under the bridge since you left. We meet no Mickey Rooneys here. As for James Steward, I had never heard of him even till you mentioned him, and you can tell him so just as he is mixing his salad. Bob and I had chops, potatoes and greens yesterday, which he cooked very well, also hock[11] and port, and then played chess. I am delighted he has taken to it, as there were rather too few things which we could do together. He came down to see me when I was ill, so did John Simpson, and so—you will scarcely credit it—did Joe. Oh but I really must mention that our local refugee committee has put me on, or rather at, the Tribunal which is going to revise the refugees' sentences. This should bring me into touch with other Germans [?]. I must really get up now. Writing to you has made me very happy. Thank you for your letter.[12] I was very glad to hear about Harvey. Get him photographed. Give Gerald my love.

Love from Morgan

*   *   *

11-9-40   West Hackhurst,
                                                              Abinger Hammer,
                                                                      Dorking

Dearest Christopher,

It is very nice to hear from you again.[13] I hadn't felt I could write to you any more, except on practical matters, never hearing: but your letter sets me off. I have heard from Gerald also. No doubt this blitzkrieg makes one odd and intimating: Morgan carries more parcels than ever, but against what a tragic sky! However *you* ought not to be overawed by a blitzkrieg, after China. You know you felt just as usual, and went on as usual unless stopped. I saw the first night of it last Saturday from my flat—I think you know I have a flat near Bob's now, that's to say overlooking Turnham Green. London burning, a grandiose spectacle. Yet I felt only annoyance and sadness. When I got back here I tried to read the second book of the Aeneid, and *that* was overwhelming. It confirms my notion that we are only equal to great situations in poetry.

But I am certainly very sad and apprehensive. I am sure that we are going to be invaded.

Up to now, we have abundance of food, drink, sleep & amusement.

I have to go up to London again next Sunday, to broadcast to the Empire. Am not looking forward to it, for the place must be in a bad mess.

Your mother has given me some news of you. She is relieved that the British Embassy understands your position, and Bob and I are glad too, though he thinks it *mis*understood it! Oh what a silly fuss! My letter in the Spectation [*sic*] wasn't a defence, though I would like it to have been: it was an offensive against the Dean of St Pauls.[14] I think the whole thing has died down now, and Mr Wilson Harris seemed a bit ashamed at having vented it in his columns.

The night as I write is full of booming bombers. I wish I was out of it all—not [in] another part of the world, which would not suit me, but dead. I am sure there is hope, but want some one else to do the hoping. What would the Swami say to that? Down on it, I doubt not.

My pamphlet is out at last.[15]

I am reading Middlemarch. I have read A Portrait of A Lady.[16]

This is not much of a letter, but I have sent yours to Joe instead of rereading it, and seem stupid. Bob, May & Robin went off for a week's holiday in Devon, but he wires this morning that he has been recalled. He has had digestion troubles again, but keeps well if he diets. May is nursing at the West London. Robin has been bombed in Berks[hire], and fell the following

day off the back of a municipal dust cart, to which he was clinging.[17] Well
fare well dearest Christopher though of course I shall write again if possible and to Gerald also. Give him my love.

Love from Morgan

*   *   *

1-1-41 (my birthday)

West Hackhurst,
Abinger Hammer,
Dorking

Dearest Christopher,

The archbishop of Canterbury has wished us all an unhappy new year,
so I had better do the same to you: Archbishop: Morgan: Christopher is a
true proportion, I should think. Also want to write because a letter from
you which had miscarried has just turned up. You wrote it in the summer
of 1939, in answer to one from me about the Burgess-Jackie imbroglio, and
I am very glad to have it as it fills up a gap and also records your earlier
impressions of Los Angeles. It miscarried not in the post, but in my
mother's writing table: she appears to have stored it there while I was away,
and has now discovered it. She is quite calm about it, in fact all is well.—
Then there is your more recent letter which I want to answer. I can't do so
in detail because *I've* lost that—lent to Joe or Bob perhaps. But you told me
in it about "yogi," very clearly: about the rooms with the clocks in them and
the garden at the end. I see that one may, or may want, to go into the garden in the future. But why do you feel you have been there in the past? It's
there I don't follow you. I long often to be at rest of course, and a good
night seems a premonition of something far better. But do I *come from*, or
belong to, sleep or a garden or any conceivable state? I don't feel so.

I have written to Gerald [Heard] lately. Shall probably send this c/o him,
as I think you've changed your address. He will have told you my news,
unless I send this by air and outstripe [?]. I have several friends and love
them—there's nothing much more to say—and I sometimes look curiously
into that love for signs of a new social pattern, but see none, not the least
sign of a sign. I am going with a very odd and somewhat marginal friend to
Norfolk on Friday—Lord Kennet. He is driving me up. I may see Johnny
Fisher up there—you may remember him at Dover. He is now in the army.
In March Bob has a week's leave, and we hope to go off together. I have not
seen much of him lately, being shut up down here with a sprained ankle.
Aunt Rosalie and Mrs Barger stay here—the latter homeless.

Well dear Christopher this is not a very thrilling letter to cross the seas, but I don't mind, and indeed remember you instructing me not to mind. I will go to bed now. With my love,

Morgan

Lady Kennet's epigram:

> What is a Communist? One who has yearnings
> For equal division of unequal earnings.

Morgan's retort:

> What is a Capitalist? One who hopes
> To gain Heaven through knowing the ropes.

Query: How is Morgan's visit likely to go?

* * *

[Letterhead:] Metro-Goldwyn-Mayer Pictures
Culver City
California

February 14th. [1941]   as from: c/o Gerald Heard.
                                            8766 Arlene Terrace. Hollywood. Calif.

Dearest Morgan,

Thank you so much for your letter of January 1st. It was a long time since I'd heard, but I didn't feel out of touch, as Gerald read me what you wrote to him. How odd, and how artistically right—that the letter about Jacky should have suddenly hatched out of your Mother's writing-desk—such a very ancient egg, Chinese almost. Jacky, I gather, is now somewhere abroad: I hope he remembers me charitably, if at all. Harvey and I are giving up our house at the beginning of next week and retiring into separate privacies—quite amicably, however. I hope to get a room near Gerald, and see a good deal more of him in the evenings—until my time at Metro is up and I can surrender myself to the Quakers. What they will do with this valuable gift is still uncertain, but I shall probably start at a forestry camp for C.O.s in the mountains near here. Sooner or later, I expect to get sent to Europe.

Gerald may have told you that a number of the leading Friends on this coast are much interested in his work. They are marvellous executives—unselfish, efficient, devoted; but they're beginning to feel that ambulance units and soup kitchens are not the whole of religion. In the summer, Gerald is planning to spend a month with them, meditating and discussing. I hope to be in on this, too.

At the moment, Willy Maugham is here, resting for a few weeks before continuing his lecture-tour. He is optimistic about the war, but very tired, I think. He reminds me of an old gladstone bag, the veteran of many voyages, covered with labels. God only knows what is inside. I wish I could unpack him, but it is forbidden. He has been sealed by the customs. Or perhaps I am only inhibited by a legend. Yesterday he came to the studio, and ran into the Marx Brothers, who have no such inhibitions. They crowded round him, slapping his back: "Hi, Willy—what say we get together Friday evening, and go see the fights?" It was so queer and touching. Willy looked slightly dazed, but happy. This, I felt, is how he wants, so terribly, to be treated. But then I remembered a passage in *The Summing-Up*, in which he says that he can't bear to be touched.[18]

After the war, Willy wants to go to India, and revisit the swamis. "But why to India?" says our own little swami, "And why after the war?" He sits curled up in a corner, wrapped in a blanket, for he has just had a series of heart-attacks, and may not live much longer. He is in his fifties, and often looks like a boy of eighteen. Women clatter around him, fussy and devoted, preparing meals and arranging flowers. At sixteen, he was a revolutionary. Then he met Brahamananda, who said: "There is no failure in the search for God." And there wasn't. There is nothing more to tell about him—no anecdotes, not a line for a gossip-column, nothing. All kinds of people have impressed me, during my life. The swami doesn't impress you—sometimes he is ridiculous—but when you are with him you know that God exists.

You questioned what I said in my letter about the house with the rooms and the passage leading to the garden. Well, I am bad at comparisons, anyway—they make me feel self-conscious even while I am writing them. But I can't feel that "the garden" is only in the future. Surely we came from it, or how would we have this awareness that it exists? O don't you agree with Wordsworth?

I needn't repeat that I think continually of you in the middle of all this mess. At present, if one can believe the newspapers, we are on the brink of war with Japan. I suppose they could bomb Los Angeles once or twice, if they didn't mind sacrificing an aircraft-carrier. There are people here who are actually considering building air-raid shelters.

Write again soon.

All my love,
Christopher

* * *

W[est] H[ackhurst]   11-10-41

I quail before preparing an Indian broadcast, and will start a letter to my Dearest Christopher instead, although I "ought not" to do so. It is not the first letter I have started. A fragment about the Chinese wine cups you gave me lies about somewhere. I got off a letter to Gerald about a fortnight back. I hope it reached him. It was partly about praying. People over here are rather silly and shy about prayer. Anyhow I find it easy to silence them when they condemn it. I believe it is much more like going to bed with someone than is generally supposed. Hence the shyness. Hence the great advantages *or* disadvantages which may ensue.—Not that, having silenced them, *I* go away and do a flop. Don't think it—!

I was not however proposing to address you about this, but rather to give you the menu of a dinner which Bob cooked in my flat last Wednesday for Joe, Stephen, and ourselves. The flat is at Chiswick now, overlooking Turnham Green, and when reached extremely nice. On the mantelpiece were two of your jade cups. On the wall opposite an "oil" by Bob, done from the water-colour sketches he made at Amsterdam when we came to stay with you there. It is said, by Joe & Stephen, to be very good—i.e. one would pick it out in an exhibition. This however was it

MENU

Hors d'oeuvres
  Oeufs Mayonnaise: with sliced cucumber, tomato, raw carrots
Joint
  Roast shoulder of mutton with mint sauce
Vegetables
  Roast potatoes, boiled potatoes, French beans, braised tomatoes. T.o.

MENU (cont)

Sweets
  Stewed blackberries and apples. Cornflower cream
Cheese
Coffee
Wines:
  Sherry: present from Aunt Rosalie, rather a failure
  Claret: Médoc

Port: Cockburns
Brandy: stolen by May from the West London Hospital: a success

So you will see that our problems are not quite what you expected or your Swami perhaps hoped. I must knock off now and have some Beefex with mother and Mrs Barger. The last named has been living with us for a year— she is the widow of a Cambridge friend, eminent scientist. I had a very nice letter from you, which I meant to reread before writing this, but can't think where I put it, and don't want further delay in sending you my love. I do miss you very much—more lately than I have done in the past. For the first year or two I felt content that you should be where you are. I probably hoped your world would spread to me. But mine seems more likely to spread to you.

The P.E.N. Congress last month was a good one. Unluckily I neither saw nor heard Erika Mann. Her speech didn't please Madariaga,[19] Thorton Wilder, or Dos Passos, but I don't know how they judge things. I met Arthur Koestler, and shall see him again, and have already seen again a young Chinese from Pekin[g], Hsiao Chien: he has offered me a banquet in London and been down here with a gift of a tea pot and tea. Oh dear how much easier and more charming are they than the Indians, and this reminds me of my broadcast.

Talking of Manns, though, did Klaus ever publish my article in Decision and if so will he pay me?

I had sometime back now, an extremely nice letter from your mother, and must answer it.

Leo and Tom, after some months with Miss Phillips & Miss Hayles at Teignmouth where Sandy remains are now back in Dover in their old flat. The Slaughters are at Guildford I believe, but I have not sought them out despite Mr Slaughter's Beethoven, which was most remarkable. William remains at the Admiralty. Mr N——[Norris] is I believe in——. John Simpson, George Thomson, are still at Birmingham. Bob has got across his superiors through refusing to cart dung to their back gardens, and, though a super driver in his qualifications, has been taken out of the garage and put on to ordinary duties. He has also been bad with what was called bursitis, but now they have called it fibrocitis instead, and he got better at once, and can do his squash and his rowing. He looks very fit, and you can take it that he is sending you fondest love. I shall see him again on Monday. Joe— but perhaps I told Gerald this—has moved to Putney: a nice flat as regards view, near the end of the bridge and on the roof of a hotel.[20] He looks a bit older. I don't think I do—since you left me, I mean. But it is hard to know.

Well dear Christopher this shall do from your

Morgan

*   *   *

824 Buck Lane
Haverford, Penna.
January 11. [1942]

Dearest Morgan,

Here's your letter of November 11 unanswered for at least a month since I got it.[21] A busy Christmas, of course, came in between—but also, with you, I have a nice leisurely feeling. The mental communication, at any rate on my side, is still very strong. Also, I feel increasingly that I shall see you before long. I don't know exactly how, but, as you say, "your" world has spread to "ours." As soon as I'm drafted as a C.O. I shall see what possibilities there are of being sent abroad. The age group to which I belong is to register on February 16. Meanwhile, I am very busy here—at a Friends' Service Committee hostel for refugees—since last October. The refugees are all teachers or lecturers who hope to fit into the U.S. educational world, a difficult but not impossible ambition. Meanwhile they study teaching methods at the neighbouring college, and also improve their English by private tuition from a number of people, including myself. Aside from this, my own job is social, menial, confessorial, advisory, interpretive, consolatory, apologetic; in fact, whatever I choose to make it; and always profoundly interesting. Thee is so little one can materially do, but so much one can understand—if only the attention is focused unwaveringly on the problem. Needless to say, mine isn't: so I'm guilty every hour of lapses, failures, minor cruelties. These people, especially the Jewish ones, register, like exquisite scientific instruments, every failure towards them in charity or understanding. They draw back quicker than snakes, and the work of weeks is spoilt in a couple of seconds. Mere pity is useless here. True charity is the intense alertness which Gerald so often writes about. Nothing less is any good.

Since the official declaration of war, we, as an "enemy alien" group, are naturally subject to restrictions.[22] The authorities have been wonderfully reasonable, on the whole—though some local interpretations of the rules seem to prevent our people form [sic] going to the post office or getting their hair cut, and similar absurdities. However, we are sure these little points will be straightened out later. In the meanwhile, many of course feel badly about being called "enemy" at all, even in official documents. They fought, when permitted to do so, during the French phase of the war, and are inclined to make obvious comparisons.

Deep snow here, which is beautiful, but I long for California, and the mountains and the desert. Also I miss Gerald and Aldous; and neither of them are much [. . . ?] at letter writing. Benjy Britten is returning to England very soon, I believe: I hope to see him before he goes, and in that case shall give him personal messages to you and other friends.

I agree with you about prayer. It *is* like going to bed: just as "getting religion" (that horrible expression) is like falling in love. And prayer, in its turn, has various consequences, like consummation. After leading this kind of life—or intermittently trying to—for about a year and a half, there isn't anything much I can say about it without embarrassment, except that "it pays," in better balance, better integration, greater contentment, and, much more important, in an increasing appetite for it and commitment to it. Anyhow, in my case, with all my backslippings, it's still a lot more satisfactory than physical marriage ever was—not that the one excludes the other. If the right person came along, that could be more wonderful than ever. At present there is nobody, and I'm quite fairly content to have it that way.

Oh dear, this is a hell of a stiff, censor-conscious letter! Chiefly because I can't gossip, which would reassure you that I'm the same old Chris you used to know. But I can't gossip about strangers, so you must just imagine that part of me functioning too, and know that my loving thoughts are very very often with you and Bob. Please remember me to William, John, Leo and Tom.

All my love,
Christopher

*   *   *

6-2-42

Dearest Christopher,

I have just got your letter of Jan. 11th, and I have just been giving Stephen a glass of sherry at the Reform Club and seeing an excessively nice letter he has had from Wystan. [B]efore which I had just been to tea with the Robin Majors, and mentioned you there, indeed this is just a row of justs, and I have just been broadcasting to India about Aldous' book, which I think very good, and now I am just going to bed. Only 11.00 P.M., but I after all am 63. It has made me very happy to hear from you and to know that I am in your thoughts, and I am glad to know about your work too. I write in my Chiswick flat—the one that has been such a success, and bears so many signs of Bob's love, energy and taste. Do you remember the sketch he made at Amsterdam? It has now become an oil painting and hangs in a Bond Street exhibition, and is to tour the provinces next month.

I broadcast a good deal and read a good deal, and as for writing, if you can get hold of the December number of *Horizon* please read an article by me in it.[23] You will then see where I stand—though it is much more a sit, modified by a *very very* slight genuflection.

I will leave this letter open till the morning. I am interested I should be right about prayer, I never minded it, and the Maharajah's gay shrieks of "Morgan—Morgan—don't come nearer [. . . ?] this morning, please, I am holy" raining in my ears, even on that morning, as profound.

Very little gossip is obtainable here. Most people are segregated in jobs and there is very little entertaining, through lack of servants, food, and petrol. Stephen Tennant, once an enormous golden mountain, is still to be discerned above the rising waters, embanked by his bad health, and Bob and I hope to go there on Saturday for a weekend. That house, and John Simpson's, are the only ones I get invited to stay at. Dear dear me, it is a solid overturn.

Well now I really must get to bed, and may even post this right away. Very very much love from your

Morgan

[continuing on same sheet of paper]

W[est] H[ackhurst]   1-3-42

This did not get posted—indeed look at the date. The best of a letter in two sections though is that one can gossip a little—gossip, as opposed to narrative, being references from section to section. Well, we got our weekend at Stephen T[ennant]'s—Peter Watson, Connolly and Elizabeth Bowen were there too. All went well until the last evening, when S.T. became annoyed because the boys would discuss a post-mortem and still more annoyed because he could not stop them, left up from the diner table, blew out the four candles which illuminated it, and rushed, switching out lights as he went, into his bed. We knew not what to do nor whither to turn. Embassies were organised. Later in the evening he dressed and reappeared in the drawing room. So even in England the Private Life can still be led. But I do not think it will be for long.

Bob loved your letter, said you were exactly the same, and it was exactly like you to pretend you were not, so as to give one a surprise on meeting. I think I am changing a little—not in affection, but three years of a war and such a war deform one's mind. It is such an awful lot one has to understand, it is too much, and too much has to be suddenly scrapped.

*   *   *

West Hackhurst
Abinger Hammer
Dorking
[early June, 1942]

Dearest Christopher,

I have just preached my first sermon, so as parson to parson may I tip you a wink? Perhaps you may not be in a position to return it, but we get the idea that everyone your side preaches sermons. Mine was on the occasion of the death of Ronald Kidd, the founder of the Council for Civil Liberties, and I took my text from Wilhelm Tell.[24] It now serves as an opportunity to chatter to you. I think you wrote last. Life goes on as usual here. The most interesting thing I am doing—but I am afraid I shall discover nothing—is to look at St Augustine and his contemporaries, and ask them how they took *their* Landslide. But they are so different from us, that even when I can catch what they say it does not sound like wisdom. And I am looking for applicable wisdom. They are partly so different because they had a sexual conscience and not a social one, whereas it is the other way round with us. I am only just tapping the thing, though. I wish I had Gerald to direct me, though I suppose he would say I was wasting my time. After the "Confessions" I am reading a little Claudian,[25] and then thinking of the Tomb of Galla Placidia, which I saw at Ravenna once in tourist days. It was certainly a very strange age, and even less of a piece than ours.

You will prefer some news of ours. The John Lehmann-Spender vista you know. Joe Ackerley is all right in his flat over Putney Bridge, where he has adopted a pigeon. William is still overworked at the Admiralty. John Simpson had not yet been called up, and stayed with me for a night in Chiswick last week. Bob is still spared to me and is rowing in a regatta this weekend. I think I told you he has burst into art (oils—of Amsterdam) and been hung. Robin, aged 9, is up for a few days, since London keeps quiet. We went to a cinema and there was a film of Dover, showing that vaulted restaurant where we might all still be eating, and a travelling shot down the high street toward the church, where nothing seemed damaged. Robin scarcely remembers Dover. He is very good company, and will soon be going to a Friends' Co-educationist school at Saffron Walden. As for new objects, the chief one is a young Chinese called Hsiao Chi'en. I wonder whether you have heard of him, or will; he has written "Etching of a Tormented Age," which is about contemporary Chinese literature, and he is well acquainted with their new ambassador to Washington.

I don't much like this letter. It is of course not easy to write friends from whom one has parted for years. One sees and knows them as well as ever, but cannot believe they will hear what is being said.

8-6-42

Since beginning this a few days ago I have heard from Gerald, but it looks a stiff and misty letter and I have not yet coped with it. We get very provincial. Since the war started, I have not even seen the sea. Our lives are interned without being spiritual, and trying desperately to balance we get exalted and false ideas of America or Europe or China. I have violent longings for fragments of my past—mostly small pieces of scenery abroad, with blurred edges—and I reconstruct partings which I hadn't at the time known would be for so long. One of the worst is the parting from Charles Mauron at Lausanne June 1939 when I scrambled into a silly mountain railway train, and he already almost blind.

Charlie (waiter Charlie), who was at the Trojan Horse near your house, has now gone to the Black Bug [?] at Nottingham. Victor's is now absurdly expensive; none of us go there, and we learn from M. Victor's confrères that it is his obstinacy. When in London I eat at the Club or at a Lyons Cafeteria, or Bob cooks down at the Chiswick flat, where we have accumulated some wine. I have plenty of money—partly because I broadcast regularly to India—and certainly it is a help. I wish I had hope, as well as tenacity and calmness. Sometimes I wish I had it [hope?] instead of them [tenacity and calmness?], for I have known the sensation in the past and it is lovely. The lights going up again, the Prince Baudouin running—one would die of such happiness.

I have just brought out my Virginia Woolf lecture. Harcourt Brace is publishing it your side. Have also been preparing A Passage to India for Everyman, with some notes, and with Peter Burra's article on me as an introduction.

Would like to hear more about your work with "aliens." I believe they are still unhappy over here, but we got Wolfgang (John Simpson's friend) back.—Did Klaus Mann ever publish my article?

With love dear Christopher from Morgan

* * *

As from: 9121 Alto Cedro Drive.
                                                                   Beverly Hills. Calif.
                                                                   July 8. [1942]

Dearest Morgan,

Such a nice letter from you, of the eighth of June, which I'm answering from the train, enroute for California and the above address. It is the house of friends and will always find me in the foreseeable future, so we'd better stick to it from now on. As a matter of fact, there has been a little spurt of news suddenly: two very descriptive letters, one from Tony Hyndman, who seems so happy and so admirably fitting into his new life; one from Benjamin Britten, who was fitting less well at the moment but very interestingly, because he could still hold England and the U.S. in some kind of relation to each other.

The train is dragging very slowly through the state of Kansas, hours and hours late: pretty woods, and fields of alfalfa (or isn't it alfalfa?) and little towns with silos, full of people who believe in the verbal accuracy of the old testament. The Middle West is so overpowering that one hardly dares think of it much, like Antarctica, or interstellar space; but soon the land will begin to tilt up and we shall climb gradually all through the afternoon, and soon after midnight we'll be in the mountains of New Mexico, seven thousand feet above this grilling heat, and some of us lying in our berths without covers will catch severe colds. The train is full of soldiers and sailors, and farm kids going out to the naval bases to be inducted: the war is still psychologically in its opening phase here. Watching them laugh and joke, or turn suddenly serious as some old hand explains the ropes, one's heart goes to lead. And then, of course, there are the newspapers, and the cartoons, and the commentators (whose forgiveness one can only commend to the mercy of an all-knowing power): but I have learnt a little from experience and try not to wallow any more in mere futile rage. Personally, I have very very much to be thankful for. I am on my way to the country I love now like a second home: far more than I ever loved any country, except the hills and moors of north Derbyshire when I was sixteen. And I shall see Gerald, and Chris Wood, and Denny Fouts, and lots of other friends. And I shall swim in the Pacific, which is like dying and turning into sunshine and foam. And I shall be able to relax for a few weeks, without correcting anybody's prepositions and tenses.

And then? Well, I have signed the necessary forms and am now registered as a conscientious objector, which means that, with more or less delay, according to the decisions of the draft tribunal, I shall probably be sent to a work-camp. I have volunteered, as I believe I told you in my last letter, to go in an ambulance unit to China, but it seems to be established as a precedent that one must spend at least some time in the work-camps first: and maybe, if public opinion wishes it, we must stay there altogether. I hope I am prepared for whatever happens along this line: I try to be: but one is generally less prepared than one thinks. However, right now, I'm hardly worrying at all.

Some day, I will try to write about Haverford. There was so much of it that I never got around to describing it to anybody in a letter. Central Europe could hardly have supplied a second such all-star team of individualistic, neurocratic [*sic*] virtuosi: there were days when I could have signed an order for total pogrom without flicking an eyelid: and yet nearly all of them were extraordinarily sympathetic, all were fascination, and, when I felt strong enough, I loved them dearly.

And Caroline Norment, our Irish directress—what was one to make of her? Superficial observers called her a phoney old ham, a Hitler, an octopus. True, it was impossible to speak to her before breakfast without unleashing a typhoon; true, she yielded to her appetite for tragedy until, in the last two months, she couldn't enter a room without playing either (i) the heartbroken mother of congenital idiots bravely fighting back her tears with a smile while the poor little slobbering things pluck at her sleeves and pester her with meaningless questions, or (ii) King Oedipus emerging blinded from the palace at the very end of the disaster, slowly raising his hands to his streaming eyeholes, slowly letting them fall. But all the same I have met very few people who could cope with very difficult tired pessimistic middle[-]aged middleclass aliens the way she can: she has an absolute genius for it. And I am really very fond of her indeed. I guess I naturally like octopi. In the midst of the tempest, I was often reminded of dear Berthold Viertel, yelling blue murder at Gaumont-British.[26] He is very happy and busy and well, bless him, organizing Goethe evenings in New York. Nobody else seems to have had the obvious idea of presenting the best of German culture to the German-speaking members of the population. It is a huge success. Not only refugees come, but very considerable numbers of second-generation German-Americans who have kept up their language and like to speak and hear it but have been inhibited from doing so lately because of the popular idea that all such meetings must be Bund-meetings, and therefore disloyal. Meanwhile Salka writes movies, and so does Peter, the second son (did you ever read his beautiful novel "The Canyon"?) but very soon he'll be in the Army.[27]

Wystan I saw last Monday: he has been staying in the neighbourhood of Haverford. He has been expecting to be drafted last week, but the board held him up another month on some technicality, and this was really heaven[-]sent luck as now he reckons he'll be able to finish his Christmas Oratorio, which I believe is the best thing he's ever done. He says his ambition is to be sent to England as an American soldier, and then behave insufferably in London literary circles, chewing gum and talking about "us Yanks."

I wrote to Klaus about your article but got no reply. I'm not sure if it was ever printed or not, but quite sure you'll get no money for it now, as Decision has packed up for good. I am hoping to get hold of your Virginia Woolf essay. Many people, including Wystan, tell me how good it was. Wish I could hear your broadcasts.

All my love to you. And to May and Bob. I'd love to see Robin again now [that] he's bigger. Why can't they ship the whole lot of you over: I'd even be content if I could choose a dozen: but no doubt I'd pick the ones Britain needs most.

As always, lovingly,
your
Christopher

*   *   *

25-7-42

West Hackhurst,
Abinger Hammer,
Dorking

Dearest Christopher,

This is not too bad for I was thinking twice of you yesterday and today receive your letter. Joe took me into a certain locality, when enter Brian Howard, looking flat [?] and thin, and we exchanged a few civilities: that always brings back Amsterdam to me, for there I first met him.[28] Later in the evening I was thinking I would ask your mother for your latest address: but I suppose this is not two thoughts but one thought. Brian told me that you were sitting in a tent in a desert. Untrue. And that Gerald and Aldous were sitting in a temple with an observatory on top. Untrue? Your letter made me feel very happy. But also very provincial, and it is part of the psychology of this war that everyone, sooner or later, will come to feel provincial; your lads in the train, going out to the great clear conflict as they thought, hadn't got to this yet.

Previous to that meeting with Joe and Brian, I called on Day Lewis in the M.O.I.[29] He wants to remain there, doing important work, and it seemed just possible I might be able to pull a string over this. I don't often see him. Lunch, previous to that, with Roger Senhouse.[30] Which brings me back to Bob the night before. He arrived with a toothache and a record called the Big Noise from Winnetken [?]. The toothache went off, and so did the record, fairly well: I complained of its thematic poverty. Bob, mashing potatoes around onions and feeling better, argued that rhythm is all that matters. Then we took to drink.

It is now decided that May gives up her job at the West London in the autumn, and that Robin comes home to them. But Bob is longing to go and fight, so I dunno. Nothing seems to fit. Luckily for me, indeed for us all, the police won't release him, so we all go steadily forward. Even Ted—dim Ted and dimmer Vi—are in the group.

I keep reading about the Roman Empire from about 370 to 450, and seeking parallels with the present. Incidentally I get a lot of fun (from the letters of St Jerome for instance) and a lot of beauty out of illustrated books (Wilpert's Mosaics; Peirce & Tylers L'Art Byzantine).[31] But I wish Gerald was here to talk about it. He would tell me where the parallels stop, and why, and he might say something illuminating on the topic of chastity. I cannot understand why, for several hundreds of years, all the more sensitive people thought going to bed was wrong.

I don't know how I am, which you will wish to know. After the news of Torquay I looked and felt like a very old man for a little, but that premonition has passed.[32] Have been away more than usual lately—weekend to Sassoon, to John Simpson[,] and the Wilsons with Bob, and to the Bells and Leonard last week—L[eonard]. is much the same, though encamped amongst piles of Virginia's bombed library from London. V[irginia] seems always in the next room. I can never get clear in my mind as to whether she was right or wrong to go: at any rate she gave us something to think about.[33] I once told you dear Christopher that I might one day go mad (running slowly in large circles with my head down—an unhelpful spectacle and easily handled by the authorities). I don't feel any extra inclination to do this, but must be beware of melancholy as you of rage. Wonder if you'll get to China. Please write again on getting this. It helps. I owe Gerald a letter. Give him my love, and lie a lot in the sea. I haven't even *seen* it (until at Leonard's, faintly) since the war began. There's provincialism! William, like Day Lewis, overworked in his office. He came here for two lovely days not long ago, and was [. . . ?] looking down at the grass at insects. [the following written in margin of front side of letter:] Yes, I read the Curyon [Caryon?] and broadcasted on it. Lovely.—Do hope that Wystan will lend me his chewing gum when he gets over here as a Yank. I wish that I, like Britten, could get America into my landscape a little.

[written on top of the front page:] *Love from Morgan* [underlined three times, twice in red ink], which would otherwise be lost in this shuffle.

*   *   *

28.12-42   As from: West Hackhurst, Abinger Hammer, Dorking

Dearest Christopher,

Your health was drunk first of anyone's at Bob's party yesterday. We had roast goose, plum pudding, and lots of wine to drink with. Later on we toasted Joe, William, John Simpson, and other absents, but you seemed uppermost in our hearts, and Ted and Vi, whom you may have forgotten, recalled how competently you nursed their baby at Dover. The party was a little marred by May developing a sick headache, but she rallied towards the close and your galloping pony from China looked down. (You have many here who love you [and count upon your love.])[34]

I have a clearer idea of your outlook (no—I mean inlook) partly from your letter, partly from your article in John Lehman's Penguin,[35] and partly from a few words with Benjamin Britten. I *say*, how nice he is. We have not fixed a real meeting yet, engagements swirl between, but I talked to him at Cambridge, and ate some food with him and Pears after their Michelangelo at the National Gallery.[36] I have also seen some photographs of you at John L's—why wasn't I given one? They are good—and a drawing of you by Paul Cadmus: not good, but I was pleased to think you were in touch with him, for he once wrote me the nicest letter any stranger ever has. Do you still see him? If so, convey kindness and cordialities.

Do you still see anyone? For all I know you are in some training camp, and this is the sort of doubt which suddenly checks a pen. It may be enquiring so widely off the mark. I'll return to myself. I know where I am: on a chair: in my (Chiswick) flat: and on the tiled mantel are: three bits of holly, two green plates, a little rowing cup of Bob's, two Chinese wine cups of yours, and a clock which has just struck 1.00. I ought to go to bed. I lunched today with William at Victor's, now confined to the ground floor but otherwise unchanged: then I bought a sponge with difficulty; then had tea with an Austrian refugee—an authority on Byzantine Mosaics. [S]o we interned him in Canada. Then I got back here—difficulty again: no trolly-bus, and black pitcher than black—and have since been conning the Beveridge Report.[37] I speak to and with a Search Light Unit about it on my way home tomorrow. I go to them every week. I am not the least suited to the subjects they want, but anything which interrupts army-routine is meritorious. Actual Christmas I spent with my mother. She is well, but of course very old, and restless. I will post this letter when I get home.

I go on broadcasting to India. I do it for George Orwell now, and am getting to like him, but he is strange and I dislike something in what he writes without being able to chase it into daylight. Stephen I don't often see. His new wife is well spoken of, but not in my judgement anything of a pianist. (Each sentence I write has a "but" in it. That is because I went to a university.) Occasionally, and in likely places, I see Mr N—[Norris]: but we do not contact.

Did I tell you I have been reading about the 4th and 5th centuries? I wondered, and still wonder, whether they resemble the times we live in now. Did they contain Christophers, Geralds, Benjamins, and Morgans? Oh by the way they did—a Morgan, I mean: Pelagius means "Morgan," and he provided a heresy to which I should not object to subscribe.

I must write to Gerald. If possible, give him my love.

Morgan

*   *   *

[early winter 1943?]³⁸

I hope no more will go during the next month or two.

Lionel Fielden, with whom I lunched lately, said the Breughels had vanished from Brussels.[39] Had you heard? Were put into a lorry by Belgians, he said, and never seen again. I remember seeing them with you, and asking you, in a larger room near them, to become my literary executor. (Released you since) I feel flustered that these Brueghels should be lost.

The cold is endless—ever since Christmas. This week I go to town to broadcast on Stefan Zweig[40]—sorry that this letter should end much as it began, but it can't be helped. Come and see me if possible—it would do me good.

Ever so much love again from
Morgan

*   *   *

7-6-43

West Hackhurst,
Abinger Hammer,
Dorking

Dearest Christopher,

Things were bad during the past month and I nearly wrote and whined across the Atlantic to you. Permitted by Police regulations, Bob volunteered for almost certain death, for the post of engineer on a bomber. May was in tears, Robin said "But Daddy, aren't you happy at home?" [T]he

Board recommended him specially, physique perfect, and then Christopher would you believe it they discovered that his eyes are of the type which go completely blind at 25,000 feet and so it has gone by like a nightmare. He will volunteer again for anything when he has the chance, but anyhow he won't be able to go up into that filthy sky. His argument—divested of some boyish frills—is that he has hated Fascism for years, and that thousands of people who don't mind it in the least have been forced to go and fight against it and be killed; so why shouldn't he fight? Not a bad argument. Well I am glad I didn't whine to you, but glad I thought of doing so. You can think now either that things are O.K. or that I have learnt how to handle them. William has been wonderful.

I don't really know what else to talk to you about besides Bob, we have been parted too long, and I reach you easiest through that deeply-cut channel. I know one can't genuinely reach anyone through anything, though. So I had better continue with some scrap of news. John Lehmann, whom I don't often see, has just been so nice to me and taken me to the Ballet. He showed me a very gay and exciting letter of yours about a book you were at, and about a book of Lincoln K (forget how the name finishes but like the man) which you had put him on to. Life here is very boring geographically—one can't move about, or rather can only move with great trouble and arrangements with hotels; and one can't, without even greater trouble, turn from a continental gadabout into a cosmic one. It is boring gastronomically also, and like our two pussies I am usually meat-hungry. Wine isn't so bad, for I never drank much and now drink all I can, and that comes to the same. Do you remember the champagne dinner in an upper room on your birthday at Ostende? That was a strange visit. It crackles up most of it like burnt paper, but here and there a word stands out.

I see it is 1.00 A.M. I have been mowing the lawns and feel sleepy. Lovely lovely garden, and the wood, much of which I planted in the twenties, has turned this summer into a wild young man who no longer needs my help. Oh, before I forget. Richard wrote me a kind and unexpected letter, telling me how you were, and what he thought you were feeling.[41] I didn't get a great deal out of it except the kindness, the much kindness. John Simpson I see as much as I can. And I have a new friend whom I like extremely— Hsiao Chi'en is his name. He is studying myself and Virginia [Woolf] at Kings. And I also have a new girl acquaintance—her name is Hazel Earelly-Wilmot—who works in the Czechoslovak Institute. Thus, thus, do I avert the cosmic. If I realised that I was penned up, a Britisher, in Britain, I should "go mad." Love to Gerald.

Love as always from
Morgan

*   *   *

1946 Ivar Avenue
Hollywood 28. Calif.[42]

June 21st. [1943]

Dearest Morgan,

Your letter, dated June 7th, just arrived: nice and quick. I must write by return, while it's "warm." That's what I did in answer to your last, but it sank with that clipper which foundered in Lisbon harbour, and tho I tried several times to communicate, the channel was somehow blocked, and I wrote stiff cold literary notes which I tore up. Today, however, it's wide open. Gosh, that must have been awful for you about Bob. Thank heavens he finally didn't go. I wish I was a real Yogi and could utter authoritative prophecies that he will die at the age of 101 in bed, though, actually, nothing would surprise me less. My experience, such as it is, all points to the fact that those who are always volunteering and plunging ahead tend to survive. As for Bob's reasons—yes, they are good ones. But, among his friends, let him not forget Heinz. One can build arguments sky-high, and very firmly, but the foundations lie deeper. Heinz is really most of mine. I begin to know this more and more. It's the old story of Sodom and G. Because everybody is Heinz to someone. The Gita says this is no argument, because "Both he who thinks the Self to be the slayer, and he who thinks It to be slain, know nothing. It cannot slay, neither can It be slain." But that, as you'd say, it too "Cosmic" for me at present. For Bob too, I guess.

Yes, my letter to John Lehmann was gay, and I am gay most of the time: but I also know quite well that this is a pleasant period, with a time-limit to it, during which I have to prepare some steel cables which won't snap when strained. I honestly believe that I now believe in "God" (can't explain what I mean by "God") and that I rely on Him, and will turn to Him next time things get tough. But, of course, I have absolutely no way of being sure of this, or of what help I'd receive in, say, a crisis like yours; or of whether this belief of mine mightn't go away just as mysteriously as it came. If you can fall out of love you can fall out of faith (but can you fall out of love?) or anyhow, William James says so.

Swami is away just now: one of his brother-monks got sick in the East and he won't be back till mid-July. I do the ritual worship most days, which is probably familiar to you: the flowers, the brass bowls, and incense, and candles and perfume and bell. And the Sanskrit mantrams. I think of you very often while I am doing it—you especially, because everything Indian suggests you to me—and sometimes I talk to the Lord about you. Sometimes you and Bob are sniggering in the background, because of the wrap I'm wearing, and the flower on the top of my head. "Look at Chris in drag!" And I can see you at lunch with us: you and Swami warming to each other; and you enjoying the curry, which is good.

I have a feeling I must know Hsiao Chi'en. Believe he wrote to me once, from Cambridge. And, oddly enough, Eardly-Wilmot is the name of one of my Mother's greatest friends. She was the wife of a brother-officer of my Father's, who was killed in the last war. Hazel is a relative, maybe? This one was Mildred, and she had two very attractive children, now grown-up, Anthony and Joan.

Gerald is down at Laguna Beach. Very busy with religious groups and gatherings. Haven't seen him in a long time. Aldous is finishing his novel in the desert at their little ranch. Willie Maugham wrote an affectionate letter from New York. He has just published a drug-store anthology of modern literature, not bad, but a few inclusions almost unbelievable, and I didn't agree with his remarks about you. Lincoln Kirstein and Pete Martinez are both in the army. Pete, you know, is co-author of the Mexican novel I like so much. He and Swami would probably be your favorite people in the U.S.

Well, goodbye for now. Do keep writing often, and I will too.

Love as always from
Christopher
And to Bob too, *much*.

*　*　*

West Hackhurst—Abinger Hammer—Dorking
23-10-43

Dearest Christopher,

The enclosed it is hoped will reach you about Christmas. You were spoken of with love. It was a party given by Bob and me in my flat to Leo and Tom whom I extricated for a couple of days from Dover. I don't think they had been to London since the war started. Joe put up Tom at Putney and I had Leo. The only other person was Margery Wilson, the sister of John Simpson's idiot, and as she did not know you she has not signed. Bob suddenly looking at the door said "if only Christopher would walk in . . . . " We are all changing, and it is not always true that a:b::a+x:b−y, but it is oftener truer of people than of ciphers. Thank goodness. The party was a big and grand one for these days. A ham in a tin, which an American lady sent me three years ago because she thought genius was starving, was opened, and found not to be bad. May made manes [?] of cheese straws, Bob potato salad, and we drank real sherry, unreal burgundy, and one bottle of champagne.

I understand your ritual and drag easily. The universe is very odd, and we do not recognise this enough. I do not understand your feeling that God will help you—i.e. I don't ever feel that I shall ever be thus helped myself. When I was so upset about Bob's being taken from me, I seemed to get through it all alone—first behaving as an Englishman should, then breaking down, and then behaving as a human being. That last stage ended when he was rejected on account of his eyes, and now I really don't know how I behave. Perhaps you will write more to me about this "trust-in-God" business, but I don't *think* I shall be able to catch on.

Dinner party at Stephen's. Tea with John Lehmann. M. Fouchet, editor of Fru [?] French *Fontaine*, to lunch, très parisien, né en Venezuela, and full of gossip about Gide.[43] Slump in Arnold Bennett. Attacks on Milton failing. Do you know anything about Mark Twain? Am rereading *Ulysses*.[44] When, where, how often, and how have you crossed (i) the Mississippi (ii) the Missouri? Have you ever visited Cairo or St Louis? This cannot reach me in time for my broadcast to India on Nov. 4th. Still I should be glad to know.

My most important news is a revisit to Rooksnest, Stevenage, Herts (the original of Howard's End).[45] It is very strange. The strength of such feelings. (I don't think you know much about them—Richard probably does.)

This house really bores me though I shall be upset when I have to quit it. I must go down now and have some Oxo [?] with my mother in the drawing room. It is pouring wet day but mild, and the leaves of the tulip tree, the guelder [rose], [. . . ?], the Japanese Cherry and the azaleas are all lovely different colours.

I will write again before long. I have not written to you for a long time, but I think of you and talk of you a lot.

Love as always from Your affectionate Morgan

[enclosed Postcard:]

Christmas 1943

With love to Christopher from:

[signed names:]

Leo Charlton
Tom Whitchelo
May Buckingham
William Plomer
Joe Ackerley

Bob Buckingham
Morgan Forster

Oct. 20th 1943

9 Arlington Park Mansions
Chiswick W.4.

*   *   *

Vedanta Society of Los Angeles
1946 Ivar Avenue
Hollywood, California
July 27 [1943]

Dearest Morgan,

If this ever reaches you, it will be by the hand of Bill Roehrich, who
needs no other introduction because you will like him, too.

As always,
your loving
C.

*   *   *

1946 Ivar Avenue

November 27. [1943]

Hollywood 28. Calif.

Dearest Morgan,

Your letter intended for Xmas arrived nearly a week ago: you were pessimistic. The mails aren't that bad. I loved getting it, and the card with signatures. Yes, wouldn't it be funny if I did walk in? I might, I suppose: if this
war goes on long enough or stops. What should I say as my opening line?
How would you answer?

At Xmas you will get a parcel from me, I hope. It was guaranteed to be
delivered then. It will probably have the most futile collection of oddments
in it—three genuine San Diego shrimps, a piece of scrapple from
Philadelphia, one Idaho potato, and so forth. Talking of geography, I have
never visited Cairo or St. Louis. (I was once in Memphis). Not counting our
journey from Vancouver down through Canada, via Chicago to N.Y. in
1938, I have crossed the continent five times, always by Chicago except
once, when we went down by bus to New Orleans and up through Texas. So
that's 5 Mississippi crossings. Am vague about the Missouri because it's at
right angles.

About God helping us. "Helping" is [a] misleading word, perhaps. Let's say, for example, that there is something inside you which is larger than your personality, and which has some kind of access to what is outside you, just as the smallest inlet of the sea anywhere has access to all the oceans. Call it your genius, if you like. You half sarcastically acknowledged its existence when you burnt those stories in order to get on with The Passage to India. (of course, that could be written off to innate Puritanism: but I think that's superficial.)[46] Well, this "genius" lives in you all the time, and it is not merely literary. Literature is only a function of it. It is there, neither friendly nor hostile, not in the least "sorry" for your troubles or "made angry" by your failures or "pleased" by your successes. It just exists, and can communicate with it or leave it alone, as you please. Communicating with "it" consists in realizing that you are it—or rather, it is you. The only "you" there is: because Morgan Forster is only real in a temporary sense, like a cloud or a storm. While you are communicating with your "genius" you lose all sense of being an individual Morgan Forster, and so you lose all Morgan's fears, doubts, desires etc. etc. You are just as much Bob, or Joe, or William, as you are Morgan—because they too have inlets leading to the ocean, and you are the ocean. And that "helps." In fact it's about the only thing in life which does help. Giving soup to Czechs, etc., is just a way of saying, by token action: I know you have a drop of the ocean inside you, too. Otherwise, to hell with the soup. It might as well be arsenic.

I wish you would write me about Stephen [Spender]. I know so little about his present life, wife, ideas etc.

Am very much occupied with our translation of the Gita, which is going to be quite curious, partly verse, partly prose. I never thought I would turn into a poet in my old age.

Later. Reading through what I've written about God etc. I feel bored. It's so badly put. Full of religious clichés. And as always I feel: how impossible to say these things *directly*, much less write them. If I saw you, maybe I could *convey* something which was nearer the actuality—while I was talking about the weather, or the poetry of Blunden, or Prague.[47] After all, what can you tell me in so many words about Bob? You can only talk around it. But I get something of what you feel.

Am reading Lorca—Spender, and La Chartreuse de Parme (which gives one a glimpse of what postwar Europe could be, if the worst comes to the worst).[48] Wystan is making a Tennyson anthology, and a collected works. We wait with the greatest interest for Willie Maugham's new novel, which is reputed to deal with mysticism in India.[49] It is alleged to be the most expensive film-property he has ever written. Isn't he a wonder? Aldous gets nicer and nicer: so truly kind and full of thoughtful attentions to everybody. He expects to finish *his* novel soon. The sun shines and shines. The gas-ration decreases. We dig new flower-beds. The dummy Santa Claus figures are up all along the Boulevard; and a plaster snow-man. I have an ingrowing toe-nail and a bad tooth: otherwise am well. The war, as Hemingway says, is there.

Excuse this lousy letter. I *must* get something off to you today. Love to everybody. And write again soon.

Always your loving
Christopher

*   *   *

14-12-43   West Hackhurst,
Abinger Hammer,
Dorking

Dearest Christopher,

You do send me good things—Bill Roehrick, and now I get a delicious food parcel: most welcome butter, and other delicacies. The dried bananas are new to me, and we shall have some for Christmas. You have sent me a letter also. But I will begin with Bill, who completely bears out your note about him, and speaks of you with affection such as goes straight to my heart. I have only seen him twice so far: we lunched and he took me to his show and Stephen took us to tea at the Ritz afterwards, and the next morning we went about to book shops. I like him immensely, we have written to each other since, and all being well shall meet in London. At present they are on tour, and as he will be in Birmingham for Christmas I have put him in touch with John Simpson. He has such good observation too: few people would have overheard one lady saying to another in the Ritz "We still manage to wash the cow all over everyday."

I wonder if a p.c. reached you, or will reach you: it was signed by Bob, May, Leo, Tom, William, Joe and self in my flat, and took you our love. "If that door would only open and Christopher come in!" said Bob, but it was a good party otherwise, and the biggest I have ever given—Margery Wilson, John Simpson's idiot's sister was there too. I had made an effort and asked Leo up for two nights from Dover, and he made a greater effort and accepted, and Joe invited Tom. Leo & Tom also managed to get down here to lunch with my mother. They were fairly well and very nice.

The friend I miss even more than you is Charles Mauron for the reason that he is working out, in his blindness and the darkness of France, some connection between mysticism and aesthetics with the help of Chinese philosophy: I should be able to absorb this, I think, better than I could absorb the connection *you* are working out, with the help of India, between mysticism and conduct. (Heavens what a sentence! Quite Geraldean in its elaboration and misleadingness.[50] It makes me say, incidentally, that I like Charles better than you, which I don't, and that I absorb connections, which I can't). Returning to you, thank you very much dear Christopher for the account you give of your ritual. That I do follow, for I know that the universe is a queer place and that ritual is a way and perhaps the best way of acknowledging this. What I don't follow is your belief that when you are in trouble, as you soon may be like all of us, God will help you. You may be right, of course, but I can't imagine the belief. It is too far beyond my powers, and I can't connect it with ritual.

I still dispose my time between here and London, and make new acquaintances still, mostly of foreign nationality. I keep pretty well—staler and older, but managing to blame both these defects on to the war. Bob looks older too. I shall get Christmas meal off their goose I hope. Robin is learning to play chess.

With love as ever from
Morgan

*   *   *

1946 Ivar Avenue.
Hollywood 28. Calif.

January 22. [1944]

Dearest Morgan,

Thank you for your letter. I am very glad to hear that the food parcel (and Bill Roehrich) arrived in time for Xmas. I would give a good deal to have seen you all at tea at the Ritz—or is the Ritz not ritzy any more? Yes, indeed, I got, and shall treasure, the signed postcard from your party. I thanked you for it, I'm pretty sure, in one of my letters, so fear this can't have reached you. It is hard to know just how much gets through nowadays—except to Mr Norris, who always begins: "I received your letter of August 1st on November 23rd. Cannot understand this delay. My letter of March 4th to you should have arrived, but you don't mention it. Please let me know about this at once . . . " and so on. In fact, most of his letter is usually taken up with discussing when and why and how the last one will, did, could, or should have arrived. His conversion to Catholicism—a theme before which Balzac himself might hesitate—is still only referred to somewhat obliquely. Do you ever see him now?

I was also much pleased to have a copy of Stephen's new poems among my [C]hristmas mail. They are very interesting, I think; though I didn't altogether follow the philosophy involved. Nor the exact tone of voice in which the title "spiritual exercises" was used. Ironical? Apparently not. S. inscribed my copy "from the untransformed Stephen," which also needs some explanation. I have written to him, of course.

I gave your address to "Pete" Martinez, the Americo-Mexican boy whose memoirs Lincoln Kirstein wrote in "For My Brother." I hope you will meet or have met him. He is something quite special—one of the really unique people I have known. He may have left by now, however.

You say you "can't imagine" the belief that God could help you. But if "God" is inside you, surely there must be some way to contact him, and surely contacting him would be "a help"? I don't have to tell a person like yourself that there is something inside you infinitely greater than what you ordinarily think of as Morgan Forster. As a matter of fact, you have asked Its help dozens of times—whenever you sat down to write anything. No artist can possibly doubt that this power exists, can he? Aren't we just misunderstanding each other in a purely verbal way?

I suppose one could argue that this power only exists in each individual for certain purposes, or to a limited extent. And of course there is still the problem of "evil" which Buddha refused to solve, and which [C]hristianity solves much too glibly. And the equally mysterious problem of "grace," or whatever you like to call it. Any theory can be exploded, because all intellectual truth is only relative. But I come back to the empirical. Aren't you, in practice, aware of this power? And how do you explain the saints? There are an awful lot of them. And such different temperaments. Are they all crazy, or mistaken?

You say that Mauron is working out a connection between "mysticism and aesthetics" and that I am working out a connection between "mysticism and conduct." But I'd say they were three corners of a triangle: or maybe it is a much more complicated figure. They all confirm each other on different planes. What is conduct, anyway? Behaving *as if* some set of values were true. And by behaving in this way you actually *make* them true. But, conversely, if you believe in a certain set of values, the appropriate conduct will follow. (I think the above are some of the most risky generalisations I have ever made: but you will perhaps get something from them impressionistically, at any rate.)

Did I tell you in my last letter how much I admire William's autobiography?[51] My Mother sent it me for Christmas. Am now just starting Willie's The Razor's Edge, but can't say anything yet. At any rate, the subject is interesting.

This weekend I saw, for the first time, D.W. Griffith's *Birth of a Nation*. Do you know it? It's still wonderful, in spite of the fascist racial nonsense about negroes. There's a kind of Tolstoyan simplicity in the contrasts: the two schoolboy friends from the North and South who meet again on the battlefield and fall dead in each other's arms; and the Southern colonel coming home from the war, and the killing of Lincoln, and the attempted rape and suicide of Mae Marsh, and Lillian Gish's romance: everything told like a story to a child, without any impressionism. And subtitles like: "True to the stern code of her Father's honour, she sought refuge within the opal gates of death." (Why *opal*?) The movies have lost all that lyrical quality now.

Aldous told me this quotation from D.H. Lawrence which I didn't know: "The dark *stinging* centrality of the duck on the muddy pond." Mother, I've been stung by a duck! A good entrance-line for a character in a play. In fact, the Nobel Prize should be awarded to anybody who could write a play in which this seemed quite natural.

Must stop now.

Very much love to you as always, and to Bob,
Christopher

∗   ∗   ∗

West Hackhurst,
10-2-44

Abinger Hammer, Dorking

Dearest Christopher,

The enclosed will partly explain itself. I have quickly become attached to Bill [Roerick], and am distressed that he is likely to go to Africa very soon. I would have liked much more talk with him: when people have so much charm I am never content until I have got to the bottom of their charm. Something solid underlies it, I doubt not, but want to know. Such heaps of lovely things you have sent me—*two* parcels, not one, arrived and at our party we had sandwiches made with your butter, ham and sardines. Robin was very good, sat on bed sorting stamps, then played chess with me. Bill and I lunched in town next day, and he sang two lovely folk songs as we walked round Leicester Square. What a turn for evil civilisation has taken. How glib I sound saying so. Bill manages to see John Simpson at B[irming]ham and Forrest Reid at Belfast. But I expect he has written to you. He has seen a good deal of the Kenneth Clarks in London.

The dolour and heaviness which invade one when writing to a friend who has been long far away—discount them when reading this letter. I was moved specially by two things you said in yours. One of them was your reminder to me how I had burned some stories in order to finish A Passage to India. That sacrifice still seems to me right, still inexplicable for I wasn't and am not ashamed of them. I will try to connect it on to "God." Your other remark was about my feeling for Bob. It made me realise that he (and he only) can make me feel a shit without saying so, or even thinking so. There does seem—in both the above—a reaching out into some sort of sea.

Paul Cadmus, who did a bad picture of you, has done a very nice one for me. He writes very pleasant letters. What sort of a chap is he? He has asked me to get into touch with Lincoln Kirstein's Mexican friend, but no success so far.

It is cold here and there is no gas[,] no electricity here, scarcely any coal, very little oil, and green wood. So war suffering is in this direction. London has plenty of everything as far as I can see, and there is no gas rationing such as you have been worried with.

My aunt Rosalie, whom you may remember from Dover, is here and she and mother send you messages. I have become a "good"—i.e. acceptable—broadcaster did I tell you, having made my reputation on the Indian service, and there is a clamour to use me on the Home [broadcasting service] to preach culture. Preaching (with me) would soon lead to compromise and falsity, so I go careful[ly]. The things I want to talk about, like the destruction in Italy, I shouldn't be allowed to say. We are all crouched around the drawing room fire, the ladies are trying to mend the knees of my drawers, but arguing so much that I am losing my sense of gratitude. I will finish and take this to the post. Best love to Gerald when you see him—yes, I owe him a letter. My good wishes to Aldous, also to Willie [Sommerset] Maugham. How is Wystan? This piece of paper is from a present given me by Miss Phillips & Miss Hayles. They live in Devonshire now.

Much much love from
Morgan

[Enclosed Postcard:]
    With love to Christopher from:

[signed names:]

May Buckingham
Stephen Spender
Joe Ackerley
Bob Buckingham
Robert M. Buckingham (Robin)

Bill Roerick
Natasha Spender
Morgan Forster

9 Arlington Park Mansions
Chiswick W.4.
February the 8th 1944

*   *   *

28-2-44   West Hackhurst,
Abinger Hammer,
Dorking

Dearest Christopher,

Yours of 22-1-44 has been with me some little time and merits answer. Your previous letter of 27-?-43 took a much longer time to come. Which brings me to Mr Norris. I had not heard of his conversion to Catholicism, but Tony Hyndman, into whom I ran in a tube, said that he was violently anti-Semitic. This, and other rumours, has caused me not to see Mr N. though I am false to myself in not doing so[.] I ought to examine his depths for myself, since I got amusement out of his shallows in the continental days. Occasionally, when I have been where perhaps I shouldn't I have been conscious of him through the reek.

Bill Roehrick has gone, missed by many, and particularly by me, for he has gone out of his way to be serious and sweet. It is long since I have felt so close to such a young person. I don't know how much the "well known writer" in me is important to him. Legitimately important in so far as he has been trying to make me write. He got down here for an afternoon and all loved him and the day before he left we spent ten hours together trailing about London and the Churchill Club, and got so thoroughly worn out that we could only grin at one another and say so. I have written at his introduction to Tommy Ryan. The other boy, with whom Tommy was, is killed or missing. As for Martinez, I have been hoping to hear from him, for Paul Cadmus also told him to look me up. But no one has any news of him, and perhaps he may not be in this country.

You will have read of the renewed raids. All whom you know are safe, so far as I know. Bob had his usual heroic gruesome time, and he's been very grave since, and has changed—come nearer to your point of view over this and to mine. No further satisfaction in smashing civilians in Germany. We are all feeling pretty serious minded. My flat shook, and the windows and door of his flew about. I hope America will never have anything as bad, and I hope Poland etc. hope that we shall never suffer as they have. It is a ladder of misery, in which each rung is tempted to keep to itself, ignore the rung below it, criticise the rung above.

Yes, I'm aware of something in myself at times which isn't myself, and which Stephen wanders towards in his poem. I don't like to call it God nor do I think it wisely so called, for the reason that the word "God" has kept such bad company and hypnotises its users in wrong directions. I even queried your saying that it was infinitely *greater* than oneself: *different*, yes, but one hasn't the apparatus for measuring size.

I returned from London the day before yesterday with one of my pleurisy threats, and since then have mostly been sitting, quite well really, in the drawing room with my mother, and getting muddled and fidgety. And I'm not content with my remarks on God. When the weather improves, and I can be alone, I will write about him again. Do you like Blake? (I do) Do you give good marks to generosity, tenderness? In what set of values are we to believe if generosity and tenderness are to colour our conduct?

Yes, William's autobiography is splendid. I have written a long thing for me (40,000 words or so) about this house, and it's amusing in parts, but dispirited and scrappy, and anyhow couldn't be published because it criticises the living. I wrote partly as a social document, partly to read to the Memoir Society.

Much love and Bob will be sending his. He is altering deeply but you would like him. I wish he would paint or even read but know by analogy that he can't go farther than gadgetting [*sic*].

Morgan

Two lovely food parcels, let me repeat, reached me from you at Christmas.

* * *

March 16. [1944]

1946 Ivar Avenue
Hollywood 28 Calif.

Dearest Morgan,

I am sitting writing this against the wall on the beach. Denny Fouts, whom you would probably like as much as I do, is studying anatomical German—part of his work at the University, where he has just started, being free of the draft with a heart-murmur. Anatomical German, incidentally, is much easier than anatomical English: the occipital, for example, is just called the Hinterkopf. I suppose this proves something—but as Denny has to learn both words anyway, the interest is somewhat academic.

It's really a very cold day, owing to a wind off the snow-mountains, but this wall is so hot that I feel quite sick. Five yards form [*sic*] it, we'd be shivering. This also proves something.

No doubt Bill has told you all about Tommy Ryan, and Bruce Wadsworth, his friend, who is missing. In fact, he says you may be meeting Tommy. I hope you do. You can help him so much—more than you realize. When I heard about Bruce, I felt miserable all day—though I barely know him: we'd met twice. He was crazy about old houses. I wanted him to see Marple, but he never got there.[52]

Twelve years last Monday since I met Heinz. He is so vividly with me, much of the time, that I'm surprised I don't *know*, telepathically, whether he is dead or alive, *somewhere*. But I still mind *where*.

Have been quite busy in a literary way. The Gita translation is finished—part verse and part prose. I'm afraid the verse isn't so hot—but the variety does seem to make the whole thing more readable. Then Aldous and I are writing a story we hope to sell to the movies. Prostitution? No—it is rather good, and the kind of story which is best told as a film. I'll let you know more about this later. Thirdly, there is a story I began to write last year, and have just reopened, about working with Viertel at Gaumont-British. This is quite a problem: it has to be written as historical fiction, and should be called: "A Tale of the '34," or some such title.[53]

Viertel himself left for New York last night. He has written a play about the Nazis—at the cost of Herculean snortings, groans and carpet-pacings—and now he hopes it will be produced. My fear is that he will be too late. Such things are so quickly out of fashion.

Auden is well, busy teaching and writing. He just sent me a most curious production—a commentary on "The Tempest," in poetry and prose. Haven't had time to digest it, yet.

Paul Cadmus you would like, I'm pretty sure. But I can't say I know him awfully well. He is gay, affectionate, talkative, intelligent—but there is a mysterious part of him which sometimes paints a picture of a massacre, a riot or rape, so hellishly ugly and *perverse*, that one doesn't know what to say or do, except vomit. On being expostulated with, he obviously doesn't understand why he does it himself, and talks unconvincingly about being influenced by Bosch, etc. The rest of his work is represented quite well by the drawing of me and the picture he sent you.

Is civilisation really decaying—or is it that, as we get older, we notice it more? The pre-1914 was an obscene mess, in a different way. And as for the 20's!

I am much worried by the news of another bad raid on London. It's so impossible to evaluate these things by the newspaper. Do take care of yourself.

Very much love, as always, and to Bob,
Christopher

*   *   *

[May 2?–9, 1944]   [Patterdale, Westmoreland, England]

Dearest Christopher,

I take up, to answer your letters of March 16 & 28, the pens of Dorothy Wordsworth and Canon Raunsleigh: that is to say, I am in the Lakes, and it is raining. It did not do so for the first days of my visit, and I had a very good time alone, walking slowly all day without fatigue. It is the first time I have been out of the London area for 2 or 3 years. Travelling is so awkward that one needs an incentive, and this was found in a lecture I undertook at Glasgow. I am at Patterdale, the head of Ullswater. It has been a lovely change from Surrey and London—the last named looks a dreadful muddle. Bob was in some bad raids—he wormed his way into a cake of rubble whose plums were human beings, cut through the back of a wardrobe, handed out the dresses, cut through the front, handed on [out?] morphis-pills from a doctor whose hand showed through the floor, and extricated an old lady and carried her in his arms to safety, and she calling on Holy Mary all the time. I took Robin a fortnight back to Natasha's [Spender's wife] recital. He sat between me and Joe, was very good and sensible over the music and shook hands or bowed to what is left of the Bloomsbury elite—Beryl de Zoete and Sybil Colefax-Wraiths[54]—offered toffee to Elizabeth Bowen, and had popped into his own mouth a spoonful of demerers [?] sugar by Stephen to steady his nerves. The concert was a success—lovely Schumann, smashing Ravel. Beethoven less successful. Oh and that reminds me, I have a bone to pick with the C sharp minor quartet—easy enough, for it consists mainly of little bones. I cannot believe that this scrappy self-willed dispirited stuff contains the secret of happiness, and expect it was an extra piece of naughtiness on B's part that made him say so.

It is so dark that Christopher Wordsworth can scarcely see the paper. The sky is lighter than the earth, so a cloud must have set down on us. I am the only guest in the hotel which I first visited nearly 40 years ago, and it hasn't much altered, except to become more comfortable and to send a grandson to Rugby.—Ought one, by the way, as one gets older, to fling about such unreturnable weights as "nearly 40 years ago"? It is a moot point, and I haven't found a ruling. I want to be thought young, and for very good reasons. Yet I combine this wish with the heaving of silencers. The truth probably is that neither youth nor age are bad, so one wobbles between them.

Oh the mists are lifting! May Hutchinson can see Helvellyn quite well. Coleridge, who should have gone up it today, would be better for a little Landanum;[55] disordered stomach; too much exercise? Too much food? Landanum not to be had. I return to London tomorrow, and shall post this letter there, and perhaps add something to it when I have seen Bob. I don't think I can write austerity stories. I did finish the memoir, rather against the grain, and the result is wry and peeved. I have now heard from Bill [Roerick]. An interesting letter, but he makes no reference to any person, thing, or incident in this country, although he was here several months. Is this "American" or is it Bill? And does one rally him on it?

I think I shall go to the Post Office, and buy some chocolate modge[?], against Southey's advice. It is strange that you and I should be writing in sceneries so different from each other and from ourselves—you amongst carrots and rattlesnakes, and I in this slightly holy upland of the English-speaking people. I wish we could meet. Could it have been a cousin of yours whom I saw in a shop in Shere? I know you have an aunt there, and he was rather like you to look at: very young: you would know him—if he exists—as a child.

I have been broadcasting on books that have influenced me. Bob said "Don't forget the negative ones" and this panned out well

NO	YES
The *goodness* of St. Augustine	v. Blake's
The *cleverness* of Machiavelli	v. Voltaires's
The *indignation* of Swift	v. Samuel Butler's whose Erewhon I was specially considering
The *strength* of Carlyle	v. Sophocles' in the Antigone

I agree with all you say about love when I read your words, but never manage to think or feel clearly on the subject. Has love an antithesis? Would its antithesis be hatred? I agree one can't determine to love. But I think one can determine to realise other people exist, and if one succeeds love may come easier. Of Heinz I have often thought, and have looked at photographs of him and Bob grinning at one another on that Dutch railway car. So you have known him since March 1932. I met Bob in 1930—also March I think—it was the Boat Race Day. The two often occur to me together. I often expect you will meet H. again—the ordinary earthly meeting—and I am glad on that account that you didn't stay here, as on other accounts.

Nothing from Tommy Ryan so far. I hope I shall see him.

I shall like to see your Gita translation. I read Mrs. Besant's and got a good deal out of it. Best luck to your Viertel novel. I liked him when we met. I don't expect I shall go to his anti-Nazi play. Most people here are fed up with them, and I am disgusted with the Lunts' change of locale from Finland to Greece, though they acted well.

The rain redescends. Not even de Quincy would have gone for a walk with a rather Doverian gunner, and I don't expect *I* shall for the gunner won't call for me this evening.[56]

Susan Glaspell—I can't remember whether she once sat on the edge of my bed at Brunswick Square or not. Norman Matson, who was closely connected with her, certainly did, and I liked him. Didn't she once have another semi-phony play about a University? Bill lent me Wilder's The Skin of our Teeth. Not phony, but sometimes foolish and expecting carelessness to do the job of charm.

9-5-44

This about a week later. Have reached home and the flat. Nice second letter from Bill, introducing personalities, but what is not so nice [is] my letter to Tommy Ryan returned to me[.] "Name rejected" is the alleged and mysterious cause. Meaning, I guess, that there are two of his name and that the naval address given me by Bill was not enough. Please write to him and give him my address, and we will hope to get into touch that way.

Must go and broadcast.

Love,
M.

*   *   *

West Hackhurst, Abinger Hammer, Dorking
Saturday, 16-6-44

Dearest Christopher,

I don't suppose that pilotless planes are more dangerous than anything else, but new forms of danger make one self conscious, and I find myself waiting to get off one more letter to you. I don't think I have written since my visit to the Lakes (Ullswater) at the beginning of May; I had been lecturing at

Glasgow, and looked in at those lovely model mountains for 5 days. So small. But I got so tired and was so happy. I thought of you amongst carrots in huge Mexico—and now it seems to me I must have written to you since, and if I did it tells you something about my life: its lack of variety. The Lakes will stick out for years. I wanted Bob and May to go, with [?] Robin, when they take their holiday in August, but they have managed to hire their motor boat again. It does not move, but stays in the water between Teddington and Richmond. You get from the bank to it and back in a dinghy. I stayed a night there last summer, and the early mists rolling off the Star & Garter were certainly striking.

The windows keep shaking, my poor mother calls down for assurance, (she is very good over this hateful rubbish) and I call up that it is guns. Probably it is. But Christopher[,] how disgusting, how difficult not to grumble in a war's 5th year, how impossible for me to create a book. I wonder whether you, by sheer willpower, will succeed, as you intend to do.

Sun.

At this point I went to bed. What a night—cold[,] starlit and restless. Everything far away, including the owls, and the voices of boys calling out excitedly. The house shaking itself gently for no reason. I didn't intend to write you this kind of letter, but perhaps it is worth preserving as a document. As for news, I hear constantly from Bill, but (as I mentioned to you when last writing) my note to Tommy Ryan was returned from its official address. William [Plomer] came to a meal in the flat with us last week. I have rather lost his acquaintanceship through his overwork, and I have lost Joe's [Ackerley] through his emotional specialisation. [R]egrettable losses, though they aren't losses of friendship. I have had another letter from Paul Cadmus, a long one. I do think he must be very nice. His horror pictures gave me the depressed feeling that impotence does—I felt the same, more strongly, when I saw the pictures of D. H. Lawrence. I did not want to vomit. Do you know his friends the Frenchs?

Best love from
Morgan

I envy you your film work, and wish I knew more about the tricks and technicalities of that trade, so that I might spot the dishonesties in a picture with less bother and be left free to enjoy its achievements or possibilities.

*   *   *

July 8. [1944]   1946 Ivar Avenue. Hollywood 28.
                                                                    California.

Dearest Morgan,

Your letter of June 16 arrived today. It had been opened by Auntie Censor (unusual these days) and was directed to the old Alto Cedro address. So, considering the delay, it was very quick.

Yes, I'd been worrying a lot about the rockets. Here, we argue about them, wondering if they are more frightening than piloted planes. I have rather a thing about the *malice* of pilots: they may suddenly take a dislike to your particular house. But the rockets must be dreadful, too. So impersonal, like roulette.

Your earlier letter told me about the lakes. (I answered it a week ago). I'm so glad that was a happy time.

Hope that you will be seeing Lincoln Kirstein. He has your address. I think you will find him very stimulating, and able to talk the language of both hemispheres, which is rare. Also, he might bring Pete. It seems he's in England still. I wrote L. and am awaiting a reply. He may also see my Mother.

Am reading George Moore.[57] I infinitely prefer his gossip to Proust's. It's about nothing much, but I like the tone. He is fearlessly preoccupied with the things he thinks important (in *Salve*) and assumes you will be too. So you are. Or at least I am. The account of his hunting for a house in Dublin—told without the slightest attempt to amuse. One *couldn't* care less, yet one reads on.

Also saw Garbo in her first big film, Gosta Berling. She isn't special—only 17 and curiously plump. But the atmosphere of the picture. Those immemorially old saga-faces. The whole smell of the North. The gloom which somehow isn't depressing. The great lakes and forests, and the neurosis and the furs, and the scowl of hopeless love. Strangely cosy. There were also some very sympathetic wolves, which, apparently, could only run on ice. As soon as Garbo and Lars Hansen reached the bank of the frozen lake, they were out of bounds, and the wolves retired and they had a love-scene in big fur mittens. Several young ladies of enormous size fainted on top of small but agile men, who bent under them but did not break. Mrs. Viertel told us that Garbo's eyelashes were so long they had to be curled up before her eyes could be photographed.

Gerald has written a life of Christ from the point of view of Gamaliel. Brilliant, I am told. The Huxley-Ish[erwood] movie story is not sold yet. I'm getting ready to write a life of Vivekananda.[58] Harvey Young is coming back to Hollywood soon, which may mean almost anything or not much. I feel more and more strongly that I shall see you before long.

                                                                    Best love,
                                                                    Christopher

* * *

7-7-44   West Hackhurst,
                                                Abinger Hammer,
                                                        Dorking

Dearest Christopher,

All whom you love are safe so far—the narrowest shave has been William's, who was keeping John Morris company in his (M's) flat. They were mainly battered by the noise. Glass broke but did not stale them. Bob injured his knee carrying a boy out of a blitzed house—returns to duty today. Leo writes cheerfully on his own behalf and Tom's from Dover. Down here it is fairly safe, though occasionally Goering doesn't put enough stuff in, and they flop on the downs. I am mostly here, so do not worry about me. I only go up to broadcast or to see Bob. I am thankful that you are away from it—not so much out of the danger, which you aren't interested to be, as out of the daftness. Only to music do I retain a first hand response. Everything else is conditioned by bombs; one is bearing up; one is setting an example; one is being kind; one is patronizing the past for its ignorance, or enjoying it for its security. Even if I could write a novel, I wouldn't; it wouldn't have integrity. Your work can have it. You are spared this unedifying worrying. One or two people are heroic certainly: Rose Macaulay plays away at a work of erudition, *Visitors to Portugal*, and won't even leave London for a weekend. But silly heroism, what. Daft like the rest of us. She is not making anything of the amazing situation which has burst on us. I do a little thinking about the Flying Bombs, though. I believe they are going to be important psychologically. They will bitch the Romance of the Air—war's last beauty parlour. Fewer films entitled Flarepath at Dawn. They are inhuman, and people can't get to grip with them in their minds, and feel thwarted, and are driven to reconsideration, and so to—?

Bill keeps writing to me. He is a grand fellow. I disappoint him with my sterility, but no matter: he must keep on being disappointed. What a lot of pleasure that rapid meeting with him has given me!

Jeanne de Casalis and Antony Asquith want to make Howard's End into a film.[59] What do you think of the idea? I think it is a dreadful idea, though I am struck by her sensitiveness. She sees what the house is and does see herself, I fear, playing Helen. I wish you were here to talk to. You would be sure to have some opinion. Umm. The house is an actual one, and during the past two years I have been going to it again. They would either shoot it [there], which I should not like, or build it which I should not want. They would do something really English, and said so, in the Ivy, and I have a vision of elm trees in the hedgerows, and of thousands of cows, such as astonished the Hardys when they saw Tess.

Popping into the Red Cross Book Sale yesterday I bought the Memoires of Saint-Simon.[60] Six volumes, which seemed to be wrong, with London Library edition contains [*sic*] forty. Still, six will be quite enough, for my main object is to find out what happened to civilisation when Madame de Sévigné left it, and before Voltaire came to it. I want also to find out which human beings have scored for the human race by having happy lives; Saint-Simon is unlikely to tell me—too cross. I think I have scored myself and I do not mean anything subtle by "scoring." I have had good friends, and have not been parted from them too soon, and health, and have gained a reputation of the sort I'm glad to have had.— How tepid this reads. Please steep it in something, Christopher. You will keep on getting letters like this from me I'm afraid, for the reason that we are not for the moment at our mental best in the London area.

Love from Morgan

*   *   *

July 29. [1944]

1946 Ivar Avenue
Hollywood 28. Calif

Dearest Morgan,

I think of you so much. There is no way of knowing just how bad the bombing is on any particular day. The newspapers are not allowed to say, and anyhow the news is not popular, because it doesn't form an harmonious peal in the victory carillon. Please keep writing very often as long as this continues, even if only postcards. (But of course I hope and even expect it will have stopped before this letter reaches you).

There seems little news. The Gita translation will be ready next week and will go off to you, to John Lehmann, to Stephen, etc. You probably won't be in the mood for it at present, but put it aside. It can wait. It has waited more than two thousand years. At the moment I've just finished a very priggish-sounding article on "The Gita and War" for our magazine. It annoys me, but there are things in it I wanted to say. The rough draft of my novelette is ready: a triumph of will rather than literature. But perhaps I can turn it into something. The present war gets in the way. One tries to choose between wisdom after the event and deliberate stupidity. I have been so very active this year, writing anything and everything: which I can't help taking as an omen that the war will end very soon. Spring coming and the nest-building instinct. If novels are nests.

I will now come right out quite frankly and say that I have no idea what Saint-Simon wrote about. Or Madam de Sevigne, either. Or, for that matter, Chateaubriand, Rochefoucault, or someone else, with an appetising name—Beavais, Bernaise, Bonpoint—oh, I remember, St Beuve. Not to mention Montesquioueuoueuouxxxxxqq. And weren't there some more Madames? Recalmier? Or did she just lie down? But I have asked you enough questions for one letter. Please answer on one side of the paper, dismissing each character with a single sentence, or silent disdain, if you prefer.

Howard's End, to my mind, is a play, not a movie—in that it is designed to induce claustrophobia rather than agoraphobia. Pictures should never be made about old or loved houses: the camera destroys all the atmosphere. But Asquith has plenty of taste. And de Casalis helped write that rather good play about Napoleon on St Helena. I agree with you in mistrusting the "really English" line. "Really English"—that's a rare bird, not to be caught by the camera: unless one photographed it by mistake for a parrot.

Strange grey lifeless weather again: as if all the sunshine had been taken over by the government and made into something explosive. Must stop and cycle over to see Dodie Smith, who, as I'm sure I must have often told you, strangely reminds me of you. Your letter didn't seem the least tepid, but if it had, you know what I would have steeped it in.

Lots of that, as always,
Christopher

*   *   *

15 Dec 1944

[telegram sent from Hollywood, CA]
How are you no news in ages worried please write
love happy Christmas Bob Buckingham family friend

Christopher Isherwood

*   *   *

18-12-44
West Hackhurst,
Abinger Hammer,
Dorking

Dearest Christopher,

I have just wired to you and this inadequate letter shall go off tomorrow. We are all of us all right. My *good* news is that I have at last news of the Maurons. They have emerged after four years from their cares and their Chinese mysticism, and Charles, now quite blind, has gone straight to the Mairie and is organising the distribution of food. Marie looks after five goats and has written five books. I find it difficult to write to them, as I do to you. Old Gerald once neatly explained why; starting to hope is painful, and we have had to practice, for so long, the better kinds of despair over here—gaiety, endurance, helpfulness, the enjoyment of art are some of those kinds.

I am just broadcasting to India, of all places, about your Gita, of all books.[61] I like the translation very much indeed, far better than Mrs Besant's, the only one I had read. (N.B. this is not my first canter though, vide Abinger Harvest). Instead of thanking you, I have cabled you to send me another copy, for I don't like to lend mine, except to Bob, and people start asking for it.—[I] Don't say much to India, of course. Quote poem about Fig Tree towards the end.

I hear constantly from Bill. Another American soldier has also been found—by Bob, and we are all getting fond of him quickly. His name is Noel Voge, from California. He is a translator, and married, in Portugal, a Yugoslav wife. Bob is going in for French, also for high class drama, and here he is supported by Robin and May: the four of us attended Hamlet and Richard III. Their party is on the 26th—we shall be thinking of you. We meet at 12.00, for roast goose. Bob's father and mother will be there, also Noel Voge, and Joe and his sister Nancy arrive for tea. Brother Ted is breeding too fiercely to make this journey.

You must be anxious as to whether we are safe, and I must write more frequently. I am so afraid of being depressing for depression's sake. Most people mind V. 2 less than V. 1.[62] I'm not sure I do, for when everything is quiet and the silence I love approaches, I sometimes start wondering whether one [i.e., another bombing raid] is coming. Certainly anyone you know in the London area may vanish entirely at any moment, not run to a corpse even [i.e., burned]. But the percentage is very small so far—that is to say among those I know. Though many houses of friends have been destroyed or damaged. William Plomer is fairly all right—in the admiralty, not too good with shingles. Joe moderate. Leo and Tom still at Dover. Please write again. What news have you of Wystan?

Best love, and I am sorry to have worried you and much [. . . ?] cable. Also I should have thanked you for that book at once.

Morgan

Just received letter from Richard.

3

The Postwar Years

9-5-45   Chiswick [London]

Dearest Christopher,

It is long since I wrote, but soon after I received your last letter my mother died, which has given me much to do, besides terrible grief. You might tell Gerald when you next write, with my love. She was not ill long—under a week, and did not suffer, or have illusions, and I have no regrets or remorses [*sic*], though all the other sorts of sadnesses [*sic*]. If I could have come straight away, say out to you, it would have been all right, but neither the state of the world nor my immediate duties permitted that, and I have to drag on at West Hackhurst destroying things—150 years of letters mostly from women to women about women, and masses of rubbish from straw fans to wardrobes which are in many cases not absolute rubbish and have a semi-life which complicates their fate. I dislike destruction, also sadness. What I shall *do* is beyond me, as it is beyond the world. I have no illusion that problems are soluble: their only use is that they show one, roughly, where one is. Everyone has been very kind, and I eat and sleep all right. The actual date of death was March 11.

I have just turned up such a pleasant photograph—you and me on beach at Ostende while Heinz in middle distance appears to be looking down his back at his toe. I expect that the sight of it got this letter going, though you have often been in my thoughts. I am in bed at Chiswick. Last night was Victory Day, you will remember, and today is another one. I came up to broadcast, also to see Bob, but of course he is on extra duties. I am feeling rather sick as I drank a good deal (for me) in an experimental way. It was not very nice in London. Isolated shrieks, no rhythm, no contacts. Six years have been too long. And we haven't yet had Vactory Day. Or Vuctory. A man in the club, whose name I do not know, grimly stood me champagne. Then I squashed [?] in pubs for beer. Buckingham Palace, seen well from sideways, was surprisingly effective, with a great decor of evening clouds, and the King lobbing words very carefully at the enormous concourse. I should have liked to be in his place, for there is great thankfulness, and he could have seen it and focused it if in possession of field glasses. I could not see him.

I must get up, dear Christopher, and settle whether to be unwell. No, I need not get up, because I have now done so, turned on the bath, and got back into bed again. It is only 8.00 A.M. so my celebrations have not been riotous. Through the windows I can see the spire of the church which William calls St Utrillo and the flag on it town hall, but dimly because of the dirt. Will this country ever be clean and tidy again? No. I was merely stating a problem. My broadcast will be on Osbert Sitwell and on a concert of Indian Music in the National Gallery.[1] Oh that reminds me, I don't think I ever thanked you for the additional Bhagavad Gitas. I was very glad to receive them. Joe sits on one of them, another is promised to Indians in Broadcasting House.

Please write again, with any news. We are so provincial here, and I have an idea that your province may be larger. The people you know here are all right—that is to say the people you knew with or through me. Bob has bought a boat and is rigging it. At present it lies inside a barge at Hammersmith Bridge, so is not very big. Bob calls the barge a dry dock. May says with resignation that she understands that there are intervals in the career of a boat when it can be used, and that perhaps one will occur before the end of the summer. Perhaps I shall look in on her this morning on my way up. It is very nice having them so near, and there is always lots of food.

Best love, dear Christopher
Morgan

*   *   *

26-8-45   W[est] H[ackhurst][2]

Dearest Christopher,

News at last, and in the Hollywood sense. Having finished my picture with the Crown Film Unit, I am flying to India to attend a conference of writers. How livelily Morgan writes—always did! No, but this is so. It is an Indian P.E.N. meeting on Oct. 20th, at Jaipur, and I have got air preference. At the last moment I may be pushed off the plane to accommodate a business man, but up to that moment it is so. And I am partly writing to ask you whether you have a message for this conference. I should be very glad of it if you have. It doesn't matter your not belonging to the P.E.N. A greeting.

Or more. And will you ask Aldous if you are near him. And Gerald if the same. Swamis can also communicate. I think the company would be thrilled and pleased if something came from your coast. I will enclose, if I can find it, all that we yet know about this curious stunt. They are my hosts in India, and the British Council is sending us out: odder still. "Us" is self and Ould, the P.E.N. Secretary in London.

All my friends want me to go, and some may be glad to get rid of me, for I partly died when my mother did, and must smell sometimes of the grave.—I have noticed and disliked that smell in others, occasionally—I do not cotton [?] to sorrow.

My old maid has been very nice at being left alone for a couple of months; has a sister who will come, and a former fellow servant, and my aunt Rosalie, and Joe, and Bob, May and Robin. And I have a good gardener. So they should get through somehow, and the house still working on my return. I have still millions of things to see to and destroy, and no visible future or bright reground. But I shall be thankful to see men and women of a different colour in the streets and India will provide that. My best friends there are all dead, and if death meant being with them I should like it. I have a romantic fantasy that I shall never come back. But events don't stage us like that. Besides, I may never start, which is more likely.

I forget if I wrote to you since my visit to Leo & Tom at Dover, but I don't want to fill the rest of this paper with small chat—except to say that Bob and May & Robin have gone up the Thames in a boat they now possess, have been away a fortnight and are now returning. I met the boat at Weybridge regatta.[3]

Very much love from
Morgan

* * *

1946 Ivar Avenue
Hollywood 28 Calif.
[September 26, 1945]

Dearest Morgan,

Just got your letter. I hope this reaches you before you leave. Look here, couldn't you possibly come back by way of California? It would be so nice, and I know you'd have a great welcome in N.Y. too. Cadmus would see to that. Here, of course, there are Chris,[4] Gerald, the Huxleys—not to mention Dodie Smith, who would love to meet you—as who wouldn't?

I haven't been able to contact the Huxleys and Gerald quick enough before writing this. But I am sure you can convey their greetings to the conference, with Swami Prabhavananda's and mine. I really don't know what message to send—as I combine the utmost goodwill with the wish that all Indians would speak Hindustani, Bengali, Urdu, etc, and stop murdering the English language. I always tell Swami that this was India's revenge on British imperialism.

No time to write more. Am just finishing a screenplay. Then I hope for a long holiday and work of my own.

All my love,
Christopher

* * *

March 26. [1946]

137 Entrada Drive
Santa Monica. Calif.

My dearest Morgan,

My reasons for writing to you have been accumulating steadily, these last few days. A letter from John Lehmann saying that you were selling West Hackhurst and perhaps going to live at King's, then a copy of your lecture on inter-war prose, a photograph in an old book, the Passage to India left in the apartment by a weekend visitor and reread—also, more indirectly, a deep deathlike sleep last night after three days of beach-picnics, gin, chatter, empty grinning and too-loud laughter—a glance at Mencius in some anthology over early coffee—most of all, perhaps, a letter from Heinz, written last August 26, form [sic] a prisoner of war camp in France. "Dear Mr Isherwood, you'll be astonished to hear from somebody whom you think will be already dead. After I had a bad time in Germany as you may know, I had to become a soldier and was caught than at the Reihn-River. Who knows what my life will look like after I get discharged. Yours affectionately . . . " I have written, of course—to one of those addresses which are all numbers and capital letters—but he must have been sent back to Germany long ago, and I don't suppose they will forward P.O.W. mail. So there's nothing to be done till he writes again. "Dear Mr Isherwood"! What do you make of that? Does he think I'm ashamed of knowing him, that I'll be embarrassed, or something?

You have never written since you got back from India. I think I understand why. There is probably too much to say. Well, you shall say it, I hope, before very long. I plan to come back this summer, in July or August. When I think of England, it all really adds up to my mother and you.

I wonder if you have read my novelette, Prater Violet. They liked it here, chiefly, I think, because it doesn't pretend to be a masterpiece, in this land of canyons, skyscrapers and epics. You will see all its weaknesses and forgive them. They are weaknesses in myself. Yes, it is quite clever, quite amusing, nearly plausible—and one then reads something like your lecture. People say you are a great writer, and I think you are, whatever that means—but it's not the point. The point is that you are incapable of telling a lie. Oh, there's so much I want to talk to you about—Hinduism, God, sex, (why a little S? The typewriter chose it), your prostate operation (I just had a minor one), India, America, England, War, Peace. I would love to see you and Swami together—the two pillars of wisdom. They can keep the other five for a public building.

But I can't write you a proper letter, Morgan dear. I can only make noises indicating love—another small letter, but it has stayed with me when so much else has been left behind in strange houses or scattered on the road in the haste of retreat.

As always,
Christopher

*   *   *

1-4-46
West Hackhurst,
Abinger Hammer,
Dorking

Dearest Christopher,

I have just received your letter of March 26th. I am very much excited about Heinz, as will Bob be, whom I shall see tomorrow. I do not fear Dear Mr Isherwood at all. It is very natural after years of oddness, also he has been through much more than you, and is bound to be strange in himself for a time. It is grand too that you will be in England this summer, and we will talk, amongst other things, of when I shall come to America.

My Indian visit probably saved my mind. I returned to more worry and sadness, for I have been given notice to leave this house—it is not mine to sell. However, I expect to get through. My mother's death has been much more awful than I expected. I am glad that no one will miss me like that. In India I found food, warmth, "fame," affection, and *space*—the mere travelling about was exquisite. I can't tell you how happy I was. I kept telling myself—e.g. in the mosque at Delhi, the Fort at Bikaner, the Fort at Agra, the Caves at Ajanta, and from the train during Diwali passing Sassaram. (How many of these words does Swami remember?) I lectured, broadcasted, talked literary—you are well known to Indians, but for *Gita* and *Goodbye to Berlin* only. I will try to get two broadcasts (done over here) out of Joe Ackerley for you. It is a nuisance that I haven't been able to settle down here on my return, and think, I like to think when I want to think, and I rather think I wanted to think.

King's [College Cambridge] has worked out fortunately. Two small rooms out of college and one very large one in, all unfurnished. So I shall be able to bring along quite a lot of stuff. I don't go till the autumn, so you will probably see this house again. Last time you arrived very late, and the cold duck was overdone. There is also the flat at Chiswick still. I could put you up there if needful. My goodness the weather has been lovely this week. Such a nice boat race—the 16th anniversary of Bob and my first meeting. He rowed in a fascinating centipede called The Head of the River, the sort of race which you don't know whether you've won until for some time afterwards.

I must leave room for one or two points which you relegate as minor. What is this operation which you mention? Prater Violet I have never read. Could you send me a copy? What is this present address of yours? I don't think I've had it before.

Bill Roehrick is very faithful, very generous. I have fed the whole of Abinger Manner School with his maple sugar. I wonder how you will find the food over here. I don't think it is any worse than it was 6 months ago, but people are not looking as well as they did—I noticed it on my return.

Morgan's Love

*   *   *

14 Jan 1947

[sent from Hollywood, CA]
STAYING WIT LEHMANN BUT LONGING TO SEE YOU 22ND OR 23RD IF POSSIBLE ALL MY LOVE CHRISTOPHER ISHERWOOD

*   *   *

K[ings] C[ollege] C[ambridge] 21-3-47

Dearest Christopher,

I ought to have written. I am never ill but sometimes becalmed. I like the Don Quixote and have been reading in it.

Thank you for your Bill's address. The Bill I can scarcely call mine is being so helpful, and I think a programme may evolve that won't inconvenience his plans. A little New York, with Red Carpet for you, then Tyringham,[5] then I go to Harvard, then Arizona, perhaps, with him, for he has to go sometime in May to Hollywood. I shall return to New York. I shall go home, which means Bob and his family for me now, as you saw.

When do you come back to London? Can I not see you before I fly on the 14th?

Also can I give you a cheque for £50? Curtis Brown have just snubbed me for making what I thought a quite legal and indeed honourable offer.

The £50 will be, you understand, payment for a copy of Don Quixote, illustrated by Gustave Doré, which you sold to me.[6]

Dearest Christopher, I have just had three very pleasant nights in town, went to the Alchemist, saw Bob, had a present of a large picture by Jamini Roy, perhaps a farmer, perhaps a god (Kama?) holding a parrot with his legs rather apart.[7] "Fancy meeting those eyes in the dark!" cried little Mrs Bolton. The picture has brought excitement and freedom to me in a way you may understand. It is something of my own, and it represents the goodness of India. The painter gave it me because I once admired it in his studio at Calcutta and did not say so; I talked about it in London and he heard of this. And it was brought to me by two other Indians, Narayan & Rekha Menon; such a trouble they took, she especially. The boy's flesh is blue: he is that mixture of the sturdy and the sacred which, if it does not repel, attracts strongly. I only had the picture yesterday. I expect to get tired of it, then I shall take it down.

I saw that wisp in the distance, Guy Burgess. His meeting with you seems to have gone as I expected it would.

Much clothing is accumulating here for Heinz and his son. Christopher, you do not like packing things up. No more do I. That is the real trouble.

I am here till next Thursday. By then I hope to have finished my Harvard stuff and to spend 3 or 4 days in town.

Is there any prospect of help for your mother? Does Richard see eye to eye with reality more? Have you tried advertising? And for a married couple?

Hoping for another letter.

Morgan

*   *   *

In train called "Exposition" (to Burlington)" in Nebraska 2-6-47

Dearest Christopher,

I seem to write to everyone but you. And you to me? It *was* a muddle over Swami. Suddenly I decided to visit an old and isolated friend, C. H.

Collins Baker, at the Huntington Museum, San Marino,[8] wrote to Chris W. and had nice telephone talk with him and Gerald, but that was all. My letter to Bill missed him. I do wish I had written to you.

I spent 9 happy days in Berkeley with Noel whom I like more and more, and with his wife whom I much liked so far as I could see her, but she is hoping to become a Doctor in Zoology and very busy. Noel and I went for two days to the Yosemite, and it even looks if I shall include Niagara. The third of the Heavies, whom I had purposed to exclude. Heading now for Chicago. I may very likely reach New York on the morning of Monday the 9th. Paul Cadmus should have left the keys of his apartment at Harcourt Brace's where I shall call for them. If I do not find them, woe and telephones, in which you will be involved.

Niagara is rather funny. In 1944 I spoke to a Canadian air officer in the tube, and since he did not know London met him next day for St Paul's—that is all I have seen him—rather "common" commercial type. He came down over Germany and we corresponded, now it turns out from the map that he lives close to Niagara Falls. He is very anxious I should stop with him and meet his wife and child, writes "life is so short that we may never be near one another again," which is enough to fetch me and most people?

There seems no reason you should need to catch me at Chicago. In fact I can think of no possible[reason]. But I shall be there until the evening of the 6th if I achieve Johnny Kennedy, and longer if I don't. Address: c/o C. F. Huth, University, Chicago.

Kindest greetings to Bill. Love to you and I hope we shall be together often. Except for visits to Bill Roehrick, Harold Barger, Archibald MacLeish, Paul Cadmus, and Asaf Ali,[9] I am expecting to settle down in New York quietly.

Morgan's Love

*   *   *

Dakar. April 12 [1948]

As you see, we are drawing inexorably nearer. We'll probably get to le Havre around April 24 and then spend a few days in Paris. We ought to be in England at the beginning of May. Our boat is an overcrowded old French tub, and crawls across the Atlantic inch by inch. The jabbering of the passengers is probably audible for miles around. Am longing to see you.

Christopher

[postscript:]
We'll be seeing you very soon. It's wonderful to be cross the Atlantic—it took forever.

Bill

*   *   *

K[ings] C[ollege] C[ambridge] 3-5-48

Dearest Christopher,

Thank you for your foreign card, and I have your arrival from Bob. When will I see you. Bill also?

I was meaning to come up on Wednesday. Could you both come to tea at my flat at about 4.00? Lunch at the Reform Club would have to be for one guest only. Could you come alone to that, and then we meet Bill? Or I could offer you both drinks.

If you have gone north Wednesday, I will cut an engagement here on Tuesday with Harvard University and come up and meet you in the late afternoon or evening. But in that case, it will be necessary for you to ring Cambridge 55006 at about 9.30 tomorrow (Tuesday) morning.

Love from
Morgan

John not there, is he?
[the following, at the bottom of the page, is a poem by Isherwood,
    written in his hand:]
He pulled up short 2 miles from the place,
Number Four stared him right in the face,
Turned to his fire boy, said "you'd better jump
'cause there's two locomotives that's going to bump!"

[written below the poem:]

O mio babbino caro.
Petite Suite Roussell.

*   *   *

[Kings College Cambridge] 25-6-48

Dearest Christopher,

Tennessee Williams got up too late to reach Cambridge. [Gore] Vidal arrived, and I wish hadn't, as I disliked him a lot. I hope anyhow he returned you Gerald's *[A] Street Car [Named Desire]*. I am looking forward to seeing it on the stage, where its colour, violence, and seedfulness [*sic*] should be effective. I did not find the characters alive (my old whimper), but that is where actors and actresses are so useful. Alive themselves, often through no wish of their own, they are compelled to vivify the dramatist's ideas. I shouldn't have thought it was a good play—with the chief character an invalid who ought to have been looked after earlier. Still the stage is always surprising me into a good deal of pleasure. The poker scene might look lovely.

What I am really writing about though is *Maurice*. I should very much like a talk alone with you during the next week or so. I am ashamed at shirking publication but the objections are formidable. I am coming up on Tuesday for a night or probably two. Wednesday morning should be all right. If you [are] able to drop me a line here, do so. Otherwise, I will ring you in London.

Lovely letter from Ben [Benjamin Britten]. Herring etc. comes to Cambridge at the end of the month.

Love,
Morgan

*   *   *

KING'S COLLEGE CAMBRIDGE [summer 1948?]

Your visits much enjoyed—though there were provincial wonderings why you had an evening engagement in town. Now I am deposited here, I think for some time. Grand if you could disclose yourself to Heinz on Liverpool St. Sta[tion] Sat. 8.30—or ring him up at Lark-crow[?] on Sunday morning at CH1 2407. Later in the morning Bob drives them away to Coventry for a couple of days.

Much love,
Morgan

*   *   *

[Kings College Cambridge][10] March 27, [1949]

Dearest no Christopher. No alas, no chance whatsoever of us taking the long trek to the Pacific seaboard. Am sure to get dazed and tired as it is and may pay but a short visit to the U.S.A.

On the other hand it is, as you know, only a little hop from the Pacific seaboard to the Atlantic one. Could you and Bill not take it during our stay?

Who you may ask but should not is "we"? Bob is coming too, all being well. He is wild about it, it is his suggestion, and all that remains now is to get some one to sign an affidavit to support him in the U.S.A. I have asked Bill Roehrick, what if it is not convenient to him shall approach Lincoln. We shall have plenty of money as soon as we land in New York, so the guarantor shouldn't be called upon. (We didn't write to you, since a N.Y. guarantor seemed best.) My own permit to travel will have to be through the Bank of England, and probably forthcoming. Bob could only stay about 10 days. I should rather like to return with him, but this is not yet decided. We shall be flying.

I have a good deal of news and all good. I have been for the last 3 weeks in Aldeburgh composing (with Eric Crozier's help) a libretto for Ben's next opera, "Billy Budd." The work went wonderfully well. I am amazed at it and at myself. I have so far only written a sort of play, but think we shall be able to break it down into libretto form. (What does break down mean and why is it so often used?) Crozier plans the thing and stuffs it with naval oddments. We are a lucky combination. I do hope it goes through. We have another session in August.

All the above PRIVATE for the moment. Ben is issuing a statement for his agents shortly.

(N.B. Peter would play Vere, not Billy)[11]

Today is Boat Race day, and 19 years ago did I meet Bob. He had a lot of duty, but I managed to see him, and he treated me, Robin, and two New Zealand women to seats at the Race itself. Hot sunshine and all very gay, and Cambridge won by 1/4 of a length. Robin is going to France.

I go to Cambridge tomorrow to write the lecture. They only want about 1/2 an hour.

Bob has just had a long and interesting letter from Heinz[,] [w]ho has received 4 C.A.R.E. parcels from you this year. He would 1/2 starve without them.

Besides love to Bill, would he send me the photos of me which he took at Aldeburgh. They are said to be so good but not a glint of them have I seen.

Love to you, and I never thanked you for your birthday letter and cable Your health was drunk, and Bill's.

Morgan's Love

*   *   *

January 16th [1950]   31152 Monterey Street. South Laguna.
                                                         California.

Dearest Morgan,

I hope you got the letter I wrote a short while ago, and I hope you had a nice birthday? I'm writing again because I've been asked to, for the following reason—

It is said, I don't know how truly, that you were "approached" recently by some Hollywood representative or agent, asking if you would consider letting them make a movie out of *Passage to India*. Your answer, allegedly, was No; because enough novels had been ruined already and you didn't see why *Passage* should be added to the list.

All right—

Now I have a friend named Frank Taylor, who used to be in publishing and has now come out here and become a film-producer. He works at 20th century Fox. When I describe him as a friend, I hope I sufficiently indicate that he is unlike the usual sort of producer. He is, in fact, a civilized person. And the *Passage to India* means to him what it means to people who care about novels, not movies. At the same time, he would like to make a film out of it, if he could do the film just exactly the way you wanted it done. What is more, his boss, Darryl Zanuck (the head of the Studio) is also interested in making a film of the *Passage*, and would therefore be very likely to let Frank go ahead and make the picture *if* Frank could get you to agree to it.

So Frank has asked me to ask you if your No was an unqualified No. Or if you would consider *any* kind of arrangement. He would suggest that you should come out here personally, and that you and I—or you and anybody you wanted—should write the film together; and that you should have absolute Last Word on how it was done. This is, of course, not an offer; because no offer can be made until Frank knows whether or not you will accept one. If you agreed in principle, then he could go to Zanuck with the idea and try to get it through.

Morgan dear, I hate even to bother you with all this; but obviously I have no right to decide without asking you that you would or wouldn't be interested. So I pass it on to you. I feel almost unwilling even to add how much I would love you to come. You know that. You would stay with us, of course, in our dear little house overlooking the ocean and Billy would make you very snug, and we'd just pop into the Studio maybe once a week, and Frank would come out to see you here, and you would be treated like a priceless jewel. Of course, I just want to get you here, no matter how. My attitude toward the project is frankly prejudiced for that reason; and now I won't say another word about it.

Our life here (since moving down to this place) has entered a phase in which everything immediately visible is perfect, and everything and everyone not here is a cause for anxiety and fear. Now we're told that everybody in England is threatened by flu...Oh dear...This certainly wouldn't stop us coming to see you all, if we had the money. But we have to live very quietly at present. I review books. Bill is taking a job with a potter.

Please write sometimes, Morgan dear. We both love you very much.

* * *

Kings College Cambridge Jan. 4, 1951

Dearest Christopher,

Is not that nice! Shall expect you Tuesday, let me know when, also whether you would like to dine in hall that night—cosy but tires one if bossy Professor Adcock presides.

Generally speaking you must organise, for though Ian and I get on nicely, I don't know him well, so that there is no point in the three of us going about together. There'll be my room here if you want to talk to him.

Must conclude, as I am wearing two spectacles which makes writing difficult. Can't get over that picture.

Morgan's gratitude and love.
Going to Aldeburgh late in month
Epigram for 1952: Women are not mysterious, merely incalculable

* * *

[At] Bob's [London]   Jan. 23[,] 1951

Dearest Christopher,

Here is your letter, here was your letter, and I love them both and was about to answer the first one.[12] Oh how I would like to be with you and Bill and *sun*, and have all three of you waiting on me! Dear human [?] friends do wait on me here, but where oh where is the sun warmth and sunlight?

All so grey, and I am weary of the modulations, delicate though they may be, inside that grey.—I fear though that I mustn't consider travel. Not quite robust enough for export yet, and more easily tired and muddled than in the past.

Now for the film. I fear my answer must be a paregoric NO. As I told 20th Century Fox when they were rushing after A Room with a View in 1947. I like films, I like novels, but I don't believe that a novel can be turned into a film without transforming its character. I gave this same answer to the man who wrote pleasantly recently to me: name forgotten, had a Roger in it I fancy, and said I had met him with you; firm called Mann. I added (to him), that sooner or later an author's name disappears from the bills: instance, Henry James' from The Heiress, which is now written by someone else. I wouldn't at all mind writing *for* the films—have indeed done so, and enjoyed yielding and cooperating and fitting in, as I enjoy it over the Billy Budd libretto. But I won't hand over what was written as a novel to an unknown number of cooks. The nearest (and dearest!) cooks I could control, should indeed be in complete sympathy with, but what of the cooks who would be unexpectedly called in—the vegetable cooks, the curry-experts, the continuation kitchen maids, the overall-contractors, the contractors in overalls? How could I control all [of] them? More grit and vigilance than I possess would be required. Bob says Bernard Shaw did successfully control. Muddled, I acquiesce, and then remember Caesar and Cleopatra.[13] With the film industry as at present constituted, I don't see an author *can* be guaranteed to have the last word. I am sad about the films, but that is another matter.

Your letters [are] not before me. I am in bed and must get up, for I am going this afternoon to Cambridge with May. She most kindly coming to overhaul my wardrobe, but will be trapped into a certain amount of festivity I hope. I did have a little influenza for my birthday, however I got here with it, and was not bad. There are two sorts of influenza, the little and the large, and the large is mainly north of the Tees.[14] Always think of us in the south, when you are inclined to be depressed.

Don Windham has been here, much nicer without "monster" Sandy.[15] He comes up to Cambridge for the day on Thursday. And there has been a long and welcome visit from Noel and Marietta Voge from Berkeley—them you don't know.

Well dearest Christopher [I] must stop. Much much love to you, much to Bill, and respects and regards to the friends with whom I should have been immediately working.

Bob may want to add a line. Much love,

Morgan

[note from Bob:]

My dear Christopher, I did my best for you but it was "no go." M. distrusts Hollywood too much. I expect he is right. I will encourage him to make another visit to America when he is really better. We all send our love,

Bob

*   *   *

King's Coll., Camb.   Jan. 14[,] 1952

Dearest Christopher,

I found your letter on my return—what you say about Maurice excites me.[16] There ought to be that extra chapter, but should it not come *before* the boat chapter at Southampton instead of after it? I mean like this: Leaving the British Museum, they go off together, we know—in surroundings not too unsuitable they talk as you say, they feel as we know, and M. says "It mayn't work but we'll give it a try"—A[lec] says I can't, I daren't, I must go as arranged with Fred, you're the only person I've ever . . . but I can't—also (perhaps) there have so often been women that I daren't—In the boat chapter he has dared, Maurice has won him. The final chapter with Clive then stands firmer than ever.

Do you think this would work? Or do you still prefer them to have it out after the boat?

I will have a try—humility my guide. I don't think though that I could write fiction—and of that type—anymore.

I enclose a precious and remarkable letter to Dear Forster, which please return.[17] It shares your fear that it may be only physical attraction. It is an enlightened letter—sometimes too much so: some great things also happen in the dark—it is there that the physical may start flowering.

It occurs to me that you may have seen the letter already. I adopted some of the criticisms when redrafting. He is the model for Risley, as he gaily suggests.

I'm sure we're right about Arctic Summer, though when I read it aloud, with cuts, it seems much better than it is.[18]

I come up on Sunday the 20th for most of the week. What can you manage?

I was not at all sure that you would still like M[aurice] and feel very happy.

Love,
Morgan

No. *Much* love

＊　＊　＊

[King's Coll., Camb. letterhead crossed out and replaced with "As from Bob's"]

Jan. 18[,] 1952

Dearest Christopher,

I could meet you Tuesday evening—dine say, or after dinner if you couldn't dine. Please ring Bob's. Monday as you suggest. I get there Sunday night and may be staying on a few days.

I have drafted out that chapter, and would like to show it you, together with the chapters before and after. British Museum—that chapter—boat at Southampton—good bye to Clive is the sequence. I'm afraid it isn't right in itself, and couldn't be after so many years, but my wanting to do it is important, and I am sure it is wanted, and may—despite the jar in tone—strengthen the stuff on each side of it. A (recorded) meeting between M. and A. *after* the boat sailed might too much resemble the signing of a protocol. As it is, A. has full license to misbehave and throw this attractive weight about, and M. to be grand. [A]nd I should like to think that they take it. I do feel so grateful to you. I have had the story much in mind these weeks, wondering whether A's entry up the ladder could be heated up without becoming hot stuff. But your query is infinitely more important.

What have you done to little Mark Boxer? Last term he called me Morgan, this term Sir. Still if you do not have a similar effect on Ken Shadbolt and Alex Kwapong[?].[19] I do not really mind. Dined with Simon Raven last night, and got a little drunk on nicely calculated wines. Both boys pleased with your messages.

Love and gratitude from
Morgan

＊　＊　＊

As from Bob's [London]   10-2-52

Dearest Christopher,

I have hammered out a technique. Alec is known to favour the Boathouse, Penge, as a trysting place. He is also known—and Maurice knows him—to have Maurice's home address for he wired and wrote there when Maurice fled. What more natural than that he should communicate there again? Maurice thinks of this (we didn't) and rings up his mother from Southampton, after the boat has gone. She, amidst babblings, reveals that a telegram awaits him. Shall she open it? Yes. It contains one word "Boathouse," which she will conjecture as to be a code-word. He goes there and it is obvious they have clicked before his interview with Clive.[20]

I deplore the neatness of this. Raggeder [*sic*] suggestions welcomed.

The hotel chapter is done.

Equally important, I come up Wednesday to Wozzeck.[21] Stop at May's till Friday and then perhaps to my own flat. Shall I see you dear Christopher?

Love,
Morgan

Let me have Lytton's letter back.

* * *

[return address of air letter: King's College, Cambridge]
[postmark date: Oct. 3, 1952]

Dearest Christopher,

Lovely to hear from you after all this time and I have much to say, but will confine my reply, or most of it, to *Maurice*.[22] I have heard from Monroe Wheeler (whom I know better than I do Glenway) and I am today writing to my Lit. Ex[ecut]or Jack Sprott, who has been away. He will own all my copyrights MSS after my death, so it's complicated and I don't know what I shall decide. In the interim, would you be willing to have a copy of *Maurice* on condition that it wasn't published until I died, and was only published by you in the U.S.A.? I am afraid that that's the most the gift is likely to amount to.

Also it would arrive without the additional chapter which I have never got into shape. Don't be angry—who has not yet finished his novel? Or shall we be angry with each other?

No you can't be equally angry with me, for I have finished the Dewes book.[23] The publishers are now peeking in it for libels.

So write again, please, and by then I should have consulted Jack Sprott and seen Monroe.

Next week I go to Belfast to unveil a plaque to Forrest Reid,[24] and next month (I hope) to Paris. The French Government has invited me, and to do nothing, it says. "Merci, madame, d'avoir existé" as they said to Rosamond Lehmann.

Bob is well, arrives here tomorrow, loves his probation job at Coventry, but May finds it all less lovely, as do I, for they will probably have to give up their London home, and they had got it so nice.

I am well enough—get a little tired and am at the moment at a loose end. My visit to Paul and the Frenchs at Florence was grand. In fact it has tinged me with grandeur.

Well I will write again and hope by then that you may have written again to me.

Give much love to Bill Caskey when you see him.

Oh and had forgot—Jans [?] had better write direct to Ben over setting the verses. I am afraid he is unlikely to say Yes and may be was used to say No. He gets so many suggestions like that and he is at present hard at work over his opera with William.[25] He's awful at writing.

Much much love dearest Christopher,
Morgan

*   *   *

King's Coll. Camb.   Oct. 15[,] 1952

Dear Christopher Isherwood,

As agreed, I write a formal letter to confirm my gift to you of one of the typescript copies of *Maurice*.

It is your property, and I assign you the right to arrange for its publication in the U.S.A. after my death. You have the right to sign the necessary contracts and to receive all royalties and other payments.

By the terms of my will, all my MSS and literary rights become the property of my executor, Professor W. J. H. Sprott, or of the executor acting in his place. Professor Sprott has, however, written you a letter which you will receive at the same time as this one, and you will see from it that he fully approves of the arrangement between you and myself, and formally undertakes to respect it.

He does however make two stipulations. (i) If the book is not published in the States within three years after my death, all U.S. publication rights must revert to him. (ii) You must not publish or attempt to sell the books in Great Britain: if you did this my executors would be entitled to take action against you.

I have had a talk with Mr Monroe Wheeler. If for any reason you do not wish to publish, he is willing to act in your place. In that case all U.S. rights would pass to him, and he would be entitled to sign contracts and to receive royalties, etc.

Yours very sincerely,
EM Forster (signed)

*   *   *

King's College, Cambridge   Oct. 15[,] 1952

Dearest Christopher,

Thank you for your sweet, also salt, letter.[26] All goes well. I have seen Monroe and have today posted a [copy of] Maurice to him, together with formal letters for you from me and from Jack Sprott, who is my ex[ecut]or, and entirely approves our goings on. You should now have a convincing enough array for a potential publisher. I know that you won't like receiving any money from sales and will refuse to use it, but it is simplest that the owner of the MS and rights should receive; otherwise such complications. What I would like is for the money to be kept in America for people from here who want to visit America, and can't. Bob specially in my mind. Alternately, to help any one who is in trouble. Would you mind receiving it now?

I've asked Monroe if he would see to the thing if you couldn't. He said he would. If neither of you acts, I would be grateful if Glenway [Wescott] would take over, but have put Monroe's name in the formal letter, since we had talked about it. Bob, May and I dined with him Sunday. She is at last more equable.

The salt overleaf is of course Bill Caskey, or part of him. Give all of him my love. Yes—what a figure.

I must pronounce on Hemlock and After another time. More important, Walter Baxter's new novel has much progressed—it sounds completely different from its predecessor and I am longing to read it.[27] We meet or correspond regularly. He has just read Maurice and is terribly upset by its sadness, but was drinking all the time he read. I hope to see him this week again. I hate him being sad. I shall read the "new" chapter to him and see how he feels then.

Bob has been fine over it. "Do you want it published?"—"Yes."—"Then I'll see it is." He stays happy about his future. I don't think of it. It is bound to be unpleasant for me. Coventry is an impossible place to be idle in, or to reach. I wish I could think of some other work for myself. I have enjoyed doing "Letters from Dewes State Senior," and miss it.—Can you think of a first name for it, a selling name?[28]

Much love & thanks and I will soon write again,
Morgan

*   *   *

[return address of air letter: King's College, Cambridge]

Nov.25[,]1952

Dearest Christopher,

I have just been rereading old letters of yours, Greece, Portugal, Luxembourg[—]all over the place, always inviting me to go and I never went, always generous, praising and helping me, always believing in what *Maurice* tried to do. Dear Christopher oh you have been a good friend.

I am more glad than ever that the typescript is with you and that Jack Sprott has behaved so well.

I see Walter Baxter once a week as a rule. I go to tea with him, no one else ever comes in, although he has masses of friends, and either he talks or I talk.

Bob spends his short weekend with me, his long weekends with May. I spend Christmas with them. I don't want a birthday or any more birthdays yet awhile.

I don't know about 1953. 1952 has been odd—that wonderful visit to Florence which I haven't yet grasped, and then a good deal of worry and sorrow. I cannot sum 1952 up.

If Bill has arrived, give him my love again please.

In one of your earlier American letters you say that the two people I should like were Pete and Swami. I never met Swami. You were right about Pete.[29]

I expect I have told you all the above already. But tonight I feel able to put it differently.

Love dear Christopher.

Love,
Morgan

* * *

July 7 [1953]   400 South Saltair Avenue
Los Angeles 49. California

Dearest Morgan,

The immediate reason for this—after how many months?—is that Swami Prabhavananda is on his way to England, and I do so hope you two will meet. So does he, and I have told him to go to Cambridge, which he will gladly do. He will only be in the country for a few days, however, around the 20th of this month. So could you send a postcard to the Countess of Sandwich (The Cottage, Hinchingbrooke, Huntingdon) with whom he is staying, saying which day would suit you? Of course, if you are in London, Swami could meet you there.[30]

The Countess of Sandwich is, improbably enough, an Englishwoman named Amiya Corbin who used to be one of the leading members of Swami's congregation and household, and whom George Sandwich met while in California recently. She is, in her own forthright way, a character worthy of the amazing George. Do you know him? You probably do.

Here I sit and will not stir until that fiendish novel is done. Two complete drafts finished already, but much still to do. I think everybody will hate it. It certainly isn't what they expect—if there is still anyone who expects anything of me. Am otherwise well and happy.

I long for your new book.

Bill Caskey has left the sea and is making bead collars for fashionable ladies with an intensity which borders on sadism. He makes them, and they are damn well going to wear them—or else. He's like those woman-haters who design fantastic hats which only the richest can afford. In the last phase, the hats are made of iron, with in-pointing spikes.

I hope you enjoyed the caves?

I still hope to get to England again before long.

Stephen was here. Such a great joy. My little garden-house has gained something in atmosphere since his visit. How I do wish you could see it!

Please give my love to Bob and May and William especially; and tell Simon Raven, if he's around, how much I've liked his reviews in the Listener.

Au revoir, Morgan dearest,
your loving
Christopher

*   *   *

[return address of air letter: King's College, Cambridge]   Sunday,
July 26 [1953]

I write to Dearest Christopher,

Incredible dictu—the Countess Amiya and the Swami have just lunched in my room at King's with myself and Bob. Quelle combinaison et quelle chance! I wrote just at the exact moment, all fitted, and I feel so happy about it and am sure you will be. The Swami (in a silver grey complet) was gentle and friendly, but I did not "get to know him" or have much consecutive talk. I felt that he had a philosophic mind and that I should have to peck at its edges as it turned round rather than expect it to poke me. Earl and another man joined us after lunch. Bit of a rush. I took them all to the Chapel, which was just before service and a parrot warren, now they are sure and Bob has gone, and fatigued and a little dazed [I write to Dearest Christopher].[31]

It is lovely to think you may be coming over. I do hope I see Bill too. Give him my love. Rob's marriage went off well and gaily, but there is this endless trouble of house-getting. Incidentally I am moving myself—but only from Trumpington Street entirely into College, where I have just been assigned a large bedroom close to my present sittingroom. It is a for-and-against situation, but I am thankful to have been assigned anything—the Wilkinsons are moving, and couldn't keep me.

I forget whether I wrote to you since my visit to S.W. France with Bill Roerick & Tom Coley: one of the treats of my life. I hope to go again (alone) to France in September, but it depends on all the movings [sic].

I doubt dearest Christopher my getting to America again. I can't tell you how often I think of it and of my American friends. It has been such a wonderful addition at an age in my life when I didn't expect to do or get more.

I half hoped to see the Swami again next week (at the Hyde Park Hotel) but he is very busy. But what luck it has been to get him to Cambridge at a moment when Bob was here. I want very much to talk about him to you.

Love from much satisfied
Morgan

* * *

King's Coll., Camb.   July 2[,] 1954

Dearest Christopher,

I am fascinated with the book,[32] despite disappointments and difficulties. I will be lending it to Bob, and will then read it again. It keeps approaching to and then receding from the world of my own experiences, like something moving in the dusk, and so is more provocative tha[n] anything else you have written. Leading ambiguity is Asparian-Elizabeth, whom I do *not* want to meet nor whose moves to read. She is very well done, with almost fiendish consistency, yet I haven't yet grasped how you [wou]ld have us react to her. Again and again—lifting her remarks out of their prevalent sauce—I've felt I should like then so much if they were your remarks and tasted sharp and straight of you.

Michael is a very naughty hero indeed, and how Stephen could have stood up against him I do not see—who anyhow had to have a bit of something, as afterwards with Jane. So that the (British) book-jacket's reference to "shameful betrayals" puzzles me. My feeling is that there is no specific moral lesson in the book, but that all the characters who are worth anything are learning something—to be simpler, to be alone, not to gloat even about sin, not to attack the hate-disease directly, to lie open to intimations of unity should they happen to come. Gerda—and of course Sarah—learn most, and though they try they never learn through the trying.

Technical item: Shouldn't pp 238–244 (English edition) come elsewhere? Your time-sequences are so intermixed that I can't say where, but it should be in some relationship to the marriage to Jane, not inserted into an Elizabeth-sequence, which it interrupts.

Bob and I are just back from Leiden where I had a degree and was addressed very movingly form [*sic*] the pulpit of St Peter's Church. Will try to send you [the] address. All went well, we thought and spoke often of you and at Amsterdam and the Hague revisited some former scenes. At the end of this month I go via Switzerland to Bayreuth, so you may deduce that I am in good health and continental. I meant to write to you when I saw your play, which I enjoyed whenever it was yours, but van Druten had vulgarised it; and had failed to convey the atmosphere of Nazism thickening outside in the street.—Well acted, and as you know still running.[33]

I am well (as in last paragraph) and have plenty of sensations and impressions. The trouble is they rush by so quickly, as in a dream. Holland is already vanishing, and the people who have been coming in and out of this room all day coalesce into a monologue and I into a civil grin. Indeed as I write I remember that I have not been here all day—arriving from London at 11.00 A.M. only, and since then going once and perhaps twice into a nap.

We had a large quiet upper room at Leiden, looking over a garden which had a great maiden hair tree in it. Sky always grey in the morning and sun later. Town hall near—very cheerful with its bells. The Dutch were at their best. It was a lovely quiet time and I found speaking publicly came easy—I never do it in England now. I shall be seeing Bob again soon, when he drives over with May and her New Zealand brother to lunch.

Love, and thank you for the book,
Morgan

* * *

King's Coll. Camb.   Jan. 17[,] 1956

Dearest Christopher,

Your titled friends have told me of your arrival, and here comes my line of love. Catch me spilling my further news, though. Plans only. I plan to be here until Thursday week (26th) and then to London. I should be free on that evening, but what is important: can you dine with me and Bob the next day, Friday? It is one of his very rare visits to town, and probably his only chance of seeing you. The mornings of Saturday and Sunday might be possible, but Friday dinner the 27th is best.

Love
Morgan

*   *   *

[postcard]
Feb. 19[,] 1956

K.C.C.   Sunday

Could I bring Nick Furbank for a drink on Wednesday at about 6.15?[34] I am writing to you both to suggest it. He would like it I know.—Send me a p.c. by return if you are able to as I may be leaving here Tuesday.

The visit of D[on] and yourself was much enjoyed by me and all.[35] Bob & May have just left.

Morgan

*   *   *

King's Coll., Camb.   Jan. 5[,] 1958

Dearest Christopher,

Love to you and Don, and I rang up the Cavendish before I left London yesterday but though expected you had not yet arrived[,] I am afraid I shall not see you again unless you manage, both of you, to run up here.[36] When how welcome you would be. I forget your sailing date.

Lots of letters to answer, including one from Heinz, which shall be treated discretely. He is at an address new to me, in a nice flat.

I did so enjoy our two evenings.

Love to Don and you,
Morgan

* * *

[postmark of air letter: Cambridge, January 14, 1960]

Dearest Christopher,

Double Envelope cannot move from John's fireside, and I read it there last week in comfort and with great interest, but too hastily as time was short. The photographs of Tom, we agreed, was a master stroke, broke up the Forrest-Leonard alliance, and created new alliances.

If it is the sort of story I think, I think it oughtn't to have gone to such lengths right away. As it is, the opening and the closing exercises vary too little, and there is scarcely anything extra left for Leonard. I would have been sketchier and more restrained earlier. But there, I may not have got your intention or the nature of the life you wish to describe. It may have been this absence of progress that made me feel sad as I left the fireside and went to open an exhibition of pictures by Mr Mukul Derz. I certainly found no progress in them.

It is difficult to tack on personal scraps when one has been concentrating on a single thing and that such an unusual one. I am well. May is well. Bob better but still far from his old self. I spent the New Year with them. Christmas at Aldeburgh. Tomorrow I am televised on the subject of the Cambridge Humanists, next week I go to Oxford to see the premiere of a *Passage to India*.[37] However that: enough. Close below me I see a spot that must have come from butter, and will stop.

With much love
[unsigned]

* * *

[postcard]   King's College Cambridge   [postmark: April 19, 1961]

Just to thank you for your card and to say, yes, I am only just out of hospital, though feeling unharmed. I look forward to seeing you and Don a bit later on.—Love to both—

Morgan
Wednesday

* * *

[postmark of postcard: Cambridge, June 3, 1961]

Behold my bird and with what curves about Coventry [the "y" connects with his drawing of a bird] it greets your suggestion[,] but I must check them until I have spoken to Bob (on Saturday) and May (on Sunday). 11 Salisbury Avenue is our address there and I should be there through the coming week.

*   *   *

Monday [June 5? 1961]   11 Salisbury Avenue
                                                                      Coventry, Warwickshire

Dearest Christopher,
   Can you and Don come up here on Tuesday the 13th or Wednesday the 14th, take a morning train[,] let us know when it arrives, and if Bob does not meet it then take a taxi up here from the station, and be with us for lunch? Sightseeing can occur in the afternoon.
   Did you know that Heinz and Gerda arrive in England on the 24th, and will be staying in my Chiswick flat?
   Hoping to see you here next week. Let me know date as soon as possible.

                                                                      Love from
                                                                      Morgan

*   *   *

King's College Cambridge   March 25[,] 1962

Dearest Christopher,
   I didn't come off with your book,[38] and this day, the first of British Summer Time, brings me warmth enough to say so. I read it all through and bits of it again and again, and with varied pleasures, but the final union was withheld. I tell myself it's because I'm too old, but that's priggish, and am inclined to another explanation—also personal—which is that I didn't want Christopher or his variants to guide me through a book by you any more. He had done all he could for me already. I wanted a yarn less conditioned by him. I had other reservations—my failure to be interested in Paul being one of them, in contrast to the immense interest he arouses in other readers, e.g. Joe. And connected with Paul no doubt, I don't feel I've had a look down there and come back. The hole in my flooring must be somewhere else in fact.—This reaction to a guide (or, to put him less crudely, to

a continuous presence) has come to me when reading other authors: e.g. Conrad with his much slighter employment of Marlowe. I don't always find him a help towards the matter in hand. And your matter is important and enormous.

I have been behaving very well to everyone lately, it seems to me, and your remarks on the perils and punishments hanging over those who thus excel their friends fall on me with particular poignancy. What have *I* been doing in the literary way may perhaps be enquired. Well a box has just been presented to me by the Public Trustee (How obtained? through good behaviour of course), and in it are papers relating to my g[rea]t g[rea]t uncle Robert Thornton who went to the bad in 1814[,] fled to France, and thence to Lancaster[,] Pennsylvania, where he can be traced up to 1820. On this date he closed his account with his solicitors and it is their box that has just come to me, in the arms of a Mrs Jackson. He is said to have died in 1826.

I hope to get to London later in the week, to see six Buckinghams, two Harewoods, and the retrospective Keith Vaughan exhibition.[39] I wonder whether there will be anything in it as good as the picture you gave me. I have been looking at it a great deal lately, and meditating on the Heroic Nude, of which it is a specimen. K. V. achieved some in an earlier period, they say. So did Michelangelo. Most nudes are defenceless and either sensuous or sexless. The heroic nude avoids all three weaknesses.

Here Ted Gillott has looked in with an American of three years old, and I have walked them down to the lodge. No, the cold is still icy and of a bitterness. No heart can yet flow in it. What a good thing I did not discover this before.

Back in room, and love from
Morgan

*   *   *

April 6 [1962]
145 Adelaide Drive
Santa Monica
California

Dearest Morgan,

Thank you so much for your letter. It was sweet of you to trouble to write about my novel, especially as you didn't much care for it. I'm sorry, of course, but not entirely surprised. There is a part of me, of my literary and personal character, which is very far from what you are and stand for, which is perhaps one of the reasons why I love and admire you so much! I don't mean by this that I am apologizing for myself or even for the book. It said exactly what I intended it to say, and now I feel a lot better. My next will be quite different, and no doubt, to some extent, the likers and dislikers may change sides over it.

Joe Ackerley's being here made us both—and indeed also Gerald Heard, Chris Wood, etc—wish sadly that you had come with him. What a joyful get-together that would have been! But Joe has told us a lot about you. He also mentioned a story you have written I long to see. And how fascinating the Robert Thornton papers sound!

I hope you enjoyed the Keith Vaughan show, but hope also that you will decide you like yours at least one of the best.

We have had wretched weather, but now it is fine and hot. Don is working hard. His struggle is to make himself paint. The Slade planted a seed of guilt in his heart about drawing. He feels he should do both. He will probably have a show on Long Island in the middle of the summer and he as arranged for a show here in the autumn. I'm in a whirl with teaching, trying to finish the Ramakrishna biography—which, entre nous, is becoming a labor of sheer willpower, and not very sheer, either—and planning a new short novel. I fear that "Christopher" may rear his head again, but perhaps only a few inches above ground.

I think I told you in my last letter how much Don enjoyed the New York production of Passage to India. It seems to be doing well? My only hope is that it will do well enough to go on tour and come to us here, because I greatly fear I won't get East to see it. I'm tied down to teaching until June, anyhow.

Don is out, but I can take the responsibility of sending you his love.

All mine,
Christopher

*   *   *

December 13 [1963]
145 Adelaide Drive
Santa Monica
California

Dearest Morgan,

At least, this year, my birthday wishes to you won't be late! I am writing this early because I am about to take another plunge into the Orient—India, in fact—Calcutta, not to put to fine a point upon it—there to take part in the birthday celebrations of Swami Vivekananda; his centenary. Why? You may well ask. Because I have been invited, of course. In that symbolic land, purely symbolic speeches by impurely symbolic figures are considered worth the price of a round-the-world airplane ticket, and the fact that there isn't one single thing I can tell them about Vivekananda which they don't know already is, of course, utterly irrelevant. I wish you were coming with us. Us includes Prabhavananda; and I suppose I am really going just because he asked me to. He dreads all this just as much as I do. And the mere sight of his native land usually throws him into a fever. Last time he went there, he was sick every single day.

I wish I could return via England, but alas there isn't enough time for that. So I shall just go hurtling on around like a sputnik.

Aldous died quietly, without any pain at the end. He was absolutely clear, mentally. The day before he died, he finished dictating an article about Shakespeare. He wasn't told of Kennedy's shooting, which happened just a few hours earlier.

Personally, I was very strongly pro-Kennedy; but I was still amazed at how much I minded. And, in this quite largely anti-Kennedy town, which has so little to unite it, it was amazing how much everybody minded. People just sat listening to the radio in their cars and sobbing. We were all in love with him, without knowing it.

Don is well and sends his love to you. He paints quite a lot, now, instead of just drawing; but it is always portraits, he has no enthusiasm for landscape, still life or abstractions. We will meet in New York where he is going to spend Christmas.

I have finished two books: a little novel called A Single Man, which is all about this place; and the long weary biography of Ramakrishna which I have been working on all these ages.

I would love to hear some news of your doings.

All my love to you, dearest Morgan—and to Bob and May, too. I think of you and talk about you so often. So please send me a loving thought—

Christopher

* * *

[postmark of air letter: Coventry, Warwickshire]   5th Jan. 1966

Dearest Christopher,[40]

What a delight to get your letter. Yes, I have not been well but am now spending a most happy Christmas & New Year at Bob's. It is indeed actually

May who is writing this letter. They encourage me in idleness & I gladly co-operate.

Bob takes me back to Cambridge at the end of the week.

I haven't much news. I am comfortable and happy but that is not supposed to be news. My love to Don. I am very glad to hear about his work.

Much love to you, naturally & to your work though I am sorry it is not bringing you to England.

I will stop now, having suggested to May that she should add something and she has accepted the suggestion.

Morgan's love.

* * *

Morgan has had 3 strokes, the last in September but he has almost completely recovered. Each one has affected his sight[;] reading & writing are difficult and you know what that must mean to him. Joe goes to Cambridge each week for a night or two to deal with his post. He is now as active as ever, walking well and his mind as bright and clear as a new penny but he does forget things, who does not.

We plan to go to Aldeburgh for the festival in June. We took him there last October when he came out of hospital and was in very poor shape and had such a nice hotel and so many good friends in the area we feel that we couldn't do better[;] whatever should happen there would be plenty of help.

Our children were also here for a week and I did wonder[ed] if they would tire him too much in such a small house but I don't think they did at all.

I was just remembering the day you came here to see Morgan, three years ago. Don was with you and we sat in the garden.

Robert is out calling on his naughty boys or would join me in sending our love and very best wises to you both affectionately,

May

Biographical Glossary

All entries are British unless otherwise noted.

Ackerley, Joseph Randolph (1896–1967). Literary editor, author, and close friend of Forster's. He was the literary editor of *The Listener* from 1935 to 1959. He is also the author of *My Dog Tulip* (1956) and *We Think the World of You* (1960).

Auden, Wystan Hugh (1907–73). Poet and intimate friend of Isherwood's. Major works of poetry include *The Orators* (1932), *The Age of Anxiety: A Baroque Eclogue* (1947), *The Shield of Achilles* (1955), and *City Walls and Other Poems* (1969). He collaborated with Isherwood on three plays: *The Dog Beneath the Skin* (1935), *The Ascent of F6* (1936), and *On the Frontier* (1939).

Bachardy, Don (1934–). American painter and Isherwood's companion from 1953 until Isherwood's death in 1986. His drawings have been published in several books: *October* (1983), *Last Drawings of Christopher Isherwood* (1990), and *Stars in My Eyes* (2000). His paintings and drawings are in the collections of the National Portrait Gallery in London, the Metropolitan Museum of New York, and other major art institutions.

Barger, Harold (1907–89). Professor of Economics at Columbia University form 1937 to 1975. He graduated from King's College, Cambridge, and the London School of Economics.

Baxter, Walter (1915–). Author of a novel, *Look Down in Mercy* (1951), which was considered controversial. He had previously owned a restaurant in London.

Beerbohm, Henry Maximilian (Max) (1872–1956). Humorist and essayist. Author of *Zuleika Dobson* (1911). His *A Christmas Garland* (1912) contains parodies of contemporary literary writers, such as Henry James, Joseph Conrad, and H. G. Wells.

Bowen, Elizabeth (1899–1973). Novelist and short-story writer. Her collections of stories include *Encounters* (1923), *The Cat Jumps* (1934), and

The Demon Lover (1945). Her novels include *The Hotel* (1927), *The Death of the Heart* (1938), and *A World of Love* (1955).

Britten, Benjamin (1913–76). Composer. His operas include *Peter Bunyan* (1941), *Billy Budd* (1951), and *Death in Venice* (1973). A major choral and orchestral work is *War Requiem* (1961). He also composed the music for two Auden-Isherwood plays, *The Ascent of F6* and *On the Frontier*.

Burgess, Guy (1910–63). British diplomat who also spied for the Soviet Union. He eventually defected to the Soviet Union in 1956. He introduced Isherwood to Jacky Hewitt (Burgess's former lover) in 1938.

Burra, Peter (1909–37). Literary and music critic. His essay on Forster's *A Passage to India* was included in the Everyman's Library 1942 edition.

Cadmus, Paul (1904–99). American artist who drew both Forster and Isherwood. He is best known for his paintings and drawings of male nudes.

Caskey, William (Bill) (1921–81). American photographer who was Isherwood's lover from 1945 to 1951.

Cavafy, Constantine P. (1863–1933). Greek poet who spent most of his life in Alexandria. He appears as a character in Lawrence Durrell's *Alexandria Quartet*.

Charlton, Lionel Evelyn Oswald (Leo) (1879–1956). An Air Commodore who was Air Attaché at the British Embassy in Washington, DC from 1919 to 1922. Friend of Forster's.

Connolly, Cyril (1903–74), Critic and Literary Editor. He founded and edited the influential monthly magazine *Horizon* from 1939 to 1950. He is also the author of several full-length works, including *The Unquiet Grave* (1944) by "Palinurus."

Crozier, Eric (1914–94). Librettist who collaborated with Benjamin Britten on several operas, including *Billy Budd* (upon which he worked also with Forster).

Dawkins, Richard MacGillivray (1871–1955). Professor of Byzantine and Modern Greek Language and Literature at Oxford University from 1920 to 1939.

Day-Lewis, Cecil (1904–72). Poet of the "Thirties' Group" that included Auden and Spender. He was active in the Communist Party from 1935 to 1938. His poetry collections informed by contemporary politics include *A Time to Dance* (1935) and *Overtures to a Death* (1938). He also wrote detective fiction.

Dickinson, Goldsworthy Lowes (1862–1932). Historian and political activist. A Fellow at King's College Cambridge and intimate friend of Forster's. He was a pacifist during World War I. His works include *The Greek View of Life* (1909) and *War: Its Nature, Cause, and Cure* (1923).

Doone, Rupert (1903–66). Theatrical producer, dancer, and choreographer who founded The Group Theatre, a cooperative. He directed Isherwood and Auden's play, *The Ascent of the F6*.

Fouts, Denham (Denny). Closely associated with Peter Watson in the 1930s, helping him solicit contributions to the *Horizon*. He and Isherwood became friends in the 1940s.

Glaspell, Susan (1882–1948). American playwright who, together with her husband, George Cook, founded the Provincetown Players on Cape Cod in 1915. She won the Pulitzer Prize in 1931 for her play, *Alison's House*.

Hamilton, Gerald (Mr. Norris) (1890–1970). Isherwood's friend who was the model for Mr. Norris in *Mr. Norris Changes Trains*. He was twice imprisoned in England, for associating with the enemy during World War I and promoting peace favorable to the enemy during World War II.

Heard, Henry Fitzgerald (Gerald) (1885–1971). Irish writer and philosopher. A close friend of Aldous Huxley, both of whom were disciples of Swami Prabhavananda. His works include *The Social Substance of Religion* (1932), *Man the Master* (1942), and *Is God Evident?* (1948).

Hewit, Jacky (1917–). Dancer who had a brief love affair with Isherwood in 1938. He was also the lover of the diplomat, Guy Burgess.

Huxley, Aldous (1894–1963). Novelist whose best-known work is *Brave New World* (1932). His other novels include *Point Counter Point* (1928) and *Eyeless in Gaza* (1936). A pacifist who emigrated to California in 1937. He collaborated with Isherwood on two screenplays: *Jacob's Hands* and *Below the Horizon*.

Hyndman, Tony. Companion of Stephen Spender's in the early 1930s. He became a Communist and, after joining the International Brigade, fought briefly in the Spanish Civil War.

Kirstein, Lincoln (1907–96). American ballet impresario who, together with George Balanchine, founded the School of American Ballet and the New York City Ballet.

Lawrence, Thomas Edward (T. E.) (1888–1935). Soldier and author, commonly known as "Lawrence of Arabia." He supported the Arab revolt against the Turks during World War I. His best-known work is *The Seven Pillars of Wisdom: A Triumph* (1926).

Lehmann, John (1907–87). Poet, editor, and publisher. Longtime friend of Isherwood's. He edited *New Writing* from 1936 to 1939, *Penguin New Writing* from 1940 to 1950, and *The London Magazine* from 1954 to 1961.

Lehmann, Rosamond (1903–90). Novelist and older sister of John Lehmann. Her works, which include *Invitation to the Waltz* (1932), *The Weather in the Streets* (1936), and *The Echoing Grove* (1953), were controversial because of their frank treatment of sexuality.

Macaulay, Rose (1881–1958). Novelist. Her works include *Told by an Idiot* (1923), *They Were Defeated* (1932), and *No Man's Wit* (1940). She is also the author of several collections of essays, including *The Writings of E. M. Forster* (1938), and travel books.

MacCarthy, Desmond (1877–1952). Literary and drama critic who had personal ties to the Bloomsbury circle. He was literary editor of *The New Statesman* from 1920 to 1927 and senior literary critic of *The Sunday Times* from 1928 until his death.

MacLeish, Archibald (1892–1982). American poet and dramatist. His poetry works include *The Happy Marriage* (1924) and *New Found Land* (1930). He also wrote several verse plays for the radio, including *The Fall of the City* (1937), which denounces totalitarianism.

Mann, Erika (1905–69). German actress and author who was the eldest daughter of Thomas Mann. She wrote several anti-Nazi plays for her satirical touring revue, "The Peppermill." She emigrated to the United States with her brother, Klaus, in 1936.

Mann, Klaus (1906–49). German novelist and editor who was the eldest son of Thomas Mann. He edited two literary magazines: *Die Sammlung* in Amsterdam in the 1930s and *Decision* during the early 1940s in the United States. His best-known novel is *Mephisto* (1936).

Maugham, W. Sommerset (1874–1965). Novelist and short-story writer. His novels include *Of Human Bondage* (1915), *Cakes and Ale* (1930), and *The Razor's Edge* (1945).

Mauron, Charles (1899–1966). French critic and translator who translated Forster's novel, *A Passage to India*, into French. He played an active role in the French Resistance during World War II.

Plomer, William (1903–73). Poet and novelist born in South Africa but educated in England. His poetic works include *The Family Tree* (1929) and *Visiting the Caves* (1936). He wrote the libretto for Benjamin Britten's *Gloriana* (1953).

Prabhavananda, Swami (1893–1976). Hindu monk belonging to the Ramakrishna Order who founded the Vedanta Society of Southern California. Isherwood studied with him beginning in 1940.

Priestley, John Boynton (J. B.) (1894–1984). Novelist, playwright, and literary critic. His works include the novels *The Good Companions* (1929) and *It's an Old Country* (1967), the plays *Dangerous Corner* (1932) and *Time and the Conways* (1937), and the critical essays in *Literature and Western Man* (1960).

Raven, Simon (1927–2001). Novelist who also wrote essays, film scripts, and television series. He is the author of a ten-volume work, *Alms for Oblivion* (1959–76).

Roerick, William (Bill) (d. 1995). American actor who was a friend of Isherwood's and, later, Forster's. His name is often misspelled in the letters as "Roehrich" or "Roehrick."

Sassoon, Sir Philip (1888–1939). Politician, art collector, and social host. He was Secretary of State for Air from 1924 to 1929 and 1931 to 1937. His cousin was the poet, Siegfried Sassoon.

Sassoon, Siegfried (1886–1967). Poet and autobiographer. His poetic works include *Satirical Poems* (1926), *Vigils* (1936), and *Sequences* (1956). He also wrote a three-volume autobiography of his childhood.

Shankar, Uday (1900–1977). Indian classical dancer and choreographer. He toured Western countries in the 1930s with his own troupe. His brother, Ravi Shankar, was a musician.

Simpson, John Hampson (1901–55). Novelist who wrote under the name "John Hampson." His most popular novel was *Saturday Night at the Greyhound* (1931). His other novels include *The Family Curse* (1936) and *Care of "The Grand"* (1939).

Smith, Dodie (1896–1990). Playwright and novelist. She emigrated to the Unites States with her husband, Alec Beesley, in 1938. Her works include the novel, *I Capture the Castle* (1948) and a four-volume autobiography.

Spender, Stephen (1909–95). Poet, critic, and editor. He was closely associated with Isherwood and Auden in the 1930s. His works of poetry include

Poems (1933) and *The Still Centre* (1939). His non-fiction includes critical essays in *The Struggle of the Modern* (1963) and his acclaimed autobiography, *World within World* (1951).

Sprott, Walter John Herbert (W. J. H.) (1897–1971). Professor of Philosophy at the University of Nottingham from 1948 to 1964. A close friend of Forster's and his literary executor. Author of *Human Groups* (1958).

Tennant, Stephen (1906–87). Artist and aesthete. Forster and Buckingham often spent weekends at his home, Wilsford Manor. He is considered to be the model for "Sebastian" in Evelyn Waugh's novel, *Brideshead Revisited*.

Thomson, George (1903–82). Professor of Classics at the University of Birmingham from 1937.

Toller, Ernst (1893–1939). German Jewish writer and political activist. He was a pacifist during World War I. His works include *Once a Bourgeois always a Bourgeois* (1928) and *Miracle in America* (1931). He committed suicide in New York in 1939.

Vaughan, Keith (1912–77). Painter and illustrator. He was a conscientious objector during World War II.

Viertel, Berthold (1885–1953). Austrian playwright and film director. He directed films in Hollywood in the 1920s and in England beginning in 1933. He hired Isherwood to write the screenplay for *Little Friend*.

Watson, Peter (d. 1956). Art collector. Co-founder (together with Cyril Connolly) and art editor of the magazine, *Horizon*.

Wells, Herbert George (H. G.) (1866–1946). Novelist. His major works of science fiction include *The Time Machine* (1895) and *The War of the Worlds* (1898). He is also the author of *Love and Mr. Lewisham* (1900), *Kipps: The Story of a Simple Soul* (1905), and *Tono-Bungay* (1909).

Wescott, Glenway (1901–87). American writer who lived in France in the 1920s. His best-known works include *The Apple of the Eye* (1924), *The Grandmothers* (1926), and *The Pilgrim Hawk* (1940). He served as President of the American Academy of Arts and Letters from 1957 to 1961.

Wilder, Thornton (1897–1975). American playwright. His plays *Our Town* (1938) and *The Skin of our Teeth* (1942) were both awarded the Pulitzer Prize. He also wrote *The Matchmaker* (1955), upon which the musical *Hello Dolly!* (1963) was based.

Woolf, Leonard (1880–1969). Author of works on politics and international affairs as well as a five-volume autobiography. He and his wife, Virginia, founded the Hogarth Press in 1917, and their home was a meeting place for the Bloomsbury Group in the 1920s and 1930s.

Woolf, Virginia (1882–1941). Novelist. Her key modernist works include *Mrs. Dalloway* (1925), *To the Lighthouse* (1927), and *The Waves* (1931). She is also the author of *A Room of One's Own* (1929) and *Three Guineas* (1938), both considered classic feminist texts.

Young, Edward Hilton (Lord Kennet) (1879–1960). Politician and writer. Friend of Forster's. He was a Member of Parliament and served as a delegate to the Assembly of the League of Nations in 1926 and 1927.

List of Correspondence

July 8. [1942]	pp. 28–29	typed
June 21st. [1943]	p. 30	typed
November 27. [1943]	p. 31	handwritten
January 22nd. [1944]	p. 32	typed
March 16. [1944]	pp. 33–34	handwritten
July 8. [1944]	p. 35	typed
July 29. [1944]	p. 36	typed
March 28. [1946]	p. 37	typed
April 6 [1962]	p. 38	typed
December 13 [1963]	p. 39	typed

The following letters were forwarded by Forster to Robert J. ("Bob") Buckingham:EMF/18/82: Correspondence between Forster, Buckingham, and other individuals. Origination: Buckingham

EMF/18/82/5	September 15, 1936	handwritten postcard
EMF/18/82/7	June 15, 1937	handwritten postcard
	June 28, 1937	handwritten note from C.I. to Bob attached to letter from EMF to Bob
EMF/18/82/19	July 27, 1943	handwritten letter
EMF/18/82/21	December 15, 1944	handwritten telegram
EMF/18/82/23	September 26, 1945	typed letter
EMF/18/82/27	January 14, 1947	typed telegram
EMF/18/82/29	April 12, 1948	handwritten postcard
EMF/18/82/33	January 16, 1950	typed letter
EMF/18/82/39	July 7, [1953]	typed letter

In folder: EMF/18/271/1

Letter from Isherwood to Jack Sprott. November 5, 1952, typed.

Letters from Forster to Isherwood

Huntington Library. Isherwood Papers.
Literature Manuscripts and Correspondence

Forster to Isherwood 1932–39. CI 778–823. Box 34
All letters from Forster to Isherwood are handwritten.

November 12, 1932 (should be October)	2 pp.	CI 779
January 4, 1933	2 pp.	CI 780

April 13, 1933	1 p.	CI 781
April 27, 1933	2 pp.	CI 782
April 1933?	1 p.	CI 783
July 16, 1933	4 pp.	CI 784
September 22, 1933	2 pp.	CI 785 (one side handwritten, one side typed)
1933?	2 pp.	CI 786
February 17, 1934	2 pp.	CI 787
April 7–17, 1934	2 pp.	CI 788
May 15, 1934	2 pp.	CI 789
August 9, 1934	6 pp.	CI 790
January 16–17, 1935	4 pp.	CI 791
May 19, 1935	2 pp.	CI 792
June 1, 1935	4 pp.	CI 793
July 28, 1935	2 pp.	CI 794
September 9, 1935	3pp.	CI 795
February 23, 1936	3 pp.	CI 797
May 20, 1936	4 pp.	CI 798
July 30, 1936	2 pp.	CI 799
September 23, 1936	2 pp.	CI 800
October 11, 1936	2 pp.	CI 801
December 29, 1936	2 pp.	CI 802
January 5, 1937	2 pp.	CI 803
January 12. 1937	1 p.	CI 804
January 28, 1937	2 pp.	CI 805
February 27, 1937	3 pp.	CI 806
March 2, 1937	2 pp.	CI 807
April 30, 1937	2 pp.	CI 808
July 4, 1937	2 pp.	CI 809
July 7, 1937	p.c.	CI 810 (writing on both sides)
February 17, 1938	2 pp.	CI 811
August 28, 1938	4 pp.	CI 812
November 14, 1938	2 pp.	CI 813
December 23, 1938	2 pp.	CI 814
May 14, 1939	4 pp.	CI 815
May 15, 1939	1 p.	CI 816
June 17, 1939	3 pp.	CI 817
July 10, 1939	2 pp.	CI 818
August 23, 1939	2 pp.	CI 819
September 1, 1939	2 pp.	CI 820
September 8, 1939	2 pp.	CI 821
October 31, 1939	2 pp.	CI 822
1939?	1 p.	CI 823 (KCC suggests 1938)

Huntington Library. Isherwood Papers.
Literature Manuscripts and Correspondence

Forster to Isherwood 1940–66 and to Heinz Neddermeyer

CI 824–74. Box 35

January 31–Feb. 11, 1940	6 pp.	CI 824
April 21, 1940	2 pp.	CI 825
September 11, 1940	2 pp.	CI 826
January 1, 1941	2 pp.	CI 827
October 11, 1941	3 pp.	CI 828
February 6–Mar 1, 1942	2 pp.	CI 829
[before June 8]– June 8, 1942	3 pp.	CI 830
July 25, 1942	2 pp.	CI 831
December 28, 1942	2 pp.	CI 832
[1942?/early 1943]	1 pp.	CI 833 (incomplete, p. 2 only)
June 7, 1943	2 pp.	CI 834
October 23, 1943	2 pp.	CI 835 (and postcard)
December 14, 1943	2 pp.	CI 836
February 10, 1944	2 pp.	CI 837 (and postcard)
February 28, 1944	2 pp.	CI 838
May 2?–9, 1944	6 pp.	CI 839
June 16, 1944	2 pp.	CI 840
July 7, 1944	2 pp.	CI 841
December 18, 1944	2 pp.	CI 842
May 9, 1945	4 pp.	CI 843
August 26, 1945	3 pp.	CI 844
April 1, 1946	2 pp.	CI 845
March 21, 1947	2 pp.	CI 846
June 2, 1947	3 pp.	CI 847
May 3, 1948	2 pp.	CI 848
June 25, 1948	2 pp.	CI 849
1948?	postcard	CI 850
March 27, 1949	3 pp.	CI 851
January 4, 1951	2 pp.	CI 852
January 23, 1951	4 pp.	CI 853
January 14, 1952	2 pp.	CI 854
January 18, 1952	1 p.	CI 855
February 10, 1952	1 p.	CI 856
October 3, 1952	3 pp.	CI 857
October 15, 1952	2 pp.	CI 858 (and letter from Sprott to Isherwood)
October 15, 1952	2 pp.	CI 859
November 25, 1952	3 pp.	CI 860

July 26, 1953	3 pp.	CI 861
July 2, 1954	4 pp.	CI 862
January 17, 1956	2 pp.	CI 863
February 19, 1956	postcard	CI 864
February 24, 1956	postcard	CI 865
January 5, 1958	1 p.	CI 866
January 14, 1960	2 pp.	CI 867
April 19, 1961	postcard	CI 868
June 5? 1961	2 pp.	CI 869
June 8, 1961	postcard	CI 870
June 3, 1961	postcard	CI 871
March. 25, 1962	4 pp.	CI 872
January 5, 1966	2 pp.	CI 873
December 22, 1936	2 pp.	CI 874 (letter to Heinz)

Notes

Introduction

1. The most thorough biography of E. M. Forster is P. N. Furbank, *E. M. Forster: A Life*, 2 vols. (New York: Harcourt Brace, 1978). See also Nicola Beauman, *E. M. Forster: A Biography* (New York: Knopf, 1994). Beauman's work focuses on the first half of Forster's life. The most recent and detailed biography of Isherwood is Peter Parker, *Isherwood: A Life Revealed* (New York: Random House, 2004). See also Brian Finney, *Christopher Isherwood: A Critical Biography* (New York: Oxford University Press, 1979); Jonathan Fryer, *Isherwood: A Biography* (Garden City, NY: Doubleday, 1977); John Lehmann, *Christopher Isherwood: A Personal Memoir* (New York: Henry Holt, 1987); and Claude J. Summers, *Christopher Isherwood* (New York: Frederick Ungar, 1980).
2. Christopher Isherwood, *Christopher and His Kind, 1929–1939* (New York: Farrar, Strauss, Giroux, 1976), 105.
3. Ibid.
4. Christopher Isherwood, *Lost Years: A Memoir, 1945–1951*, ed. Katherine Bucknell (New York: HarperCollins, 2000), 94–95.
5. Beauman, *E. M. Forster*, 347.
6. E. M. Forster to Robert J. Buckingham, *Selected Letters of E. M. Forster*, 138.
7. Isherwood, Unpublished diary 1935–38, May 26, 1937, p. 25.
8. Ibid., October 13, 1937, p. 26 verso.
9. Isherwood, *Christopher and His Kind*, 126.
10. Ibid., 126–27.
11. Quoted in Furbank, *E. M. Forster: A Life*, 2:177.
12. When Forster expresses his dislike of Isherwood's novel, *Down There on a Visit*, published in 1962, Isherwood is unapologetic about his novel and merely thanks Forster for taking the time to read and write about a novel he disliked.
13. Isherwood lived in Berlin from the fall of 1929 to the spring of 1933.
14. Isherwood, *Christopher and His Kind*, 177.
15. Fryer, *Isherwood*, 149.
16. Ibid., 150.
17. Ibid., 146.
18. Isherwood, Unpublished diary 1935–38, July 2, 1936, p. 21 verso.
19. Parker, *Isherwood*, 303

20. Quoted in Samuel Hynes, *The Auden Generation: Literature and Politics in England in the 1930s* (Princeton: Princeton University Press, 1972), 176.

21. Stephen Spender, *World within World* (London: Faber and Faber, 1951), 250.

22. Stephen Spender, *Letters to Christopher: Stephen Spender's Letters to Christopher Isherwood, 1929–1939*, ed. Lee Bartlett (Santa Barbara: Black Sparrow, 1980), 122–23.

23. Quoted in Hynes, *The Auden Generation*, 176.

24. Isherwood, *Christopher and His Kind*, 293.

25. Furbank, *E. M. Forster*, 2:192. Furbank notes that Gide had recently declared himself a Communist and André Malraux, the unofficial organizer, sought to take advantage of Gide's prestige.

26. Quoted in Furbank, *E. M. Forster*, 2:193–94.

27. E. M. Forster, *What I Believe* (London: Hogarth, 1939), 5.

28. Ibid., 8.

29. Ibid., 14. Reviewing Forster's essay, Philip Toynbee, a young journalist, applauds Forster's strength and fearlessness in uttering beliefs that have become irrelevant: "He is one of the very few members of the pre-war generation who have honestly confronted and recognised the limitations imposed on them by their period. He is a Liberal in every sense of the word and he has no illusions about the sad condition of Liberalism in the modern world" (quoted in Hynes, *The Auden Generation*, 302).

30. Isherwood, Unpublished diary 1935–38, September 24, 1938, p. 53 verso.

31. Christopher Isherwood, *Down There on a Visit* (New York: Avon, 1959), 154.

32. Christopher Isherwood, *Diaries, Volume One: 1939–1960*, ed. Katherine Bucknell (London: Vintage, 1997), 6.

33. Ibid., 5.

34. Isherwood, *Christopher and His Kind*, 335–36.

35. Quoted in Fryer, *Isherwood*, 190.

36. "Comment," *Horizon: A Review of Literature and Art* 1, no. 2 (1949): 69.

37. Quoted in Peter Parker, *Isherwood*, 401–2.

38. Ibid., 404.

39. Quoted in Furbank, *E. M. Forster*, 2:237–38.

40. Ibid., 2:238.

41. Ibid.

42. E. M. Forster, *Selected Letters of E. M. Forster: Volume Two, 1921–1970*, ed. Mary Lago and P. N. Furbank (Cambridge, MA: Harvard University Press, 1985), 190.

43. E. M. Forster, *Commonplace Book*, ed. Philip Gardner (Stanford: Stanford University Press, 1985), 129.

44. E. M. Forster, "The New Disorder," *Horizon: A Review of Literature and Art* 4, no. 24 (1941): 379.

45. Forster, "The New Disorder," 384.

46. Christopher Isherwood to John Lehmann, October 31, 1941.

47. Ibid., December 26, 1941.

48. Isherwood, *Christopher and His Kind*, 186.

49. In the final chapter, Maurice confronts his first love, Clive, who is now married and successful, in order to close that earlier, unresolved period in his life.

50. Isherwood, *Christopher and His Kind*, 215.

51. Furbank, *E. M. Forster*, 2:295.

52. This remark was made during an informal conversation I had with Don Bachardy in February 2006.

Chapter 1

1. Christopher Isherwood's first two novels, *All the Conspirators* and *The Memorial*, were published in 1928 and 1932, respectively. Both novels demonstrate Forster's literary influence on Isherwood.

2. *The Seven Pillars of Wisdom: A Triumph* is an autobiographical work by T. E. Lawrence, which was published in 1926.

3. "The Orators" is a long poem by W. H. Auden that was published in 1932.

4. Isherwood's first attempts at writing a memoir of Berlin, which he titled, *The Lost*. He eventually gave up this project, electing instead to focus on one character from this work, "Mr. Norris."

5. Autobiography of the Irish writer, Maurice O'Sullivan. See note 9 in this chapter.

6. They spent the day at the home of Forster's friend, Leo Charlton.

7. Forster showed Isherwood the manuscript of his unpublished novel, *Maurice*, in April.

8. The home of Leo Charlton and his companion, Tom Wichelo.

9. *Twenty Years A-Growing*, published in 1933, is a memoir by the Irish writer, Maurice O'Sullivan (1904–50). Forster wrote the introductory note to the English translation.

10. The novel, *Ambrose Holt and Family*, by the American novelist and playwright, Susan Glaspell, was published in 1931.

11. Isherwood is probably referring to one of Forster's BBC Radio broadcasts in the series "Conversations in the Train."

12. Sir Archibald Armar Montgomery-Massingberd (1871–1947) was a British field marshal; Lord George Joachim Goshen (1831–1907) was a British statesman.

13. *Behind the Smoke Screen* by Brigadier-General P. R. C. Groves, published in 1934, warns Britain about the threat of Nazi Germany.

14. Isherwood, together with Margaret Kennedy, wrote the screenplay for Berthold Viertel's 1934 film, *Little Friend*.

15. The Woolf's invited Forster to join the Memoir Club, where members read frank autobiographical accounts to each other. The club met several times a year in restaurants and in the homes of members (Furbank, *E. M. Forster*, 2: 66).

16. Jules Romains's (a.k.a. Louis Henri Jean Farigoule) twenty-seven volume work, *Les Hommes de bonne volonté* (*The Men of Goodwill*), written between 1932 and 1946, traces the story of two friends: one a writer, the other a politician.

17. Forster's biography of his close friend, Goldsworthy Lowes Dickinson, was published in 1934. Their friendship developed when Forster was elected to the elite "Apostles" society during his fourth year at Cambridge in 1901.

18. Forster wrote the text for a pageant to be staged on the grounds of Abinger Hall. It was intended to aid the restoration of the village church.

19. As a result of this meeting, Mrs. Myslakowska undertook the translation of Forster's *A Passage to India* into Polish.

20. The Sedition Bill targeted Communist literature, making it an offense to propagate literature "liable to seduce soldiers or sailors from their duty or allegiance" (quoted in E. M. Forster, *Selected Letters*, 2:124n. 3.)

21. Leopold Stennett Amery (1873–1955) was the Secretary of State for the Colonies from 1924 to 1929.

22. Isherwood is working on what will become the first of his Berlin novels, *Mr. Norris Changes Trains*. (The title in the U.S. edition is *The Last of Mr. Norris*).

23. The National Council for Civil Liberties was founded in 1934 by Ronald Kidd, a freelance journalist. The council was originally formed to monitor police misconduct at the Hunger Marches. Forster, who had become involved with the council because of his fears of growing fascism in Europe, was chosen to be president. The first major campaign of the Council was against the Sedition Bill. (Furbank, *E. M. Forster*, 2:186–88).

24. Forster's biography of Goldsworthy Lowes Dickinson.

25. The French poet, François Villon (1431–ca.1463), whose poetry drew on his sordid life as a thief and drunkard. "Honte" (French) means "disgrace" or "shame."

26. Dr. Norman Haire (1892–1952) was a leading figure in the British Society for the Study of Sex Psychology and was president of the Sex Education Society. He supported the reform of laws against homosexuality.

27. Claud Cockburn (1904–81) was a journalist for *The Times* from 1929 to 1932 and for the leftist newspaper, *The Daily Worker* from 1935 to 1946.

28. Paul Kryger was a Danish friend of Stephen Spender's.

29. Isherwood and Auden's first collaboration, *The Dog Beneath the Skin*.

30. Isherwood's novel, *Mr. Norris Changes Trains*.

31. The top corner of the back page of the letter is covered over, obstructing the last word in each line.

32. William Congreve (1670–1729), British playwright, whose most famous play is the comedy of manners, *The Way of the World* (1700).

33. British poets, Siegfried Sassoon and Edmund (Charles) Blunden. Sassoon's anti-war poems were published in *The Old Huntsman* (1917) and *Counter-Attack* (1918). Blunden's poems dealing with the First World War are collected in *The Shepherd and Other Poems of Peace and War* (1922). He also wrote an autobiographical account of the War, *Undertones of War* (1928).

34. Siegfried Sassoon's mansion in Wiltshire.

35. Forster's speech at the congress, which warned about Fascist-like developments in England, such as the Sedition Act, was rather tame for an audience that consisted mostly of young French Communists.

36. Forster had recently returned from a visit to Isherwood in Amsterdam and he is perhaps referring to Isherwood's attempts to obtain residency for Heinz outside of Germany.

37. Forster had the first of two operations on his prostrate in December 1935. The second operation was performed in February, 1936.

38. Stephen Spender and his companion, Tony Hyndman, are staying in Portugal with Isherwood. Spender's brother, Humphrey is also there.

39. *The Dog Beneath the Skin*, published in 1935, opened in London on January 30, 1936.

40. T. E. Shaw is another name for T. E. Lawrence (who was also popularly known as "Lawrence of Arabia").

41. The article appeared in the first edition of *Abinger Harvest* but was subsequently deleted.

42. Oscar Wilde's letter of reproach to Lord Alfred Douglas, which he wrote while imprisoned in Reading, England. An edited version was published in 1905.

43. D. H. Lawrence's novel, *Lady Chatterley's Lover*, shocking at the time for its explicit descriptions of the sexual act, was not published in unexpurgated form in England until 1960. An edited version, without the overt sexual passages, was published in 1932.

44. H[erbert] E[rnest] Bates (1906–74), a British writer whose novels include *Two Sisters* (1926) and *Fair Stood the Wind for France* (1944). Most of his works are derived from his RAF service during World War II.

45. Elinor Glyn (1864–1943) was a British author whose romantic novels of the early twentieth century, such as *Three Weeks* (1907), were controversial because of their erotic content and frank depiction of female sexuality. Glyn eventually relocated to Hollywood where she wrote scripts for silent movies.

46. Isherwood is referring to the collection of short pieces that will become *Goodbye to Berlin*. John Lehmann published "The Nowaks," one of Isherwood's early Berlin stories, in the first issue of the literary magazine, *New Writing*, in the spring of 1936 (Parker, *Isherwood*, 269).

47. Maurice Magnus (1876–1920). His *Memoirs of the Foreign Legion*, published in 1924, contains a one hundred-page introduction by D. H. Lawrence.

48. Forster is probably referring to the Scottish novelist, Neil Gunn (1891–1973), whose works include *Morning Tide* (1930) and *The Silver Darlings* (1941). He makes a case against fascism in *The Green Isle of the Great Deep* (1944) and in other later works.

49. Frederic Alexander Lindermann (1886–1957), Professor of Experimental Psychology at Oxford and later an advisor to Churchill during the Second World War; Sir Arthur Salter (1881–1975), Professor of Political Theory at Oxford and M. P. for Oxford University from 1937 to 1950. One of these men was probably sitting on Forster's right.

50. Basil Henry Liddell Hart (1895–1970) was an English military historian. His works include *T. E. Lawrence: In Arabia and After* (1934) and *The Defence of Britain* (1939).

51. Lionel George Curtis (1872–1955), a barrister who was an influential supporter of British imperialist policy. He was Adviser on Irish Affairs in the Colonial Office from 1921 to 1924.

52. Rexism was a fascist political movement in Belgium. The Rexist party (officially, Christus Rex), founded by Léon Degrelle, a Walloon, supported the abolishment of democracy and strict adherence to Church doctrine. In the 1930s, the Rexist party aligned itself with the interests of Nazi Germany.

53. *The Witch of Edmonton* is a tragicomedy that was published in 1658 but first performed in about 1621. The title page of the published edition lists as the authors: William Rowley, Thomas Dekker, and John Ford.

54. Furbank suggests that Forster is referring to the following passage in *War and Peace*, describing the Russians after the fall of Moscow: "Those who were striving to understand the general course of events, and trying by self-sacrifice and heroism to take a hand in it, were the most useless members of society; they saw everything upside down, and all they did for the common good proved to be futile and absurd." (quoted in Furbank, *E. M. Forster*, 2:215).

55. The co-author, together with Isherwood, of the screenplay for *Little Friend* (1934).

56. Forster is probably referring to Gerald Hamilton who had, at that time, orchestrated a plan for Isherwood's companion, Heinz, to obtain a Mexican passport.

57. Because of the recent libel case brought against him for his article "A Flood in the Office," Forster was very anxious about possible libel cases that could arise as a result of his editing the letters of T. E. Lawrence. He decided, therefore, to give up the Lawrence project. (Furbank, *E. M. Forster*, 2:211).

58. Forster is writing comments about Auden and Isherwood's play, *The Ascent of the F.6*, which opened in London on February 26, 1937.

59. Forster continues his comments on *The Ascent of F.6*.

60. Gerald Hamilton's Mr. Norris-like plan was to obtain Heinz Mexican nationality. Isherwood had persuaded his mother to pay Hamilton's lawyer £1,000 for this service. The plan does not succeed. (Forster, *Selected Letters*, 2:150n. 2).

61. Salinger, the lawyer Hamilton had engaged, advised Heinz to travel into Germany in order to renew his visa to remain in Belgium (while waiting for the decision regarding Mexican nationality). Heinz was arrested by the Gestapo in Trier, Germany (Parker, *Isherwood*, 301–2).

62. Forster's poem is a parody of a poem by Walter Savage Landor (1775–1864): "I strove with none, for none was worth my strife. / Nature I loved and, next to Nature, Art: / I warm'd both hands before the fire of life; / it sinks, and I am ready to depart" (*The Poetry Connection*, ed. Gunner Bengtsson [http://www.poetry connection.net/poets/Walter_Savage_Landor]).

63. An Indian student club at Cambridge University.

64. *Guy Mannering*, published in 1815, is a novel by Sir Walter Scott (1771–1832). Some of the action occurs in colonial India, which might explain Forster's interest in the novel.

65. Isherwood outlines his theory of the "The Test" and "The Truly Weak Man" in his autobiographical novel, *Lions and Shadows*, which he was currently working on: "the Test exists only for the Truly Weak Man: no matter whether he passes it or whether he fails, he cannot alter his essential nature." Unlike the Truly Strong Man, who will take a "reasonable" path, the Truly Weak Man will put himself through impossible challenges. (163–64).

66. Oliver Low was the brother of Humphrey Spender's wife. Isherwood had a brief affair with him in 1937 shortly after Heinz returned to Germany.

67. Forster is staying with the Hilton Youngs (Lord and Lady Kennet).

68. Forster is referring to the book, *Journey to a War*, Auden and Isherwood are working on based on their recent trip to China. Lago and Furbank suggest that "[t]he technical problem may have been that of gracefully combining Auden's poems and Isherwood's prose" (E. M. Forster, *Selected Letters*, 2:160n. 5).

69. Wayland Hilton Young (b. 1923) is the son of Edward Hilton Young (Lord Kennet).

70. The English translation of Evariste R. Huc and Joseph Gabet, *Travels in Tartary, Tibet, and China During the Years 1844–56* was published in 1928.

71. Sir Richard Thomas Dyke Acland, Fifteenth Baronet (1906–90) was one of the founders of the British Common Wealth Party; Forster is possibly referring to Frederick Charles Bartlett (1886–1969), the first Professor of Experimental Psychology at Cambridge University.

72. Jacky Hewit, with whom Isherwood had a brief affair in 1938.

73. *On the Frontier* was the third and final play written by Auden and Isherwood. It opened at the Arts Theatre in Cambridge on November 14, 1938, and later played in London.

74. Forster's large script is difficult to decipher. He is possibly signing the name: J. A. Symonds. John Addington Symonds (1840–93), British poet, translator, and essayist. He wrote on homosexual themes and translated, among other works, *Wine, Women and Song* (translations of Goliardic songs), which relates to Forster's comment prior to the signature.

75. He is writing this postscript on the back of a daily planner.

76. The actual name of the committee is The Committee on the Law of Defamation.

77. Anthony Frederick Blunt (1907–83), was an English art historian who was one of the "Cambridge Five" spy ring (which included Guy Burgess) working for the Soviet Union.

78. American writer, primarily of screenplays. His works include *Gilda* (1946) and *Night and the City* (1950). He also wrote books for several Broadway plays, including *A Point of Honor* (1937).

79. "Blackamoor" is an archaic term for a dark-skinned person ("Black" plus "Moor").

80. Latin phrase: "salaputium" means "a little man"; "dissertum" is an adjective meaning "dexterous or skilled in speaking or writing." Forster is drawing on Catullus 53.5: "dimagni, salaputium dissertum!"

Chapter 2

1. Forster is quoting Rose (Emilie) Macaulay (1881–1958), a British novelist whose works include *I Would Be Private* (1937) and *The World My Witness* (1950). She had recently written a book about Forster, *The Writings of E. M. Forster*.

2. Forster reviewed Gerald Heard's book, *Pain, Sex and Time: A New Outlook on Evolution and the Future of Man*, for *The Listener*. Forster's friend, Joe Ackerley, was the literary editor.

3. Forster has moved from central London (near Bloomsbury) to a neighborhood in the far west section of London.

4. Bumpus was a notable London bookshop on Oxford Street.

5. Parentheses in the original.

6. Marie de Rabutin-Chantal, marquise de Sévigné (1626–96), a French writer of letters was married briefly to Henri, marquis de Sévigné. Her husband died in a fight over another woman in 1651. Madame de Sévigné never remarried.

7. Harvey Young is Isherwood's current companion.

8. In a letter to Gerald Hamilton, Isherwood commented on émigrés living in California: "The refugees here are very militant and already squabbling over the future German government. God help Germany if some of them ever get into power! Others are interested, apparently, in reconquering the Romanisches Café [a popular meeting place for intellectuals in pre-War Berlin], and would gladly sacrifice the whole British army to make Berlin safe for night life" (quoted in Parker, *Isherwood*, 392). Hamilton apparently handed the letter to Tom Driberg who had it published in a gossip column in the *Daily Express*. The refugees living in southern California were greatly offended when they learned of the comments. (Parker, *Isherwood*, 392).

9. Paul Morand (1888–1976), French novelist and poet. He was a member of the Academie française.

10. This letter from Isherwood is not in the Forster papers and is, presumably, lost. For an excerpt of the article that appeared in *Horizon*, see the introduction in this book.

11. German white wine from Hockheim on the river Main.

12. This letter from Isherwood is not included in the Forster papers.

13. This letter from Isherwood is not included in the Forster papers.

14. Forster is responding to an epigram, signed "W.R.M." (W. R. Matthews, Dean of St. Paul's), appearing in the *Spectator* on June 14, 1940, which critically targets Auden and Isherwood's desertion of England. Forster wrote a lengthy response that appeared in the *Spectator* on July 5, 1940. (Furbank, *E. M. Forster*, 2:238). For the epigram and an excerpt of Forster's response, see Introduction.

15. Forster's pamphlet, *What I Believe*, originally titled, *Two Cheers for Democracy*, was published by the Hogarth Press. (The Hogarth Press was founded by Leonard and Virginia Woolf.)

16. George Eliot's novel, *Middlemarch: A Study of Provincial Life* (1871–72); Henry James's novel, *A Portrait of a Lady* (1881).

17. Robin is the son of Bob and May Buckingham and is attending school in Berkshire.

18. In his nonfiction work, *The Summing Up* (1938), Somerset Maugham expresses his personal views on a variety of topics.

19. Salvador de Madariaga y Rojo (1886–1978), was a Spanish writer, historian, and pacifist. Living in England during the 1930s, he organized a resistance to Franco's dictatorship in Spain.

20. Putney is a neighborhood in southwest London.

21. Forster's letter is actually dated October 11.

22. The "enemy aliens" were German refugees, most of whom had professional careers in Germany. Isherwood taught English at the Quaker operated hostel, which assisted refugees in finding work in the United States. (Parker, *Isherwood*, 431).

23. Forster's essay, "The New Disorder," an overview and negative assessment of current society, appeared in the December 1941 issue, vol. IV, no. 24 of *Horizon*.

24. *Wilhelm Tell* (1804), a play by the German poet and dramatist Friedrich Schiller (1759–1805), is based on the Swiss legendary hero of the early fourteenth century.

25. Claudian (Claudius Claudianus), Roman poet, who lived from approximately 370 to 402 CE. Some of his works record the turbulence of the late years of the Roman Empire.

26. Gaumont-British Picture Corporation was a major film production company in Britain during the 1930s. It produced Berthold Viertel's film, *Little Friend*, in 1934.

27. Salka Viertel (1889–1978), Berthold Viertel's Polish-born first wife, was an actress (in Vienna) and a screenplay writer. *The Canyon*, the first novel by Peter Viertel (b. 1920), was published in 1940 and offers an adolescent boy's view of life in Santa Monica Canyon. He later collaborated with John Huston and James Agee on the screenplay for *The African Queen* (1951).

28. Brian Howard (1905–58) was an English poet who, like Isherwood during the 1930s, was seeking a safe country for his German companion.

29. During the war, Cecil Day-Lewis was a publications editor at the Ministry of Information.

30. Roger Senhouse (1899–1970) was a British writer, publisher, and translator of French works by Colette and others. He was also Lytton Strachey's lover.

31. Josef Wilpert, *Die römischen mosaiken und malereien der kirchlichen bauten vom IV. Bis XIII jahrhundert* [*Roman Mosaics and Paintings of the Church Buildings of the 4th to 13th Centuries*], Freiburg i. Br., 1924; Hayford Peirce and Royall Tyler, *L'Art Byzantine*, 2 vols., Paris, 1932.

32. Torquay was a town on the south coast of England where many children who evacuated from London attended boarding schools. In June 1942 several bombs were dropped on a crowded beach.

33. Virginia Woolf committed suicide in March 1941.
34. This bracketed phrase is Forster's.
35. John Lehmann's literary journal, *The Penguin New Writing*, published from 1940 to 1950.
36. Benjamin Britten's *Seven Sonnets of Michelangelo*. Britten's life partner was the tenor, Peter Pears.
37. William Henry Beveridge (1879–1963), British economist and social reformer. His report (published in December 1942), *Social Insurance and Allied Services* ("The Beveridge Report"), formed the basis for the post-World War II Labor government's Welfare State and National Health Service programs.
38. Only the second page of this letter survives.
39. Lionel Fielden (1896–1974) was a British journalist and senior producer of the BBC during the 1930s and first Controller of Broadcasting for the Indian State Broadcasting Service, whose name he changed to All India Radio in 1935. Pieter Brueghel the Elder (c. 1525–69) was a Flemish painter whose best known works are of landscapes with peasants. Auden's famous poem, "Musée des Beaux Arts," ruminates on Brueghel's painting, "The Fall of Icarus."
40. Stefan Zweig (1881–1942) was a Jewish Austrian writer whose works include biographies of Mary Stuart and Marie Antoinette. Not wishing to live in a world increasingly overrun by Nazi Germany, he and his second wife, Lotte, committed suicide in Brazil in 1941.
41. Richard Graham Bradshaw Isherwood (1911–79) was Christopher Isherwood's younger brother.
42. Isherwood is residing at the Vedanta Society Center in Los Angeles.
43. Max-Pol Fouchet was the editor of the French literary journal *Fontaine: revue mensuelle de la poésie et des lettres françaises* from November 1942 to May 1946. The publication ceased in 1947. André Gide (1869–1951), French novelist.
44. *Ulysses* (1922) is the monumental modernist novel by James Joyce (1882–1941).
45. The parenthetical comment is by Forster. "Herts" is an abbreviation for Hertfordshire.
46. In 1922, Forster burned some indecent stories he had written in order to devote himself fully to writing *A Passage to India*. Forster maintained that he did this "not as a moral repentance but out of a feeling that the stories 'clogged' him artistically. They were 'a wrong channel' for his pen" (Furbank, *E. M. Forster*, 2:106).
47. Edmund Blunden (1896–1974) was a British poet who published several volumes of poetry in the 1920s.
48. *La Chartreuse de Parme* is a novel by the French writer, Stendhal (1783–1842).
49. Somerset Maugham's novel, *The Razor's Edge*, was published in 1945. The film of the book, starring Tyrone Power and Gene Tierney, was made in 1946.
50. "Geraldean" refers to Gerald Heard.
51. *Double Lives: An Autobiography of William Plomer* was published in 1943.
52. Marple Hall was Isherwood's ancestral home in Cheshire, England.

53. It eventually becomes the novel, *Prater Violet*, which was published in 1945.
54. Beryl de Zoete (1879–1962) was an English ballet dancer and translator of the Italian novelist, Italo Svevo; Sybil Colefax (1874–1950) was a society hostess and interior decorator.
55. Landanum was used as a pain reliever and to induce sleep. It also contained opium hence Forster is making a connection with the Romantic poet, Coleridge, who used opium to combat illness and depression.
56. Thomas de Quincey (1785–1859) was a British writer and great admirer of William Wordsworth.
57. George Moore (1852–1933) was an Anglo-Irish novelist and writer of autobiographical works. He is the author of *Esther Waters* (1894), *Reminiscences of the Impressionist Painters* (1906), *Salve* (1912), and numerous other works.
58. Swami Vivekananda (1863–1902) was the chief disciple of the Hindu holy man, Ramakrishna (1836–86).
59. Jeanne de Casalis (1897–1966) was a British actress; Anthony Asquith (1902–68) was a British film director whose films include *Pygmalion* (1938) and *The Winslow Boy* (1948).
60. Louis de Rouvroy duc de Saint-Simon (1675–1755). His famous memoirs record life at the court of Louis XIV.
61. *The Song of God: Bhagavad Gita*, translated by Isherwood and his Guru, Swami Prabhavananda, was published by the Vedanta Press in 1944. It contains an introduction by Aldous Huxley.
62. Forster's abbreviations for World War II and World War I, respectively.

Chapter 3

1. Sir (Francis) Osbert Sitwell (1892–1969) was an English writer and the brother of Dame Edith Sitwell. His most notable work is his five-volume autobiography (1945–50).
2. This letter is written on stationery that contains a drawing of Logan Rock, a picturesque rock formation extending out into Mount's Bay in Cornwall, England. The reason Forster chose to use this stationery is not clear.
3. Weybridge, on the River Thames in Surrey outside of London, is the site of the boat races.
4. Christopher Wood was a wealthy British friend of Isherwood's with whom Gerald Heard lived for some time.
5. Tyringham is a town in the Berkshires of Massachusetts where Forster visited Bill Roerick.
6. A two-volume French edition of Cervantes's classic, *Don Quixote de la Mancha*, was translated by Louis Viardot and published in 1863. It contains 370 drawings by the French artist and illustrator, Paul Gustave Doré (1832–83).
7. *The Alchemist* is a comedy by Ben Jonson that was first performed in 1610. Jamini Roy (1887–1972) was an Indian painter who, after achieving success

with portrait painting, began infusing his work with stylistic elements found in Bengali peasant art. Kama is not really a god but rather the term for "desire"—as in the *Kama Sutra.*

8. C. H. Collins Baker (1880–1959) was a British art historian whose works include *Catalogue of William Blake's Drawings and Paintings in the Huntington Library* (1957). Baker was at the Huntington evidently working on this project at the time of Forster's visit.

9. Asaf Ali (1888–1953) fought for Indian independence from Britain and was the first ambassador from India to the United States (1947–48).

10. Although the return address of the air letter is King's College Cambridge, Forster wrote the letter in Aldeburgh. Forster was residing at the home of Benjamin Britten, collaborating with Eric Crozier on the libretto for Britten's opera *Billy Budd.* They completed the first draft of the libretto in sixteen days (Furbank, *E. M. Forster,* 2:283–84).

11. Peter Pears was Britten's longtime companion.

12. The first letter is evidently Isherwood's letter dated January 16 (1950); the more recent letter is not included in the Forster papers.

13. The film George Bernard Shaw did "control" was *Pygmalion* (1938), based on Shaw's 1912–13 play for which Shaw won an Academy Award for the screenplay. The film that Forster considers an unsuccessful adaptation is *Caesar and Cleopatra* (1945), which was based on Shaw's 1901 play, starring Claude Rains and Vivian Leigh in the title roles.

14. A geographical division of England: north or south of the Tees. The Tees is a river in Cumbria (in the north of England), flowing from the east to the North Sea in the west.

15. Donald Windham (b. 1920) is an American writer and friend of Paul Cadmus. His stories on homosexual themes caught Forster's attention and Forster became his friend and literary mentor. Forster wrote an introduction to Windham's collection of stories, *The Warm Country,* which was published in 1960 (Furbank, *E. M. Forster,* 2:275). Sandy Campbell is Windham's companion; it is not clear why Forster considers him a "monster."

16. This letter is not included in the Forster papers and is presumably lost.

17. This letter is unidentified.

18. *Arctic Summer* is an unfinished novel Forster worked on intermittently from 1911 to 1914.

19. They are evidently students at Cambridge.

20. Forster eventually revised the penultimate chapter so that Maurice and Alec are reunited at the boathouse. The chapter closes with the reassuring words of Alec (who was sleeping when Maurice arrived): "And now we shan't be parted no more, and that's finished" (*Maurice,* 210).

21. *Wozzeck,* the atonal opera by Austrian composer, Alban Berg (1885–1935), was first performed in 1925.

22. This letter is not included in the Forster papers.

23. *The Hill of Devi*, published in October 1953, is an autobiographical work in which Forster records his visits to the Indian princely state of Dewas Senior in 1912–13 and later in 1921. As private secretary to the Maharaji during his first visit, Forster was well positioned to observe daily life at the court.

24. Forrest Reid (1875–1947) was an Irish novelist. His works include *Peter Waring* (1937) and two autobiographies: *Apostate* (1926) and *Private Road* (1940).

25. William Plomer was collaborating on the text for Benjamin Britten's opera, *Gloriana* (1952), which was intended as a celebration of the coronation of Queen Elizabeth II.

26. This letter is not included in the Forster papers.

27. Walter Baxter (b. 1915) is a novelist. Forster is referring to Baxter's novel, *The Image and the Search*, published in 1953. Baxter's previous novel was *Look Down in Mercy* (1951).

28. Forster's autobiographical work was published as *The Hill of Devi*; see note 23.

29. Swami Prabhavananda was Isherwood's Guru; Pete Martinez was a Mexican ballet dancer and friend of Isherwood's.

30. Forster forwarded this letter to Bob. In a handwritten postscript addressed to Bob, Forster writes: "Have invited them [i.e. the Countess and Swami] both to lunch with us next Sunday. Madness?"

31. Forster connects "I write to" with "Dearest Christopher" at the top of the page with an arrow.

32. Isherwood's latest novel, *The World in the Evening*.

33. John van Druten (1901–57) was an English dramatist. His play, *I am a Camera*, is based on Isherwood's *Goodbye to Berlin*. Van Druten took the name of the play from the famous opening passage in Isherwood's novel: "I am a camera with its shutter open, quite passive, recording not thinking. Recording the man shaving at the window opposite and the woman in the kimono washing her hair. Some day, all this will have to be developed, carefully printed, fixed" (*Goodbye to Berlin*, *The Berlin Stories*, [New York: New Directions, 1945], 1).

34. Philip Nicholas Furbank was a British writer and literary scholar. He wrote a two-volume biography of Forster, *E. M. Forster: A Life* (1977–78).

35. Isherwood began his relationship with Don Bachardy in 1953.

36. The Cavendish is the hotel in London where Isherwood and Don are staying.

37. An Indian writer, Santha Rama Rau (b. 1923) adapted Forster's novel for the stage. The play was directed by the Indian director, Waris Hussein. *A Passage to India* was later adapted for television by John Maynard and broadcast on the BBC in 1965.

38. Isherwood's novel, *Down There on a Visit*, published in 1962.

39. Keith Vaughan (1912–77) was a British artist who often painted male nudes in landscapes.

40. This entire letter is written in the hand of May Buckingham but the first part is apparently dictated by Forster.

Bibliography

Auden, W. H., and Christopher Isherwood. *Journey to a War*. 1939. Reprint, New York: Paragon House, 1990.

———. *Two Great Plays: The Dog Beneath the Skin and The Ascent of F6*. New York: Random House, 1937.

Beauman, Nicola. *E. M. Forster: A Biography*. New York: Alfred A. Knopf, 1994.

"Comment." *Horizon: A Review of Literature and Art* 1 no. 2 (1940): 68–71.

Finney, Brian. *Christopher Isherwood: A Critical Biography*. New York: Oxford University Press, 1979

Forster, E. M. *Abinger Harvest*. New York: Harcourt Brace, 1936.

———. *Commonplace Book*. Edited by Philip Gardner. Stanford, IL: Stanford University Press, 1985.

———. *Goldsworthy Lowes Dickinson*. New York: Harcourt Brace, 1934.

———. *The Hill of Devi*. New York: Harcourt Brace, 1953.

———. *Maurice*. Harmondsworth, England: Penguin, 1972.

———. "The New Disorder." *Horizon: A Review of Literature and Art* 4, no. 24 (1941): 379–84.

———. *A Passage to India*. New York: Harcourt Brace, 1924.

———. *Selected Letters of E. M. Forster*. Edited by Mary Lago and P. N. Furbank. Vol. 2. Cambridge, MA: Harvard University Press, 1985.

———. *What I Believe*. London: Hogarth Press, 1939.

Fryer, Jonathan. *Isherwood: A Biography*. Garden City, NY: Doubleday, 1978.

Furbank, P. N. *E. M. Forster: A Life*. 2 vols. New York: Harcourt Brace, 1978.

Hynes, Samuel. *The Auden Generation: Literature and Politics in England in the 1930s*. Princeton: Princeton University Press, 1976.

Isherwood, Christopher. *All the Conspirators*. London: Jonathan Cape, 1928.

———. *The Berlin Stories: The Last of Mr. Norris and Goodbye to Berlin*. 1935. Reprint, New York: New Directions, 1945.

———. *Christopher and His Kind: 1929–1939*. New York: Farrar, Straus, Giroux, 1976.

———. *Diaries, Volume One: 1939–1960*. Edited by Katherine Bucknell. London: Vintage, 1997.

———. *Down There on a Visit*. New York: Avon, 1959.

———. *Lions and Shadows*. New York: New Directions, 1947.

———. *Lost Years: A Memoir, 1945–1951*. Edited by Katherine Bucknell. New York: HarperCollins, 2000.

————. *The Memorial: Portrait of a Family*. London: Hogarth 1932.

————. *Prater Violet*. New York: Random House, 1945.

————. Unpublished diary 1935–38. Huntington Library CI 2751.

————. *The World in the Evening*. London: Methuen, 1954.

Lehmann, John. *Christopher Isherwood: A Personal Memoir*. New York: Henry Holt, 1987.

Parker, Peter. *Isherwood: A Life Revealed*. New York: Random House, 2004.

Spender, Stephen. *Letters to Christopher: Stephen Spender's Letters to Christopher Isherwood, 1929–1939*. Edited by Lee Bartlett. Santa Barbara: Black Sparrow, 1980.

————. *World Within World*. London: Faber and Faber, 1951.

Summers, Claude J. *Christopher Isherwood*. New York: Frederick Ungar, 1980.

Index